SHUNNED AND DANGEROUS

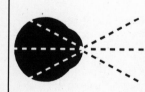

This Large Print Book carries the
Seal of Approval of N.A.V.H.

Shunned and Dangerous

Laura Bradford

THORNDIKE PRESS

A part of Gale, Cengage Learning

GALE
CENGAGE Learning·

Farmington Hills, Mich • San Francisco • New York • Waterville, Maine
Meriden, Conn • Mason, Ohio • Chicago

GALE
CENGAGE Learning®

Copyright © 2014 by Laura Bradford.
An Amish Mystery.
Thorndike Press, a part of Gale, Cengage Learning.

Thorndike Press® Large Print Mystery.
The text of this Large Print edition is unabridged.
Other aspects of the book may vary from the original edition.
Set in 16 pt. Plantin.

LIBRARY OF CONGRESS CATALOGING-IN-PUBLICATION DATA

Bradford, Laura.
  Shunned and dangerous / by Laura Bradford. — Large print edition.
    pages ; cm. — (An Amish mystery) (Thorndike Press large print mystery)
  ISBN 978-1-4104-7084-3 (hardcover) — ISBN 1-4104-7084-9 (hardcover)
  1. Amish—Fiction. 2. Family secrets—Fiction. 3.
  Murder—Investigation—Fiction. 4. Amish Country (Pa.)—Fiction. 5. Large
  type books. I. Title.
  PS3602.R34235S56 2014
  813'.6—dc23   2014014743

Published in 2014 by arrangement with The Berkley Publishing Group, a member of Penguin Group (USA), a Penguin Random House Company

Printed in Mexico
1 2 3 4 5 6 7 18 17 16 15 14

For my family,
I love you.

ACKNOWLEDGMENTS

While writing is certainly a solitary profession in many ways, I draw strength and smiles from the people around me — both during and after the process.

A big thank-you goes to Kevan Deardorff, who sends some great Amish-related news clippings my way. Thanks to him, my plot folder is growing!

I'd also like to thank my editor, Michelle Vega. Her encouragement and support is deeply appreciated.

A warm thank-you goes to Sam and Todd at Aaron's Books in Lititz, Pennsylvania. They've worked tirelessly to help spread the word about my series and have welcomed me back to their store time and time again.

And, finally, a thank-you to my readers. It's because of you that Claire, Jakob, Benjamin, Aunt Diane, and the rest of the crew have a home.

CHAPTER 1

She tucked her hands into the front pockets of her cardigan sweater and smiled at the faint squeals and screams that punctuated the otherwise quiet countryside of Heavenly, Pennsylvania — sounds she knew would only intensify as night descended.

All week long Claire Weatherly had been hearing about Mose Fisher's corn maze from the man's granddaughter. In fact, Claire almost wished she'd had the presence of mind to take notes during Esther's many tellings. She could have supplemented her shop's rapidly dwindling bottom line by printing a foolproof tip sheet and selling it to the masses expected to flock to the intricate series of trails throughout the weekend.

But she hadn't.

Instead, she'd covered her ears time and time again as her Amish employee and friend unknowingly threatened to ruin the kind of interactive puzzle Claire had enjoyed since she was old enough to navigate the seasonal challenge issued by unending rows of golden-hued stalks. The fact that this particular labyrinth was designed and run by a member of the Amish community she'd come to love only served to raise her nearly lifelong intrigue to a whole new level.

A *clip-clop* at her back made her step to the side of the road to allow the gray-topped buggy used by the Old Order Amish in Lancaster County to pass. The friendly nod of the driver, coupled with the shy smile of the man's wife beside him, warmed Claire from the inside out, prompting her to return their quiet acknowledgment with a wave.

In Heavenly just shy of nine months, Claire knew a number of the Amish in her newly adopted hometown as friends — people like Esther and her beau, Eli Miller, as well as Eli's twin sister, Ruth, and their older brother, Benjamin.

Benjamin.

She forced her thoughts from the gentle blue-eyed man and the promise he'd made that prevented them from ever being more than friends, and she focused, once again, on the orange triangle affixed to the back of the slow-moving buggy and the sandy-haired boy that peeked out at her with a hint of curiosity. She didn't know the child's family, didn't know which farmhouse they inhabited, but thanks to her deepening friendship with Esther and her own fascination with the Amish, Claire was capable of filling in some of the blanks herself. She figured the little boy, who eventually smiled as the buggy flaps slowly drifted closed, to be about six years old. Judging by the length of the driver's beard, the man had been married a good ten years or so, making the youngster he transported one of probably four or five. The woman who sat so stoically beside her husband handled the children and her daily work with little respite and nary a complaint.

Releasing a quiet sigh, Claire watched the buggy disappear around an upcoming bend in the road, the now common sight enveloping her in a welcomed sense of calm. In any other place, Claire's assessments would be nothing short of conjecture. But there, in Heavenly, they were a virtual certainty — rare givens in a world of few.

The unmistakable hum of an approaching engine cut through her thoughts, and she turned once again, the buggy of moments earlier replaced with modern technology and a dashboard-mounted dome light. The passenger side window slid open as the sedan slowed to a stop beside Claire, the familiar face behind the wheel bringing a smile to her lips.

"Where are you off to with that spring in your step?" Jakob Fisher leaned across the seat of his police-issued car and raised her smile with his always endearing set of dimples. "Is there a Schnitz and Knepp sampling I'm unaware of?"

"Ha-ha. Very funny." Stepping forward, she leaned her arms against the open windowsill and assumed the role of interrogator. "So what brings *you* out here?"

The slightest hint of crimson rose in his cheeks before disappearing behind a suspiciously timed rub of his face. "Just doing the detective thing, I guess."

"Detective thing?" she teased. "What, exactly, is *the detective thing*?"

"I keep my eyes open, make sure everything is okay. You know, that sort of thing."

She considered poking holes in his answer with a reminder of the handful of patrolmen tasked with that exact job but opted to let it go. Jakob's obvious discomfort at her question was a dead giveaway to the real reason he was there — a reason that had nothing whatsoever to do with his professional persona and everything to do with his personal life.

Yes, Jakob was headed toward the Amish side of town for one reason and one reason only — to catch whatever glimpse he could of his childhood family, a family he lost the day he left his Amish upbringing in favor of donning a police uniform. His brief yet welcomed contact with his sister, Martha, only weeks earlier had ceased the day Rob Karble's murderer had been apprehended.

The step backward clearly hurt Jakob if the renewed dullness in his amber-flecked eyes was any indication. But, still, the chance to interact with Esther's mother, albeit briefly in the grand scheme of things, had given his perpetual hope a fresh set of legs. The nod of acknowledgment he now received from his sister, Martha, whenever she stopped by Claire's shop certainly didn't hurt, either.

"How good are you at puzzles?" she asked.

Jakob's brows arched. "I can hold my own. Why?"

"Care to put that claim to the test?" She knew she was teasing, maybe even bordering on flirting, but after hiding her heart behind a wall for the past year, it felt right. Fun, even. "Because I'm fairly certain I can find my way from one end of the maze to the other far quicker than you."

At the mention of the word *maze,* Jakob

sat up straight, all lingering signs of his infamous knee-weakening dimples gone. "I can't do that, Claire, and you know that."

She drew back, her head hitting the top of the sill as she did. "Ouch!" Rubbing at her part line, she kept her gaze firmly on Jakob's. "The maze is open to the public. That means you're every bit as welcome there as I am."

"I'm quite certain my father would disagree." The hint of anger in Jakob's tone did little to cover the hurt Claire knew to be the true reason behind the man's quip. All the longing the detective exhibited for even the tiniest sighting of his family — his mother, Miriam; his sister, Martha; his brother, Isaac; his niece, Esther; and her many siblings — stopped shy of his father, Mose. And while any attempt at conversation regarding the man was quickly changed, Claire had pieced together enough to know bad feelings between the two ran deep.

For Mose, she knew it was anger over his eldest son's decision to leave his Amish roots post baptism, a sin punishable by excommunication. But for Jakob, the anger ran far deeper, to mumbled encounters that depicted a childhood of low self-esteem groomed at the hands of Mose himself.

"But you have a right to be there," she protested around the lump that rose in her throat. "Just like anyone else."

"It's a right I don't choose to exercise," Jakob countered before softening his tone and finding a smile she knew was difficult to muster at the moment. "But I'd like to hear about it when you're done if that's —"

A long, slow moo from just over Claire's left shoulder cut the detective's sentence short. She turned around to find a slightly larger than average Holstein staring at her with deeply troubled eyes. "Whoa there . . ."

"It's okay, it's okay — she won't hurt you." Jakob stepped out of his car and came around the hood for a closer look. When he reached Claire's side, he greeted the wide-eyed dairy cow with a soothing hand. "Hey there, sweetie. You missed your late-afternoon milking, didn't you?"

Claire looked from Jakob to the cow and back again. "How do you know she missed her milking?"

Jakob stepped closer to the animal and offered what she imagined was a word of comfort spoken in Pennsylvania Dutch before providing an answer Claire could understand. "You can see it in her eyes and her udders. She's engorged."

Glancing past the cow, she raised a hand

in the direction of the Amish men working in a distant field, but to no avail. "If you wait with her, I'll head over there and let them know their cow got loose."

Jakob took in the tab on the cow's ear and shook his head before dropping into a squat and manually relieving some of the cow's discomfort. "This isn't Hochstetler's cow."

"How do you know?"

"Because of this" — he pointed at the *Z* etched into the plastic tag — "which lets me know it's Zook's. *Harley* Zook's." He stopped milking the cow long enough to meet the animal's soulful eyes and inquire as to its name. "So are you Jennie? Or Maggie? Or perhaps Julia?" Then, to Claire, he said, "If Harley still does things the way he always did when his brother was alive, her name starts with a *J* or an *M*. Not sure why, but that's how he always named them."

She squatted down beside Jakob and ran a hand along the side of the cow. "Is this Harley Zook a friend of yours?"

Jakob turned his attention back to the udder between his fingers, his focus no longer on the cow or Claire. "Ally would be a better word."

"Ally?" she echoed in confusion.

"He was the only person who didn't shun me for leaving the Amish to be a cop."

16

"So this Zook fellow isn't Amish?"

He gave a half shrug, half head shake. "Nah, he's Amish."

She tried to make sense of what she was hearing, to rationalize the man's words with what she knew of the Amish, but she came up empty. "Then why would he support you leaving after baptism?"

Jakob seemed to weigh her question against an invisible pull, his words, when he finally spoke, catching her by surprise. "Because it was Harley's brother's murder that prompted me to leave. It was John's death I wanted to help solve."

She cast about for something to say but was saved from the futile task when Jakob filled in the blanks, unprompted. "Course you now know, by the time I made my choice and walked away from my upbringing, the murder was solved — chalked up to a crime of ignorance-inspired hate by an English guy named Carl Duggan."

At her nod, he continued. "Anyway, it would have been too late to go back even if I'd wanted to, but that didn't stop Harley Zook from standing nose to nose with my father and telling him I was an admirable man, someone to be respected and admired, not treated as the outcast I'd become."

Pulling her hand from the side of the cow,

she rested it, instead, on Jakob's upper back, the tension she felt there heartbreaking. "I agree with Harley."

"My father didn't. He stood by his disgust in me and added a healthy dose of disgust for Harley, as well. In fact, from what I was able to glean from my sister earlier this month, my father actually holds Harley responsible for my decision to leave . . . as if it was *Harley* who cost him the son that was never good enough rather than that son's own beliefs and convictions."

Oh, what she wouldn't give to be able to wave a magic wand and make things right for Jakob. If she had one, not only would she allow him to have real relationships with his family again, she'd also erase all the pain in his heart where Mose Fisher was concerned.

In the absence of any magical powers — wand or otherwise — Claire simply swallowed and changed the subject. "If you tell me where Harley Zook lives, I'll walk out there and tell him about his cow."

Jakob rose to his feet then assisted Claire up to her own. "I got this. Really. You head on over to the maze and have a good time. Call me when you're done and I'll give you a ride home."

She felt her cheeks warm at the notion of

Jakob picking her up and escorting her back to Sleep Heavenly, her aunt's bed-and-breakfast that doubled — at least for the moment — as Claire's home. "I can't ask you to do that. It's Friday night. Surely you have plans."

Slowly, he looked from the cow to Claire and back again, the hint of a smile twitching at the corners of his mouth. "Aside from getting this beauty back to Harley's, I've got no plans. Except, hopefully, to sit outside on your aunt's porch with you, enjoying what may very well be one of the last relatively pleasant evenings we'll have before winter rears its head."

She tried to think of something to say that would remove Jakob from the hook he was voluntarily putting himself on but came up empty-handed. The truth was, she liked the notion of Jakob coming out to get her, liked the image of sharing Diane's porch swing with the handsome detective. If nothing else, his presence would keep her from poring over her gift shop's books, searching for the financial life jacket she needed to keep Heavenly Treasures open.

Tilting her head upward to meet his gaze, she gave in to the smile that surely mirrored the dimple-laced one making its way across his face with lightning-quick speed. "You're on."

Turn by turn, Claire made her way through the first part of Mose Fisher's maze, each step she took sending an amusing chill skittering down her spine.

In all her years of navigating mazes, Claire had never succumbed to the creepy factor that had sent so many of her childhood friends back to the starting line before they'd completed even a quarter of the course. Granted, cornfields had been the backdrop of many a horror movie and thriller novel, but to her, mazes were all about the challenge — one she'd never been able to walk away from.

Yet, there she was, not far from the starting point, and her heart was beginning to pound, the isolation of her current path fraying her nerves.

"Stop it, you sissy," she scolded herself as she lifted the flashlight Mose had handed her upon payment and flipped it on. The circle of light it cast confirmed the maze was, indeed, crafted from rustling cornstalks rather than the paper-thin people her mind had almost convinced her were whispering.

Shaking away her momentary bout of stupidity, Claire turned to her right and then her left only to stop and turn back at the familiar sound of Esther's voice.

"I'm over here, Esther," she called out, turning the beam of light in the direction from which she, herself, had just come and waiting for her friend to appear. Hired to assist Claire at the shop, Esther King had quickly earned a place in Claire's heart.

More than a handful of times, Claire had tried to put a finger on what, exactly, it was about Jakob's niece that had left such an indelible impression on her heart. After all, they'd only known each other just a little over three months — a drop in the bucket compared to so many others who'd come and gone throughout Claire's life. Yet, each and every time, she came back to the same thing. Esther was true in every sense of the word. And, as a result, Claire appreciated the simpler things in life more than she'd ever imagined prior to meeting the young Amish woman.

"There you are." Esther stepped around a break in the cornstalks and waved. "Dawdy said you were inside the maze."

Claire nodded at the mention of Esther's grandfather. "I just started a few minutes ago if you want to come with me. But if you do, you can't tell me when and where to

turn, okay? I want to figure this out myself
—"

"It happened, Claire! It finally happened!"

"What happened?" The words were no sooner out of her mouth than she knew. The sparkle in Esther's eyes that magnified tenfold whenever her beau, Eli, was within a mile radius crackled beneath the thin white cap covering her hastily pinned head of soft brown hair. And her skin, which had never known a lick of makeup, boasted a lovely shade of crimson befitting the almost-twenty-year-old's unmistakable happiness.

"Oh, Esther . . ." She closed the gap between them, reaching for Esther's hands as she did. "Eli asked you to marry him, didn't he?"

The healthy red glow in Esther's cheeks deepened still further. "He asked Dat, and Dat gave his blessing."

"Oh, Esther . . ." she repeated, the enthusiasm emanating from her friend duplicating itself inside Claire. "I told you this day would come. I told you Eli would do everything he could to win your father's trust and respect."

And she had. Even when Eli himself threatened to make Claire eat her own words with his bouts of anger, an emotion that was not acceptable among the Amish.

"So when will it happen? When will you get married?" she asked.

"In early December."

"You mean *this* December? As in five weeks from now?"

Esther's gaze dropped to the soft earth beneath their feet then returned, shyly, to meet Claire's. "Yah. There is much to do to get ready, but I will still work with you until that time."

Releasing her hold on Esther's hands, Claire noted her friend's tied kapp strings with a touch of nostalgia then pulled her in for a quick embrace. "I want to help in whatever way I can, Esther. I can cook. I can set up benches. I can help with invitations . . . I can do whatever you need me to do. Just say the word, okay?"

When Esther said nothing, Claire stepped back for a better look at her friend's face. "Esther? Is something wrong?"

Seconds turned to minutes before Esther spoke again, her words barely more than a whisper eked out between hurried glances in the direction from which she'd approached. "W-would you please tell my uncle? I . . . I think he would like to know."

Claire blinked against the tears her answering smile couldn't erase, the excitement over Esther's need for her uncle to know battling against the reality that necessitated Claire's involvement in the first place. To Esther, though, she simply nodded. "I'll tell him this evening, Esther. I promise."

"Thank you, Claire." And, just like that, Esther was gone, her basic ankle-high black boots making nary a sound against the earth as she disappeared between the cornstalks, her destination surely involving one very happy groom-to-be.

For a long moment, Claire simply stood there, her heart and her thoughts filled with the kind of hope one wished for themselves and the people they loved. Marriage hadn't worked for her and Peter, but she knew it would be different for Esther and Eli. Different because the Amish didn't believe in divorce and different because Eli had taken the time to get to know Esther, treasuring all that he'd discovered in the process.

Yes, Esther and Eli would have a long and happy life together; of that, Claire was sure. Squaring her shoulders, she turned back toward the body of the maze, her enthusiasm for its unknown trails noticeably dimmed in light of Esther's news.

"Claire?"

She spun around in time to see Esther reappear between the stalks. "Esther! You scared me!"

"I did not mean to scare you, Claire. I want to help you."

"Help me?" she echoed.

Esther's slender finger led Claire's focus and flashlight to a small cutout in the stalks. "Every year Dawdy makes a harder maze inside the main one. He says it is for those who find the big one too simple."

Claire felt her brows arch in curiosity. "You mean like an expert trail or something?"

At Esther's slow nod, Claire clapped her flashlight against her empty hand and squealed.

"I did not tell too much, did I?"

She retraced her steps back to Esther and planted a gentle kiss on her friend's still flushed cheek. "You told me exactly what I wanted to hear. Now go . . . find Eli. Give him a hug from me and tell him how pleased I am at your news."

This time, when Esther left, she didn't return.

And this time, when Claire turned back toward the maze, she kept going, her instincts guiding her feet around one line of cornstalks after the other with very few course corrections along the way.

Here, in the depths of a section few knew about, Claire was able to navigate the clever web without distractions, each foot of progress she made entirely her own. Slowly, she rounded one bend and then another, until the beam of her flashlight jogged across the first sighting of a person she'd had since parting ways with Esther nearly thirty minutes earlier.

"Hello there," she called, transferring the beam of light from the man's bearded face down to his simple pale blue shirt and black suspendered pants. "It's nice to see someone else trying their luck at the harder course."

When the man said nothing, Claire stepped closer, lowering the flashlight still farther in an attempt to minimize its blinding effects. "If you're lost, I can help you find your way out. I'm pretty good at these kinds of mazes."

At his continued silence, she decreased the gap between them to mere inches. Her gaze found and then followed the thick rope as it traveled up the man's chest and around his pasty white neck, his bulging eyes and protruding tongue telling her everything she needed to know and nothing she'd ever forget . . .

CHAPTER 2

If she'd been thinking with a head that wasn't trying to process the notion of coming face-to-face with a dead body, Claire might have marveled at the speed with which Esther and Eli had managed to find her deep inside the expert maze, but she wasn't. Instead, all she could really focus on was steadying her breath the way Eli was cautioning.

"Claire, it is to be okay. You must breathe slowly."

She tried to heed the young man's words, but knowing a corpse was propped against a shovel handle less than five feet away made it difficult.

"Eli, we must get help," Esther pleaded from the shoulder-patting position she'd claimed within minutes of Claire's post-scream collapse. "Perhaps, if my uncle hurries, Mr. Zook will be okay."

Zook . . .

Zook . . .

Claire tried to pull the semi-familiar name from the fog in her brain and fit it inside the vague recollection that kept surfacing behind it, but to no avail. She just couldn't seem to focus on anything besides the face of death that had stared out at her from beneath an Amish hat.

"Jakob will come soon. But to hurry would make no difference." Eli squatted down beside Esther long enough to cover his fiancée's hand with his own, the warmth of their layered touch reaching through the fabric of Claire's shirt. "Harley is with the Lord now, Esther."

Harley . . .

Zook . . .

Suddenly, Claire was back on the side of the road, standing next to Jakob and a mooing dairy cow. She struggled onto her elbow, looking up at Esther and Eli as she did. "Did you say *Harley Zook*?"

Esther nodded along with Eli's verbal confirmation. "Yah."

Claire swung her gaze in the direction she'd silently vowed never to look again and shuddered. Sure enough, there, propped upright among the cornstalks, was the man who would need no help in finding his way through Mose's or anyone else's maze ever again. "That's Harley Zook?" she whispered.

"Yah," Eli repeated. "That is Zook."

"Claire? Eli? Am I getting close?" Jakob's voice, strong and clear against the otherwise too-quiet backdrop, emerged from the row of cornstalks beside Claire just before the detective himself. "Where is he?"

Eli lifted his finger to guide Jakob's gaze from Claire to the body that had necessitated the Amish man's use of a cell phone. "He is dead."

A long, low whistle escaped from between Jakob's lips as he approached the body with a high-powered flashlight of his own, his steps slowing as he covered the final foot or so. "Did you see anything?" he asked, reaching into his pocket and extracting a pair of rubber gloves. "Anyone running from this area?"

"Children run through the maze all day." With Eli's hand, Esther rose to her feet. "But they do not run from this spot. There is no map to make it so."

Jakob pulled his radio from his belt and raised it to his mouth. "I need the ME at Fisher's maze. We've got an active crime scene. Send accordingly." When he was done, he looked back at his niece and offered an encouraging smile. "This place isn't on a map?"

Esther's kapp shook along with her head. "Dawdy says this" — Esther raised her arms outward — "is to find without maps."

Sitting all the way up, Claire chimed in. "It's more for the maze experts, for lack of a better word."

"What is to happen now?" Eli moved closer to Jakob, his gait showing little hesitation.

Jakob's gaze lingered on Esther a moment longer before focusing, once again, on the body of a man who'd stood by him when no one else had. "We close things down here and investigate."

"Close things down?" Esther echoed.

"We have to. It's the only way to keep the scene from being contaminated any more than it already has been." Jakob reached out, touched the end of the rope with his gloved hand, then let his arm fall to his side in obvious frustration.

"I . . . I didn't touch anything." Claire struggled to her feet beside Esther. "As soon as I saw the rope and his tongue" — she stopped, steadied her breath, then continued on — "I knew it was too late."

"Dawdy will not be pleased to close the maze. He is already angry at Mr. Zook. This will not help."

Jakob's head snapped upward at the same time a strangled cry erupted from somewhere deep inside Esther's chest. Instinctively, Claire wrapped an arm around her friend and pulled her close. "Shhh, Esther, it's okay —"

"Dat — I mean, *Mose,*" Jakob quickly corrected himself, "may not have been fond of Harley Zook because of my choice to leave, but that was sixteen years ago, Esther."

"But Isaac is just one week."

Esther buried her head in Claire's arm, forcing Jakob to turn toward his niece's beau. "*Isaac?* What does my brother have to do with this, Eli?"

Eli looked from Jakob to Esther and back again, the light from the detective's flashlight illuminating the sudden prick of red in the young man's cheeks. "Zook offered Isaac work. With him. He said Isaac would do better working for him than making toys for Daniel and farming with your dat."

Jakob clapped a gloved hand to his face then let it slip slowly back to his side. "And Isaac? Did he accept?"

Casting a helpless look in his bride-to-be's direction, Eli hesitated.

"Did Isaac accept the offer?" Jakob repeated, his voice more gruff the second time around.

31

"Yah."

With obvious effort, Jakob raised his gaze to the sky above, a flash of something Claire couldn't identify in the absence of direct light making its way across his face and stance. Whatever it was, though, it wasn't good. That much was evident in the air that hovered around them on the heels of Eli's reply.

Swapping places with Eli, Claire took advantage of the young man's concern for Esther to offer Jakob a semblance of the support he so obviously needed. "Jakob? I'm sorry about Eli having to be the one to call you about this. But I wasn't really thinking when he asked for my phone."

Slowly, Jakob lowered his chin until he was looking down at Claire, the expression she'd missed only moments earlier now on full display. He was worried, scared even. But of what, she wasn't sure, as his response addressed her worries rather than his own. "No, Eli did the right thing in calling me. I'm just sorry you had to come across something like" — his gaze flitted in Harley's direction before returning to study her from head to toe — "*this* all on your own . . . and in the dark, no less. Are you okay?"

"I'll recover." She heard the residual shake to her voice and worked to eliminate it completely. "But I'm worried about you. You look as if you've seen a ghost."

"That would be preferable at this moment."

She allowed herself one last look at the face she knew she'd see in her dreams for many weeks to come, a silent prayer for the man's soul preceding the hand she laid across Jakob's arm. "I know his support and kindness meant a lot to you all those years ago. I'm sorry this happened to him, and I'm sorry you have to see him this way now."

Widening his stance ever so slightly, Jakob stared down at the hard packed earth, his haunting response delivered via a choked whisper. "Harley Zook tried to bring my father and me back together. Problem was, there wasn't much to bring back together. Long before I left my life with the Amish, my father decided I wasn't up to par . . . not next to Benjamin Miller, anyway."

Benjamin Miller . . .

Eli's big brother . . .

The man whom Mose Fisher used as a yardstick for his own son and who wrested the heart of an Amish girl whom Jakob himself had once loved . . .

Claire mentally culled her limited knowledge of the strained relationship between two men Claire counted as friends, and remained silent, waiting for Jakob to say the rest of his piece.

He did not disappoint. "Needless to say, Zook's efforts were wasted. There was nothing that man could say, no case he could plead, no injustice he was capable of righting, that would have convinced my father to *look* at me let alone utter a word in my direction."

The emotion with which Jakob spoke spawned a mist in Claire's eyes that she quickly blinked away. "I'm sorry about that, Jakob, I really am. All I know, though, is that it was — and is — Mose's loss."

When Jakob said nothing, she hooked a finger beneath his chin and nudged it upward until their eyes met. "You're a good man, Jakob."

"All Zook wanted was for Dat to talk to me. To acknowledge me as a person, if not a son. And now, sixteen years later, he will finally have his wish."

She searched Jakob's face for something that would explain his words, but there was nothing. Not the hurt that always accompanied mention of his father, not the fear she'd seen when she stepped away from Esther, not the excitement she'd have figured as a match for his last sentence. No, there was simply blankness.

"Jakob?"

"I wonder if Harley knew, at the end, that his own murder would make it so my father would *have* to talk to me again . . ."

CHAPTER 3

Letting her nose guide her feet, Claire reached the bottom of the steps and turned right, the telltale aroma of her aunt's blueberry pancakes calling to her as much for the normalcy they represented as for the mouthwatering good taste that was a given.

By the time she'd returned to the inn the previous night, Diane and the guests had all retired behind closed doors in anticipation of a new day. Initially Claire had been disappointed, her need to talk through the trauma of finding Harley Zook's body virtually overwhelming. But by the time she'd slipped off her shoes and flopped onto her bed, the peace and calm that was Sleep Heavenly had begun to work its magic all on its own.

Sure, she'd woken up several times throughout the night, the image of the man's tortured expression leaving her in a cold sweat. But somehow she'd managed to settle herself down each time with the knowledge that she was safe in her bed, the worry she had for Jakob firmly tucked away for examination at another time.

Unfortunately, with the dawn of a new day and the absolute certainty that word of another murder in town would unleash a resounding cry for answers, "another time" had arrived on her doorstep with a graceless thump.

"Good morning, Diane." Claire pushed her way through the swinging door off the back hallway and stopped, the sights and sounds of her aunt's kitchen embracing in their familiarity. "Mmmm, it smells amazing in here."

Emerging from behind the refrigerator door, her father's oldest sister hoisted two butter dishes into the air and smiled. "There you are! I tried to stay up and greet you last night, but I faded early. Next thing I knew, it was two o'clock in the morning and I was still in my apron and shoes!"

Claire sidled up to the breakfast bar and peeked into the bread basket, the corn muffins and giant-sized biscuits her aunt had made that morning kicking off a series of growls deep inside Claire's stomach. "Wow."

"I set aside an extra one for you over there." Diane put the butter on the counter beside the basket, pointing the way toward the solitary corn muffin on a nearby warming tray as she did. "So, did you have fun with the maze, dear?"

With no need for a second invitation, Claire crossed to the counter space beside the oven and retrieved the waiting muffin, the still-warm treat a perfect — yet temporary — answer to the call of her stomach. She bit into the muffin, sans butter, and felt her eyes roll back in her head. "Oh my. This is really, really good, Aunt Diane."

"It must be if it's winning out over a play-by-play of your first Amish maze."

She stopped chewing, swallowed, and returned the uneaten portion of muffin to the tray, the brief escape from reality over. "Oh yes, that."

Diane returned to the griddle and the pancakes that had alerted Claire to the morning menu before she'd even left the second floor of the pristinely kept Victorian. Flipping one pancake after the other, the woman chuckled. "By your response, might I assume that Mose Fisher's corn maze is harder than the ones you've conquered on an annual basis since you were five? Because if it was, I tried to warn you . . ."

"He has an expert trail inside the regular maze," Claire offered before grabbing the muffin once again and finishing it off. "Esther told me about it."

"Was it hard?" Diane reached for a third butter dish, cut a dozen or so thin slices from its stick, and deposited each one on top of a pancake before scooping them off the griddle and transferring them to a waiting plate.

There was a part of Claire that wanted to keep the details from Diane. Tales of murder, after all, had a way of dampening one's mood. And the presence of a frown on Diane's normally happy face wasn't something Claire relished.

But Heavenly was Diane's adopted hometown. She loved its people and its landscape with such genuine conviction and unwavering loyalty that it simply wasn't fair to keep her from the truth. Especially when it was only a matter of time before the news reached the woman's ears, anyway. At least this way, if Claire was the one to break the news, the facts would be accurate . . .

"I was actually making good time in that section when I found it — I mean, *him,*" she finally said.

Diane looked up from the plate of pancakes. "Him?"

Inhaling deeply, Claire searched for the most delicate way to steal her aunt's smile. "Harley Zook."

Diane's smile widened still further before she turned back to the griddle and the pitcher of waiting batter. "Ahhh, Harley. That loose shutter outside the parlor window is hanging much better now because of him."

She stared at her aunt. "Excuse me?"

"Harley Zook. He fixed that shutter I was telling you about last week. He showed up around lunchtime, nodded and smiled at me from the window, and made everything right again. He was here and gone in under twenty minutes."

Eight circles of batter formed into pancakes on the griddle as Claire dissected her aunt's words. "Did Harley fix stuff around here often?"

"All the time, dear. He's so quick and thorough it's really not any surprise people are lining up all over town and beyond to hire him for all sorts of fixes. And the way he's taken that young man under his wing? It's inspiring, really." Diane took a moment from the almost-bubbling circles of batter to liberate the glass pitchers of syrup from the refrigerator and pop them in the microwave for a quick warming.

"Young man?"

"Patrick. Patrick Duggan."

Claire plopped onto one of the two cushioned stools at the breakfast bar and eyed her aunt across the room. "And who is that?"

"The young man Harley has working for him as an apprentice, of sorts."

"Okay . . ."

Diane removed the pitchers from the microwave in time to flip the latest round of pancakes. "Patrick is the son of Carl Duggan."

"Carl Duggan," Claire repeated softly, the name ringing a bell she couldn't quite pinpoint. "Why does that name sound familiar? Have we met?"

"He's the man who killed Harley's brother, John, all those years ago. And that's the crime that —"

"Prompted Jakob to leave the Amish in favor of becoming a policeman," Claire finished for her aunt. "Wow. Harley hired the guy's kid?"

"The day after Carl's arrest, members of the Amish community tried to pay his wife and son a visit. They wanted Rita and Patrick to know that there were no hard feelings." Diane paused, pre–pancake flip, and pointed a spatula at Claire. "The outside world could certainly learn a thing or two about forgiveness from the Amish, wouldn't you say?"

She had to laugh. Only it was laced with sarcasm she didn't bother to hide. *"Forgiveness?"*

Diane returned the spatula to the griddle. "The Amish are pacifists, you know. They believe in turning the other cheek."

"And what about Jakob? They haven't turned the cheek where he's concerned, unless you count turning it *away* from him." She saw her aunt's raised eyebrow and knew it was a reaction to the hint of bitterness in Claire's voice. Her shoulders slumped. "I'm sorry, Diane. I just don't understand how they can work beside a murderer's son, yet they can't forgive their own for leaving to pursue a noble calling. I mean, think about it . . . Jakob became a policeman, not an axe murderer. Though, from what you're saying, he might have been better off in that pursuit."

Diane added the latest round of pancakes to the plate, her lips drooping in an uncharacteristic frown. "The decision to be baptized for the Amish is a commitment. One they hold in the highest regard. If Jakob had left before baptism, he would still be allowed to have a relationship with his family. But he didn't. He chose to be baptized, to become a true member of the Amish community, and *then* he left. That is why they turn their backs. He broke his word."

Claire held up her hands as she slid off the stool. "I hear what you're saying. I even get the idea in its most basic form. I just don't agree with it is all. Especially not for someone as good and decent as Jakob Fisher."

Wordlessly, Diane lifted the pancake platter and pitcher of syrup and made her way toward the dining room, Claire close behind with the juice pitcher and coffeepot. "It's nice to hear you be so passionate about Jakob."

Her aunt's word choice and the poorly disguised hope with which it was spoken brought an instant warmth to Claire's face, a warmth she rushed to extinguish for both herself and Diane. "Any passion you're picking up, Aunt Diane, is for what's right and wrong . . . not a particular person."

Yet even as the words left her mouth, she couldn't help but silently acknowledge the protective feelings the conversation had stirred up inside her heart.

For Jakob.

Any response Diane may have considered was negated by the sound of footsteps coming from the opposite side of the dining room, the six guests who were currently staying at Sleep Heavenly ready for breakfast. Claire would have to tell her aunt about Harley's fate after the meal.

"Good morning," Diane said in greeting as she stepped aside to afford each guest easier access to their spot at the table. "I hope everyone slept well?"

"We've vacationed in many places over the years, wonderful places I shall always remember fondly." Carolyn McCormick took the chair to the right of her husband, Will, and draped a white linen napkin across her lap. "But honestly? I've never felt a greater sense of peace drifting off to sleep than I do here."

The Arizona couple had checked in to Sleep Heavenly two days earlier and both had worn a smile ever since.

"I feel exactly the same way." Roger Claymore gestured toward his wife, Callie. "Why, I just said to Callie last night that Heavenly is so quiet at night you could hear a pin drop one county over."

"It's nice to know *someone* got some sleep around here."

All eyes turned toward the end of the table and the thirty-something couple from Chicago. "Was there something wrong with your accommodations?" Diane rushed to ask while simultaneously sending the platter of pancakes down the far side of the table, followed by the pitcher of syrup.

Megan Reilly paled at the question then rushed to correct an impression she obviously hadn't meant to give. "Oh. No. The room is wonderful, Diane! And that bed is the most comfortable bed I've ever slept in." Shaking her head ever so slightly, she peered at her husband, Kyle, and laughed. "My husband's lack of sleep was because of me, and my constant tossing and turning."

"You'll get no argument from me." Kyle made a face then reached for the juice Claire poured. When he was done, he draped an arm over his wife's shoulder and planted a quick kiss at her temple.

Megan extracted three pancakes from the platter that had reached her hands. "As for why *I* was tossing and turning? That's because all I want to do is find the ideal house for all of us, right here in Heavenly. The kids have spent the first few years of their lives in an apartment with not a lot of room to play. Here, there's room, but I want it to be perfect."

Swapping the now-empty juice pitcher for the coffeepot, Claire took a second lap around the table, filling each and every ceramic mug indicated by its owner. "I would imagine, in this economy, you'd have lots of homes to choose from," Claire said.

"In fact, if I remember from a walk I took last week, there are a few nice homes for sale about four blocks from here. And they all have big yards."

Kyle handed the platter to a waiting Diane, then took the pitcher of syrup from Megan and poured a liberal amount over his pancakes. "That's exactly what I've been saying. And we've seen some really nice houses."

"True," Megan agreed between bites of her breakfast. "But most of my must-have features have been spread out over different houses. If we build something new, all those must-haves and wish-we-coulds would be in one place."

"So then build," Will McCormick mused through the steam that rose from his coffee mug.

Diane disappeared into the kitchen only to return seconds later with a plate of crisp bacon in one hand and the basket of rolls in the other. "New home developments are rare in Heavenly. In fact, there are only three I can think of off the top of my head."

Megan's eyes lit up. "Three?"

"Two here on the English side of town. One on the Amish side."

"That must be the one from yesterday morning," Kyle said, looking at his wife.

"You know the one I'm talking about . . ."

Claire looked up from the bacon distribution she'd silently undertaken and studied her aunt on the opposite side of the table. "There's *land* on the Amish side?"

"Technically, it's not inside the city limits of Heavenly, but it's still within the school district boundaries and those of all public services," Diane explained. "Quite a few of the Amish have tried to buy it over the years, but after a slight glitch with the sewers, the owner is confident it'll make more money being divided and sold for custom homes."

"The location is perfect," Megan gushed.

"Not perfect enough," Kyle corrected. "Which is why we're still looking, remember?"

Megan set her fork beside her plate and addressed Diane with slightly slumped shoulders. "The Realtor didn't show us the other two developments. Are they for custom homes, too?"

At Diane's nod, Megan turned to her husband with obvious excitement in her voice. "Can we ask Alan to show us those today?"

"I don't see why not." Kyle broke eye contact with his wife long enough to look up at Claire in visible appreciation of the three large pieces of bacon she placed on his plate, all vestiges of fatigue suddenly gone from his otherwise handsome face.

That settled, Will McCormick pushed his empty plate forward and leaned back in his seat. "I'd like to ask you something, Diane, if I may?"

"Of course, Will." Diane took one final glance around the table then surrendered her full attention to the balding retiree. "What would you like to know?"

"The wife and I went for a ride through the Amish countryside yesterday and noticed two different farmhouses undergoing renovations. Both appeared to be adding an entire room." Will looked to his wife for confirmation of his observation, her nod letting him know he was on the right track. "What I wonder is whether the Amish have to go through the permit process the rest of us have to go through when we add so much as a shed to our properties."

Diane smoothed her hand down the sides of her simple white apron then lowered herself to the edge of an extra chair not far from the table. "If they were truly adding on, with a new bedroom or larger kitchen . . . sure. They'd be expected to follow the same ordinances as everyone else in Heavenly. But, in light of it being nearly

November, I think it's safe to say those were temporary structures that you saw."

Will's brows furrowed. "They were constructing them of wood just like a regular home addition."

"At this time of year — known as wedding season in the Amish community — you'll see additions like that being added to homes all the time. They are, however, temporary, added for the sole purpose of accommodating what will sometimes be as much as several hundred people for a wedding."

"They have the wedding in their home?" Carolyn asked around an audible intake of air. "Does that mean the mother of the bride has to cook for all of those people, too?"

Diane smiled. "Yes, it does. A wedding is a time for celebration within the Amish community. Food and visiting go hand in hand."

"Wow." Callie Claymore waved a hand in her husband's direction and giggled. "And your mother thought *our* wedding at the club was hard work . . ."

"So the structure will come back down once the wedding is over?" Will asked. At Diane's nod, he continued. "And how does the whole farm thing work? Does the oldest son get his father's farm when he marries?"

Claire chimed in, the answer one she herself had learned fairly recently. "Actually, it's the *youngest* son who gets the farm. They do this because more times than not, there are still a slew of siblings at home when the oldest child gets married."

"Hmmm. I never thought of that, but it makes perfect sense." Will motioned to his empty coffee mug and rewarded Claire's quick response with a warm thank-you and a wide smile. "So then what? The oldest son has to buy his own farm?"

"If there's one available in the area, yes. If not, he must decide whether to move out of state to a different Amish community with more readily available land, or pursue a different occupation altogether."

"And the wife?" Callie interjected. "Does she have a say?"

Diane shrugged then rose to her feet to begin the process of gathering dirty plates from the table. "I imagine they talk about things together. But once an Amish girl marries, she does not work outside the home. Her attention is to be focused on her husband and the children they will soon have."

Claire heard the gasp as it left her lips, sensed the questioning eyes that followed suit. Yet all she could truly focus on was Diane's words and the rush of sadness they started.

"So . . . when Esther and Eli marry, Esther won't be able to work at Heavenly Treasures with me anymore?" she whispered past the lump forming in her throat.

"When that day comes, no, she won't be able to keep working with you. But like anything else in life, dear, we'll cross that bridge when we come to it."

Claire blinked rapidly against the tears that pricked the corners of her eyes; the quiet and steady friendship she'd found in her Amish employee was on the verge of being tested by the strains of real life.

It was a test many friendships faced, yet theirs had the added twist of having formed across, and in spite of, two very different worlds. With the common ground of Heavenly Treasures removed from the equation, what would happen?

"Claire? Are you okay?" Diane hurried around the table. "Is there something wrong?"

Inhaling deeply, Claire brought her aunt up to speed on Esther's news, the implication of her friend's engagement igniting a foggy haze around her heart. "Six weeks from now, if I'm still lucky enough to even

51

have a bridge, we'll be on the other side of it."

CHAPTER 4

She was just tossing a bag of trash into the container behind Heavenly Treasures when she heard the telltale *clip-clop* of Eli's buggy as it turned into the alley separating Claire's gift shop from the Amish-owned bake shop next door. Looking over her shoulder, Claire raised her hand in greeting only to let it fall back down to her side at her incorrect assumption.

Nearly four weeks had come and gone since Eli's older brother, Benjamin, had made any of the half-dozen or so daily runs between the Miller's farm and Shoo Fly Bake Shoppe. Milk was still delivered each morning, pie boxes were still assembled each evening, and Ruth — Eli's twin sister — was still looked after and assisted during Shoo Fly Bake Shoppe's busiest spurts, but lately, those tasks had fallen completely on Eli.

Sure, she could chalk Eli's stepped-up

presence to the young man's desire to see Esther as many times throughout the day as possible, but when he still showed up again and again on days Esther wasn't working, Claire knew it pointed to more. Much more.

She forced her breathing to remain steady despite the near Pavlovian response to Ben's presence that had her heart beating faster and her hands growing damper by the minute. Somehow, she'd hoped the time apart would have dulled her senses where the handsome Amish man was concerned, but reality, and the way the late-morning sun shimmered off his deep blue eyes, was rapidly proving otherwise.

Wiping her moist hands against the sides of her formfitting black trousers, Claire willed her feet toward the buggy and her mouth into some semblance of a natural smile. "Ben! It's so good to see you."

The tall, lanky man with the clean-shaven face, high cheekbones, and scrap of dark brown hair visible beneath his hat jumped down from his seat behind the horses and held out his hand to Claire. "Yah. It is good to see you, too."

Her hand disappeared inside his strong, callused counterpart, the tingle of his touch solidifying the fact her heart hadn't completely caught up with her head where Benjamin Miller was concerned. Oh, she'd made the right choice turning down his suggestion of a life together. One only had to look at the rippling effects across Jakob's life to know what leaving the Amish community after baptism would do to Ben and the relationships he treasured with his siblings. But just because her head — and even some of her heart — knew she'd done what was best, it didn't mean she stopped wondering from time to time.

Ben was thoughtful in a way few people were. He was kind in a way that made everyone feel like they mattered. And, even more importantly, he cared enough to ask *and* to listen — a winning combination in Claire's book after coming from a marriage where any and all of those traits fell a distant second to climbing the corporate ladder.

"Nice day we are having, yah?"

She followed his finger upward, the warmth of the sun on her face momentarily chasing the autumn nip from her skin. "Beautiful."

Feeling his gaze shift in her direction, she cast about for something to say that could lead them back to the quiet friendship they'd forged and she still cherished.

"I imagine the Miller family is thrilled at

the notion of Eli and Esther getting married," she said, wincing inwardly at the audible hitch to her voice.

For a long moment, Ben said nothing, his eyes searching her face with a calming intensity. Then, finally, "You do not *want* them to marry?"

Shaking her head against the notion, she rushed to explain the potpourri of feelings Esther and Eli's engagement had stirred inside her. "Oh, Ben, I couldn't be happier for Esther and Eli. There's a tenderness between them that makes me happy every time I see them together. It's as if the way they look at each other now is some sort of magical window that allows me to see thirty years into their future . . . and they're still smiling, still in love."

"This is good, yah?"

She wandered over to the back stoop of her shop and lowered herself onto the top step. "It's wonderful, Ben. I was beside myself with excitement when Esther told me last night."

"What changed?"

Slowly, she lifted her gaze until it mingled with his, the way in which he was able to see straight into her heart as surprising as ever. "I don't know how you do that."

His dark brows rose ever so slightly beneath the rim of his hat. "I do not know what you mean, Claire."

She considered explaining, pointing to his ability to read her as one of the many reasons why her heart still fluttered every time she saw him, but, in the end, she opted to get to the point. "I didn't realize, until my aunt pointed it out this morning, that I'd lose Esther here at the shop. I . . . I guess the thought of her not being here hurts a little."

"Hurts?"

"During those first six months I was here in Heavenly, I pretty much stayed inside the inn — helping Diane, getting acclimated to her daily tasks, and sharing countless heart-to-heart talks. Sometimes, I'd go for walks by myself, but other than Diane and the guests that came and went from the inn, I didn't really have any friends here." She fiddled with the sleeves of her teal green blouse as her thoughts traveled backward along with her words. "But it wasn't until I opened this place and hired Esther that I truly felt as if Heavenly was my home, too. Suddenly, I had my dream job *and* my first real friend. And now, three months later, I'm poised to lose them both."

"Both?"

Realizing her mistake, she rushed to

clarify her words before she revealed too much. "No, no . . . just Esther."

"Esther will not be far. Eli is to stay in Heavenly if it is God's will."

She closed her eyes against the image of Eli and Esther having to move north or west to find a farm, and focused on the only aspect she could fathom at the moment. "Even if she's down the road, I won't be seeing her nearly every day the way I do now. She'll be busy with her new life, and I will be . . ." Her words petered off only to return with a defiant shake of her head. "When she is off and married, we won't be able to laugh at the day's funny moments together. She won't be able to teach me Pennsylvania Dutch the way I've been hoping she would."

Ben claimed the empty step beside Claire, propping his forearms against his thighs as he did. "I do not work at shop with you."

"I know that," she said, shooting a quizzical look in his direction.

"Jakob does not work in shop with you."

She shrugged. "No."

"Ruth works there" — he jutted his chin in the direction of Shoo Fly Bake Shoppe across the alleyway, the aroma of a freshly baked apple pie wafting through the bakery's screened door — "not here with you."

"If she did, I'd be big as a house from all those delicious treats she makes," Claire said, laughing. Then, turning her body to the side, she reestablished eye contact with Ben. "I don't understand where you're going with all of this."

Ben cleared his throat once, twice. "Ruth is your friend, yah? Jakob is your friend, yah? *I . . . I* am your friend, yah?"

At the unexpected hesitation in his voice, she reached for his hand and gave it a quick but gentle squeeze. "Yes, you are all my friends."

He looked down at the place where her hand had been moments earlier, then looked away, his Adam's apple bobbing.

"Ben?"

Finally, he looked back, a hooded effect across his otherwise clear blue eyes. "Esther does not need the shop to be your friend."

She smiled through the day's second round of tears, Ben's simple yet heartfelt words proving to be exactly what she needed to hear. "Thank you, Ben," she whispered.

"It is nothing." He rose to his feet, the snort of his horse stealing his attention long enough for Claire to compose herself. "Eli was hitching up the buggy to look after Ruth, but I said no, I would do it today."

Jumping to her feet, she nodded. "Then

I'll leave you to it." She reached for the handle of her own screened door. "It was good to see you again. I've missed you."

He held up his hand, his eyes wide. "You do not understand. I told Eli I would come this time so I could check on *you*, too."

"Me?" she asked, releasing her hold on the door. "But why?"

"Eli said you found Zook's body in maze. He said you screamed."

"Oh. That." She took in a deep breath then let it go, slowly. "I'm surprised the whole town didn't hear me scream when I found him like that."

"And now?"

"It's not something I'll soon forget, I'm sure, but I'm okay." She met his worried expression with what she hoped was a re-assuring smile then felt it fade as the events of the previous night took center stage in her thoughts. "It is disheartening to hear of any murder. But to learn it is the brother of another murder victim is hard to compre-hend."

"Duggan is in jail. He could not have murdered Harley."

"I know, but I'd be lying if I didn't say it would be easier on Jakob if this murder could be hung on this Duggan fellow, too."

Ben's head snapped up. "I do not understand. Does Jakob not have suspects?"

She stepped down to the cobblestoned alleyway, Jakob's failure to return her call from that morning sending a renewed shiver down her spine. Jakob was struggling. That, she knew already. But, in the cold light of day, the task of finding Harley's killer and bringing him to justice had to be weighing on the detective in a way no previous case ever had. Especially when the most likely suspect shared not only his last name but also his DNA.

"He has one. But it's not one even an excommunicated son would ever want to consider."

A dark cloud of emotion rolled across Ben's face just before he fisted his hands and turned toward his waiting horse. "I must go."

"Ben?" She half walked, half ran after him, the abrupt change in his demeanor catching her by surprise. "Ben? What's wrong?"

He hoisted himself onto the driver's seat of his buggy and grabbed hold of the reins. "It is as I told Eli and many others in my community last night. Mose Fisher did not kill Harley Zook."

She stared up at him. "How can you be so sure?"

"Mose Fisher would not murder. It is not

the Amish way."

"Is it the Amish way to be angry?"

He softened his grip ever so slightly. "We do not show anger."

"Eli said Mose was angry at Harley for extending a job offer to Isaac."

"Eli should mind his tongue!"

Claire shifted from foot to foot under the weight and force of Ben's words. "Eli was asked a question by a detective, Ben. He did not take joy in answering, but he did so with the truth. I commend him for that. Besides, if Mose is not guilty, nothing Eli said will make a difference."

Again, Ben firmed up his hold on the reins, gently guiding the horse and buggy down the alley toward Lighted Way — the quaint shop-lined thoroughfare that connected the English and Amish sides of Heavenly, melding the two worlds in almost seamless fashion. When he reached the end, he stopped. "Mose Fisher did not murder Harley Zook. It does not matter that he was bitter about so much. It does not matter that he had bursts of anger. Mose Fisher would not play God for any reason." Pulling his gaze from Claire, he fixed it, instead, on the fields in the distance. "I will prove this to my community. I will prove this to

Jakob. And I will prove this to you, Claire, as well."

CHAPTER 5

"Oh, Esther, this footstool is exquisite!" Claire bent over the hand-painted wooden step and marveled at the winter scene. The snow-covered bridge that graced the surface looked so real, she found herself wishing for a sweater and a mug of hot chocolate. "I can't imagine anyone actually stepping on it."

Smoothing her slender hand down the sides of her pale blue, white-aproned dress, Esther merely pointed to the next item on the counter. "I made the dolls this time."

Claire stepped to her right and scooped up two of the dozen faceless Amish dolls into her arms. "You made them?"

"Yah. When she is not painting, Mamm has been busy canning. I saw that we had only two dolls here, so I made these, instead. Do you like?"

Slowly, Claire turned each doll over in her hands, the traditional Amish dress and kapp soliciting a smile from her lips despite the doll's lack of one. "They're every bit as good as your mom's."

Esther's eyes widened. "You think so?"

"How could I not?" Swapping the two dolls in her hands for the two still on the table, Claire was pleased to find the attention to detail every bit as good as the first pair. "You do beautiful work, Esther. With *everything* you make for the store."

Dropping her head ever so slightly, Esther stared down at the floor, her uncharacteristic silence prompting Claire to set the dolls down. "Esther? Is everything okay?"

"I do not want to be ungrateful."

She drew back. "Ungrateful? You? Why would you say something like that?"

Esther looked up with eyes that glistened. "All I have wanted is to marry Eli. For my father to see him as a good man."

"Okay . . ."

"Both things have happened," Esther whispered, her voice choked with emotion. "I should be happy, but I am not."

Claire felt her mouth gape and rushed to close it for fear her reaction would be the thing that pushed a teetering Esther off the edge. Instead, Claire tucked her hand inside her friend's arm and led her to the pair of stools on the other side of the counter. For now, the shop was quiet thanks to the lunchtime lull that transferred the tourist traffic to the handful of cafés and quaint eateries along Lighted Way. "Did you and Eli have a fight?"

Esther slapped a hand to her own mouth and shook her head, the muffled effect on her words making Claire lean closer. "No. No. Eli and I, we do not fight. Ever."

She tried not to look at all of the tasks she needed to do around the shop — the pricing of Martha and Esther's new items, the changing out of the front window display for the upcoming Thanksgiving season, and the letter to her landlord she dreaded writing — and focused, instead, on the troubled girl seated on the next stool. "Then why aren't you happy, Esther?"

Dropping her hand into her lap, Esther picked at an imaginary piece of lint rather than answer.

"Esther?" Claire nudged her friend's chin upward with her forefinger. "Talk to me."

"I . . . I am eager t-to be Eli's wife," Esther stammered, "but I will miss being here . . . with you each day."

Claire willed herself to remain upbeat, to squelch the like-minded feelings she had been inwardly moping about all morning. Somehow, someway, she and Esther would remain close just as Ben had said. She had to believe that. For Esther and for herself.

"I will still make things for the store, of course," Esther rushed to add. "But I will not be here to work and to laugh."

"That makes two of us." She hadn't realized she'd spoken aloud until she looked up and saw Esther eyeing her curiously.

"Claire?"

"We'll figure something out, Esther . . . no matter what happens. I promise." It was a promise she knew she shouldn't be making, but she couldn't help herself. The last thing she needed to throw on Esther at that moment was the reality of Heavenly Treasures' pending demise.

The faintest hint of a smile appeared at the corners of Esther's mouth. "Perhaps you could come to dinner sometimes. I know Eli would be pleased if you did."

"Then we can laugh together there, right?"

The smile moved to the young woman's large hazel eyes, igniting the amber flecks that underscored her kinship with Jakob. "Yah!"

"Then we'll be okay, Esther." She took a moment to catch a much-needed breath, the sentiment Ben had shared only hours earlier resurfacing in her heart at just the right time. "We're friends, Esther. The only thing that can change that is us."

"Then it is settled. We do not need this shop to be friends."

"No, we don't," Claire rasped.

"You will come to the wedding, yah?"

She pushed the fog of emotion from her throat and smiled at her friend. "I wouldn't miss it for the world."

"It will be the second Tuesday in December."

Claire liberated a red marker from the can beside the register and marked the date on the calendar with a big heart. "Can I ask a question?"

"Of course."

"Why a Tuesday? Isn't that a work day for your community?"

Esther clasped her hands together in her lap and sat up tall. "Wedding season happens after the fall harvest. That is why it does not interfere with work. The reason we marry on Tuesdays and Thursdays is for benches."

Claire returned the marker to the can and faced Esther once again. "Benches?"

"Yah. Monday and Wednesday is when the benches travel in the bench wagon to the home where the wedding will be. On Saturday they are to travel again for Sunday worship."

It made sense. Basic, common sense.

With the Amish, there really wasn't any other way.

"There will be much to do to get ready."

"How many people will be there?" Claire asked.

"Mamm thinks it will be three hundred."

This time, she didn't shut her mouth in time. "Uh . . . three hundred?"

Esther shrugged. "It could be less, it could be more."

"And Martha will be expected to feed all of those people . . . in your home?"

"Yah. But I will help. My sisters will help. Neighbors, too."

"Three hundred people eat a lot of food!"

Esther reached into her satchel and retrieved a sheet of folded paper. With careful fingers, the young woman unfolded it and handed it to Claire. "Mamm and I made a list last night."

"List?" Dropping her gaze from Esther to the paper, Claire gasped at the sheer volume of food. "Thirty-eight chickens for the roast? Thirty-eight loaves of bread for the filling? Four buckets of mashed potatoes? Three-fourths of a bushel of cabbage for coleslaw?" She followed the list with her finger, the enormity of the task facing the Kings on Esther's wedding day mind-numbing at best. "Twenty-two dozen donuts? Ten pounds of confectioner's sugar to dip the donuts in? Thirty custard pies?"

"We will be busy," Esther mused, nodding along with the list Claire continued to narrate aloud. "Only, there is also worry."

She looked up from the paper and made a face. "If I had to prepare all of this, I'd be worried, too."

"Not for food. For Dawdy."

And just like that, Esther's wedding faded from Claire's thoughts. She quietly folded the list and handed it back to her friend. "I don't really know what to say about that, Esther. Is your mom holding up okay?"

Esther slid off the stool and wandered around the counter, her destination obviously unclear. Midway across the shop, though, she turned around. "Mamm does not want to believe her dat could do something like that, but she saw his anger. Dat saw his anger. All saw his anger. Dawdy did not think kindly on Mr. Zook."

"Was your grandfather ever shunned for that anger?" she asked, curious.

"Yah. But Benjamin always made it right. He calmed Dawdy into seeking forgiveness for his ways. He did this again and again."

Esther's words didn't really come as any big surprise. Ben himself had alluded to a

70

close tie with Jakob's father, but, still, Claire couldn't help but cringe at the rippling effect such a bond would have across the investigation. Looking to the father he hadn't spoken to in sixteen years as a murder suspect would be hard enough on Jakob. Having the man he considered a rival for his father's respect throughout his childhood playing the role of champion was sure to make things worse.

It was a subject she felt best to keep from Esther. What, exactly, Esther knew about her uncle's relationship with her grandfather, beyond the excommunication part, she didn't know. But whatever the case, it wasn't Claire's place to fill in blanks or offer opinions. She wasn't Amish. She didn't understand all the ins and outs.

But she had to say *something.* Something to keep Esther's focus where it should be . . .

"I do not know what happened to Harley Zook, Esther. But I do know that Jakob is a fair man. He is not one to rush to judgment. On anyone."

The door-mounted bell at the front of the shop let them know their alone-time was over. The lunch crowd was slowly heading toward the street and the various stores that lined it, their stomachs satisfied. "Good afternoon. Welcome to Heavenly Treasures . . ."

The shy greeting Claire had come to associate with Esther trailed from her employee's lips as Jakob stepped into the shop, his shoulders heavy. "Esther," he said with a slight tip of his head before turning to greet Claire. "How are you feeling this morning? Did you get any sleep?"

More than anything, she wanted to reach out, smooth the worry from the man's face. But she couldn't. Not there. Not in front of Esther. Instead, she did the only thing she could. She gave an answer she hoped would alleviate at least some of his tangible anguish. "It took a while. But I did manage to fall asleep." She swept her hand toward the back of the shop that led to a tiny stockroom, her even tinier office, and the door to the alleyway. "Would you like a cup of coffee? Or maybe a donut? I picked up a half dozen at Ruth's place this morning and there are still four left."

He waved off her request, adding a dimple-free smile to his response. "No, thank you, Claire." Then, standing in the same spot, he cast an uneasy glance in his niece's direction, as if he was afraid the events of the previous night had set them back from their place of tentative smiles and quick waves.

Esther took in the floor, then Claire. "Did you tell my uncle?"

"Tell your uncle?" she parroted in confusion before the meaning behind her friend's words grew clear. "Oh! No . . . Things were crazy last night with finding Harley . . ." She shook her head, redirecting the conversation from a path none of them wanted to go down at that moment. "Shall I tell him now?"

Jakob looked from one to the other, his brow furrowed. "Tell me what?"

At Esther's quick nod, Claire closed the gap between herself and Jakob, the change in tone one she was anxious to share with a man who was in dire need of a little happy news. "Eli has asked for Esther's hand in marriage."

The dimples that had, only moments earlier, been missing in action sprang to the surface of Jakob's cheeks. "And?" he asked Claire while focusing entirely on his niece.

Esther's answer came by way of the tiniest hop and the shortest, faintest squeal Claire had ever heard. But it was enough. Jakob clapped his hands with pleasure. "Esther, that is wonderful news! Absolutely wonderful! Congratulations! Eli is a lucky, lucky man."

For a moment, Claire didn't think Esther

was going to say anything, but, in the blink of an eye, Esther's smile was followed by a whispered thank-you and a split second of heartfelt eye contact between the pair. Then, Esther was gone, disappearing out into the alley as Eli's horse drew to a stop outside the shop's side window. Claire watched her go, reveling in the beauty of a moment that had Jakob looking happier than he had in weeks. Yet when she turned back to enjoy the smile for a second time, she found that it had been dulled by the visible mist in his eyes.

"Jakob? What's wrong? I thought you'd be happy that she spoke to you, that she wanted you to know her big news."

He swiped a hurried hand across his eyes and did his best to re-create the smile that only moments earlier had been so genuine. "I am happy for Esther and for Eli. The love they have for each other is plain as day. For that, I am grateful."

"Then why am I sensing you're sad, too?"

Seconds passed before he finally answered, the huskiness of his voice a dead giveaway to the emotion he was fighting to keep in check. "Because of my choice, I will not be invited to share in Esther and Eli's day."

CHAPTER 6

Diane Weatherly was many things. She was caring, generous, welcoming, and loving, to name a few. But subtle? That she wasn't. When it came to Claire's romantic future, Diane was like a Mack Truck driving through Claire's confused thoughts and emotions with one singular suitor in mind.

What Claire had been thinking, then, when she invited the detective to dinner at the inn, was mind-boggling at best. Especially when the look Diane still sported nearly an hour after the meal's conclusion was enough to send shivers down her niece's spine.

Still, though, she'd done the right thing. Jakob could use a friend, someone who'd listen when he needed an ear, smile when he needed a distraction, and offer a few heartfelt words of encouragement amid the internal debate she knew raged inside. If stepping in to fill that role added fuel to the

Claire-belongs-with-Jakob fire Diane had been stoking for months, then so be it. Claire could always toss dirt on it at a later date.

Or so she told herself . . .

"Dinner was fantastic, Diane." Jakob dropped onto the center of the rose-colored couch and smiled at the now-beaming woman on the other side of the candlelit parlor. "I can see why this place is booked nearly three hundred and sixty-five days a year."

"You're welcome anytime, dear," Diane enthused before pointing Claire toward the empty cushion beside Jakob. "Claire, please sit. You look tired."

She considered protesting — the woman's true intentions were far more about placing Claire within close proximity of Jakob than providing relief from a long and trying day — but, in the end, she did as she was told. After all, Claire's main concern at that moment was Jakob.

"I was shocked when Claire finally told me about Harley Zook this morning," Diane continued, her focus shifting back to Jakob. "I can't imagine anyone wanting to hurt such a good and decent man. Are there any suspects?"

Claire cringed inwardly at the question,

instantly regretting her tell-and-run following breakfast that morning. If she'd had more time to walk her aunt through the aftermath of finding Harley's body, she could have explained the feared connection to Mose Fisher. But if Jakob was thrown off by the question, it didn't show, the detective merely leaning forward to address at least part of the sixty-something's statement. "Did you know Harley well?" he asked quietly.

Returning her coffee mug to the end table, Diane nodded slowly. "I did. He has been helping me keep things in order here at the inn for a few years now. He was a hard worker. Quick, yet thorough."

"What kind of work did he do around here?"

"Anything and everything." Diane scooted to the edge of her lounge chair and stood, the built-in bookcases that lined nearly half of the room taunting her with a speck of missed dust only she or Claire would notice. "Last week, he was out here fixing *that* window." She pointed toward the large plate glass window that looked out over the darkened fields of Heavenly. "Yesterday morning he replaced a warped step by the back door. Whatever I needed, he fixed — broken hinges, wobbly chairs, creaky steps, you name it. In fact, without Harley, I'm not sure what I would have done except go broke using a contractor from Breeze Point."

"So Harley was a fix-it man?" Jakob reached for the coat he'd draped across the arm of the couch and rustled around in the pocket for a small notepad and pen.

Diane pulled a dust cloth from her apron pocket and ran it along the middle shelf, turning back to Jakob with a shrug when she was done. "I think it was about three years ago when he first showed up here with a toolbox in tow. He'd heard through the grapevine that I wanted to add window boxes around the inn. He listened to what I wanted in terms of size and quoted me a good price. I hired him on the spot. By the end of the day, I had flower boxes."

"Harley made those?" Claire echoed.

At Diane's nod, Jakob continued. "And that's when you started hiring him to do odd jobs around here?"

"He'd done such wonderful work, it made perfect sense." Diane wandered around the room, her earlier angst upon hearing the news of Harley's murder returning, in spades. "It got to a point where it became obvious that *this* was what he should be doing."

Jakob looked up from his notepad. "You mean working here at the inn?"

"No." Diane stopped in front of the window and gazed out at fields she'd seen a million times before. "Working with his hands . . . fixing things . . . building things. For people like me — people who simply don't have the ability or the time to tackle those kinds of jobs."

Claire opened her mouth to speak only to shut it again as Diane turned and sighed. "One only had to watch that man for five minutes to know he was much happier with tools in his hand than he was carting milk around."

"Milk?" Claire echoed.

It was Jakob's turn to nod. "Harley's brother, John, was a dairy farmer. Harley took over the operation after John's murder." At the memory, Jakob's shoulders hunched forward. "That's what the Amish do in the wake of tragedy. They step forward and shoulder whatever needs to be shouldered."

"But his shoulders grew weary after sixteen some odd years," Diane said as she perched on the edge of her chair once again. "The days of milking a cow straight into a can for drinking are long gone. Regulations and advances in technology have changed many things for Amish dairy farmers."

"So he did both?"

"For a while, yes. But eventually the notion of working out of his buggy and going from house to house fixing things won out for Harley." Diane fidgeted with the simple design along the hem of her skirt, her words beginning to pick up speed. "So, he started a mobile carpentry business mostly on my word of mouth. He got so busy so fast he ended up hiring an apprentice last month. Then, when they were here the other day working on the back step, he told me your brother, Isaac, had decided to come on board as a partner."

Jakob's gaze dropped to his notepad, yet he wrote nothing, Eli's take on Isaac's decision no doubt circling around in the detective's thoughts.

"It is funny how a few window boxes could lead to such a booming business, isn't it?" Diane mused as a slight smile played across her lips. "But Harley always made sure to fit me in when I needed something. He said I was his first customer and that entitled me to special treatment for life."

"And knowing Harley the way I did, he'd have made good on his word." Jakob dragged his pen across the spiral edge of the pad and released a pent-up burst of air.

"Zook was nothing if not loyal."

Diane paused mid-nod. "What will happen to his cows now that there's no one around to see that they get home?"

"His cows?" Jakob parroted, looking up.

"For such big animals, they sure can be stealthy, can't they?"

"Stealthy?"

"One or the other was escaping from Harley's field all the time." Diane sandwiched her face between her hands. "I think it was Jackie who was the last to sneak off the day he fixed my shutter."

"Actually, if Jackie was a few days ago, then that honor would have to go to Mary now," Jakob corrected before rising to his feet and staring up at the ceiling.

"Mary — wait!" Claire, too, stood, the pre-maze portion of the previous evening finally pushing its way to the foreground of her thoughts. "You're talking about the cow we found on the side of the road yesterday, aren't you? You said that was Harley's cow."

Jakob cupped a hand to his mouth then let it slide slowly down his chin. "That's right. I found out, after you left, that her name is Mary. At least that's what one of Hochstetler's boys told me when he walked through the field and voluntarily relieved me of cow-watching duties."

"So you didn't bring her back to Harley yourself?"

"No. Though now I have to wonder if Harley might still be alive if I had."

Claire took hold of Jakob's forearm and turned him. "Stop that. Harley was in the middle of the maze when I found him. You and I both know that even if you *had* been on his farm as much as an hour or so earlier, it wouldn't have made a difference."

"Claire is right, Jakob. There is only one person to blame for what happened to Harley. And with you on the case, that person will be in jail soon."

Claire saw Jakob swallow once, twice, and knew his thoughts had moved on to his father, the lines around his eyes deepening by the second. She rushed to change the subject. "So how could two cows go loose in less than a week?"

"Holes, I think."

Jakob's focus snapped back toward Diane. "Holes?"

"That's the only reason I can figure those cows would keep getting out. That or he failed to secure his fence on a near-daily basis. He laughed it off most days, saying his girls could use a little change of scenery once in a while. But he lost valuable work hours every time he had to go round one up and walk it home."

"Well, then, I guess I'll be doing a little fence patching myself come morning." Jakob retrieved his coat from the armrest and slipped it on, the smile he flashed at first Diane and then Claire stopping just short of his eyes. "I can't thank you enough for dinner tonight. It was delicious."

"You're welcome anytime, Jakob."

"Thank you, Diane." Turning to Claire, he hooked his thumb toward the front hallway. "Walk me out?"

She fell into step beside him, an unending lineup of unasked questions filtering through her thoughts as she did. "I was kind of hoping we'd have a little time alone this evening."

Jakob stopped halfway across the entryway and turned, his brow cocked upward in restrained surprise. "Oh?"

"I . . . I've been worried about you. How are you holding up?"

He raked a hand through his crop of blond hair and stepped closer to Claire. "Aww, man, I never called you back this morning, did I?" At her half head shake, half shrug, he reached for her hand and held it gingerly inside his own. "I got the message from the dispatcher but I was out at the crime scene most of the morning . . .

83

hoping to find something, anything, that will keep me from having to question my father."

"It'll be okay, Jakob."

"Last night, in my bed, I tried to tell myself that same thing. Even managed to do a fairly decent job convincing myself, too. But then, out at the scene this morning, I realized I was being naïve when Amish men — men who have known my father for years — are whispering my father's name in conjunction with news of Harley's murder."

"Benjamin said something to that effect this morning." As soon as the words left her mouth she regretted them. Jakob was a fair man and a good detective, but when it came to the mere mention of Eli's older brother, he reverted back to memories of a childhood where he'd never measured up to Isaiah Miller's boy. The fact that it was Jakob's own father holding the yardstick only made it all the more painful.

"You spoke to Ben this morning?"

"He'd heard what happened at the maze and he wanted to make sure I was okay."

Rolling his eyes, Jakob released her hand and stepped back. "Anything else?"

"Not really. He's convinced your father had nothing to do with what happened to Harley Zook, though."

"From what I gathered this morning, he

might be one of the only Amish in Heavenly to believe that." Like a balloon that had suddenly met its fate against a needle, Jakob's shoulders sunk in defeat. "I don't know how to do this, Claire. I don't know how to find the answers I need without confronting a man who wants nothing to do with me."

This time it was Claire who reached for Jakob's hand and held it tightly. "I'm here to help in any way I can. I could talk to Mose, I could ask Esther and Eli some more questions if you'd like, or I could simply listen when you need to vent. Just let me know what you need and I'll be happy to do whatever I can to help."

She glanced up only to look away at the intensity she saw in his eyes. Had she said too much? Tipped her hand — whatever hand that was — too far?

"How are you with patching fences?" he finally asked.

"Excuse me?"

"When I left the Amish, Harley Zook was the only member of the community who refused to turn his back on me. The least I can do — aside from finding his killer — is look in on his cows until a new owner is found."

CHAPTER 7

The sun was just rising into its mid-morning position when Jakob turned onto the long dirt driveway belonging to the late Harley Zook. Claire pressed her forehead to the passenger side window and peered out at the line of trees separating the Amish farm from the outside world.

"You don't think Esther and Eli will end up moving north or west, do you?" she asked, taking in the occasional rusting metal box visible through breaks in the foliage. "Eli is a go-getter for sure, but he's also a farmer at heart."

The car slowed as they approached a bend in the path, Jakob's attention flitting between the deceased's property and Claire's question. "I don't know. I really don't. I sure hope they stick around for Martha and Abram. But when there's no farmland to be had, it certainly makes that option a bit tougher to exercise."

"Maybe they could buy *that.*" She pointed through gaps in the trees to a stretch of vacant land on the other side. "It certainly doesn't look like it would be missed."

"Won't happen. There's more money to be had in building homes. Add to that the fact that more homeowners bring more tax revenue for the county and, well, suffice it to say Eli will need to consider other income-producing options if he and Esther hope to stay in Heavenly."

Jakob was right. Her sitting there, brewing over the unfairness of things, wasn't going to change anything. Except, perhaps, her mood . . .

"Sorry. I didn't mean to get all mopey on you like that." Claire straightened in her seat, changing her view to the simple yet sturdy fence that lined the edges of Zook's farm. In the distance, Holsteins grazed, their mouths moving constantly despite the lack of any discernible food source. Ahead and to their left stood a long, white, meticulously kept building Jakob referred to as the cows' milking quarters — the bread and butter of the victim's farm.

"Looks like the girls lived well out here . . ." His words morphed into a long, low whistle as he slowed to a stop beside a not-so-meticulously kept farmhouse. "Certainly better than Zook, it seems."

She felt her jaw slack open as she, too, took in the peeling paint around the windows, the sagging roof atop the front porch, and the rotting stairs that led to the misshapen door. Along a rural road anywhere else in the country, she wouldn't have batted an eye. But an Amish farmhouse? In Lancaster County? It didn't fit . . .

"Harley *was* still Amish, wasn't he?" she finally asked, the question rather rhetorical against the haunting memory of the body she found propped against a shovel barely thirty-six hours earlier. "I-I didn't know there were Amish who lived so" — she stopped, swallowed — "so . . . *sloppy.*"

"Harley always was one to march to a different drum. But somehow, he was still respected. By everyone but Mose Fisher, anyway." Jakob began shaking his head even before he finished uttering his father's name aloud, his hand guiding her focus away from his pained expression and back to the house. "Good thing he worked his fix-it business from his buggy, huh? Because I'm thinking this place probably would have scared off any and all prospective customers."

And it was true. If a potential client had seen Harley's house, they'd have doubted his prowess with a hammer and nails. Yet, according to items Diane had pointed out around the inn, the man was talented with his hands. Some might even say gifted if you took into account items he built rather than fixed.

"I knew a reporter once. He wrote all sorts of articles — crime, features, hard news, you name it. But ask him to write a letter or anything outside his work hours, and it was like pulling teeth. He used to say the last thing he wanted to do on his own time was write." Claire reached for the toolbox she'd set on the floor between her feet. "Maybe that's how Harley felt about fixing things. He could do it for work, but on his own time he'd rather take care of his cows."

She moved the toolbox to her lap then shifted in the seat to afford a better view of Jakob. "I mean, if you think about it, running a dairy farm is a full-time job for many of the Amish in this area, isn't it? But for Harley it was one of two jobs."

"True." He liberated the box from her lap and jerked his head toward his door and the metal fence beyond. "So? Should we find Mary's escape route and seal it off?"

Answering by way of opening her car door, Claire stepped onto the dirt driveway and lifted her chin to the early-morning sun, an unexpected odor assailing her senses with an immediate punch. "Ewww! What on earth is that?" she asked from behind her hand. "It's . . . it's *rancid.*"

Jakob lifted his nose into the air as he, too, stepped from the car and sniffed, once, twice. "That, Claire, is the telltale smell of spoiled milk."

She lowered her hand to her side, opting to breathe through her mouth rather than her nose. "I've smelled spoiled milk before," she protested.

"From the confines of your refrigerator, perhaps. But that's the smell of many, many gallons of spoiled milk." Tightening his grip on the handle of his toolbox, he motioned for her to follow as he crossed the driveway and headed toward a large troughlike contraption with several dozen smaller containers inside. The closer they got, the more intense the smell became. "Yep, that's spoiled milk, alright."

"Why would he leave it out here in the first place?"

"The bigger dairy farms use bulk cooling tanks with agitators to keep the milk moving. Harley's obviously wasn't one of them."

"And people drink that?" she said, pressing down on her nose once again in an unsuccessful attempt to blot out the smell.

"Farms that store milk in cans like these" — he swept his free hand toward the trough — "can't sell for the same higher price as the ones with the bulk cooling tanks. Instead, the milk is classified as Grade B and used for cheese."

"I'm not sure I ever want to eat another piece of cheese if this is where it comes from," she murmured.

"The only reason it smells this bad is because the trough is dry. Normally, the Grade B producers store their milk cans in cold water — hence, the trough — as it waits to be picked up by whatever company they're selling to." Jakob ran his hand across two or three milk cans, shaking his head as he did. "Pickups never take place on Sunday for the Amish, but that doesn't explain this smell or the fact these are still sitting here at all."

"Harley's dead now, Jakob."

"True. But I doubt the company who picks up his milk is aware of that yet." Jakob stepped back and eyed the rest of the cans with casual interest. "Then again, if Harley was in the habit of letting the trough go dry, I imagine the driver wouldn't bother loading the cans into his truck if they even stop by at all, anymore."

She removed her hand from her nose and

mouth to speak but got a gulp of spoiled milk–laden air instead. Coughing, she pointed toward the fence in the distance and waited for him to take her cue.

"Oh. Yeah. Sorry." He looped his free hand through her arm and led her as far from the assortment of milk cans as possible. When they'd reached a breathable distance, he stopped and looked from side to side. "Do you see any holes anywhere?"

With a deep, cleansing breath or two under her belt, Claire examined the fence that lined the farm, its shiny metal railing reflecting the late October sun with a brilliance that defied the morning's autumn temperatures. "No, I don't see any — wait!" She stepped to the right and then the left, bobbing her head from the path of the sun as she did. "Down there . . . The gate is open."

"Ahhh. So Mary didn't *escape,* she simply accepted an open invitation, eh?" Jakob fell into step beside Claire, his head shaking side to side. "I don't care what kind of animal it is, if you leave a gate open, they're going to wander off. Even the Amish ones."

It felt good to laugh. And it felt good to do it with Jakob. "Maybe Mary didn't know she was Amish."

"Maybe . . ." When they reached the gate,

Jakob pulled it shut and slipped the impressive latch into place. "There. Now, whoever takes over the herd will actually *get* a herd."

At the sudden downward turn to Jakob's voice, Claire's smile disappeared. "You really liked him, didn't you?"

"He not only understood my choice sixteen years ago; he respected it, too." Jakob rocked back on his heels and looked up at the clear blue sky. "Since he was the only one able to do that, I guess you could say I kind of had a soft spot for Harley Zook."

"He had the capacity to be open-minded, that's for sure." Claire backed against the fence, her focus drawn to the pensive quality of Jakob's face and stance. "I'm not sure how many people would be able to disassociate someone from their sibling's killer the way he did. And to give the kid a job? I'm not sure I could ever be a big enough person to do something like that."

Jakob pinned her with a stare. "Excuse me?"

"Harley hired the guy's son as an apprentice for his carpentry business."

"*Guy?*" Jakob echoed.

"I think Aunt Diane said his name was Patrick." At Jakob's blank stare, she revisited his question. "Wait. You mean the father? I can't remember his name. You'd know it far better than I would."

When it was still apparent Jakob was lost, she tried again. "Carl Duppan . . . Ducken . . . I don't know, but it was something like that."

"Carl Duck— ?" Jakob's face drained of all color. "Do you mean *Carl Duggan*?"

"Duggan?" She tried the name on for size, Diane's voice in her head confirming its match. "Yes! That's it! That's the man who killed Harley's brother, right?"

At Jakob's nod, she continued, repeating the basic sentiment that had brought them to this spot in the first place. "Can you imagine hiring that man's son as your apprentice sixteen years later?"

This time, instead of reacting with a mere look and a dose of confusion, Jakob took off in a sprint toward the car, his footfalls nearly silent against the hard-packed earth. "C'mon. I'm gonna have to take a rain check on that post-fence-fixing coffee I promised you."

CHAPTER 8

She took advantage of the midday lull in customers to nibble away at the ham and cheese sandwich she'd hastily tossed in a bag a mere four hours earlier. Yet just as her early morning outing with Jakob hadn't lived up to her expectations, neither had her lunch.

Part of that, she knew, was the overwhelming desire she had to close up shop early and plant herself in the middle of the Heavenly Police Department. Maybe if she did that, she'd have a better handle on why Jakob had felt it necessary to drop her off at Heavenly Treasures a good hour before they'd planned. She didn't like being out of the loop, especially when it was obvious her tidbit about Patrick Duggan was behind the detective's abrupt departure.

The other part, she suspected, was the intense loneliness that had attached itself to her heart the moment she let herself into the shop. Sure, she'd known Esther wasn't on the schedule to work — it was Sunday; the Amish girl never worked on Sunday. But somehow, knowing that Esther's days at the shop were numbered, the weekly ritual was far less innocuous. Suddenly, instead of being able to focus her full attention on the handful of tasks still remaining on her to-do list, the lack of chitchat seemed to suck away her motivation to do anything besides mope.

Deep down inside, she knew she should see Esther's pending marriage as a bright spot amid an otherwise bleak canvas. After all, Esther's elected departure meant Claire could bypass the whole pink slip debacle and the guilt that would surely follow.

Still, the thought of losing Esther — whether in six weeks or twelve weeks — was painful. She brightened the shop in a way no overhead light or sun-drenched picture window ever could. And something about Esther always had a way of cutting through life's little hiccups and convincing Claire to look past them with her chin held high.

Rewrapping the sandwich she'd unwrapped just moments earlier, Claire placed it back in the brown paper sack from which it had come. There was no use trying to eat; she simply wasn't hungry. Besides, a lull in customers meant a chance to look at the books one more time. Maybe, just maybe, she'd subtracted wrong along the way, or forgotten to record a deposit or twenty . . .

She slipped off the cushioned stool behind the counter and made her way toward the back of the shop, the certainty of what she'd find in the books pulling on her resolve with each step she took. Glancing at her wrist-watch, she couldn't help but sigh. Three more hours until she could call it a day. Three more hours until her self-thrown pity-party would be forced to an end by the nonstop busyness that was dinnertime at the inn.

The jangle of bells from the opposite side of the shop elicited a sigh of relief from her throat and she turned. The momentary pleasure ushered in by the promise of a much-needed distraction quickly morphed into surprise.

"Isaac?" Then, realizing she sounded more shocked than friendly, she altered her tone and added a more proper greeting. "It's good to see you. How have you been?"

He nodded, his brilliant emerald green eyes disappearing momentarily behind the brim of his black hat. "I am well, Claire. And you?"

She smiled at the man Esther called uncle and Jakob called brother — a man who'd embraced the Amish life based on nurture rather than nature. "I'm good, as well. So what brings you by?"

A long pause had him shifting from foot to foot under an invisible weight that was as plain as day.

"Isaac? Is everything okay?"

"I do not know. That is why I am here." He glanced back at the sidewalk and the tourists who traveled it alone on this Amish day of worship and visiting. "Is there any news?"

"News?"

"Of Harley Zook."

She drew back, surprised. "You haven't heard?"

All color drained from the man's otherwise healthy pallor as he stumbled back a step or two. "So it is true? Mose is a suspect in his death?"

"No . . . I . . . I just wasn't sure if you knew Harley was dead."

"Yah. I know. Everyone knows." Clearing his throat, Isaac noticeably tried to regroup. "Zook was a good man. An honest man."

She moved to the paneled upright in the middle of the shop and leaned against it for support. "You were working for him, weren't you? In his carpentry business?"

"For one week, yah. I still make toys with

Lapp, but with Zook I will do more. On Thursday I fixed a porch railing at a home in Breeze Point, and on Friday I made a cabinet for a woman in Heavenly. She was pleased with my work."

Squaring her shoulders, she dove into the subject he'd touched on only moments earlier, the insight she'd gleaned from Esther and Eli at the murder scene making the question virtually rhetorical in nature. "And Mose? He wasn't happy that you were working with Harley?"

A cloud skittered across Isaac's face just before the slight nod of agreement. "He did not like Zook. But I did not know my decision to take work for Zook would push him to . . ." His words trailed off as his gaze traveled to a spot somewhere over Claire's head.

"Push him to what?"

Slowly, Isaac lowered his chin until his focus was on Claire once again. "Such anger."

"But if you knew the history there, how could you think taking a job from Harley wouldn't upset Mose?" The second the words were out, she gasped. "Oh, I'm so sorry, Isaac. I have no right asking such a question. Please forgive me."

"I do not agree with Dat's anger toward

Zook. It was not Zook's choice for his brother to be murdered. And it is not a crime for him to respect my brother's decision to want to solve that murder. It was Jakob's choice to leave the Amish, not Zook's." Isaac took a deep breath then released it slowly. "It was nice to work beside someone who does not pretend my brother does not exist."

Finally, Isaac's choice made perfect sense. Yes, he'd been working with his hands in Lapp's Toy Shop. But with Harley Zook, he worked with his hands and could talk of the brother he was forced to shun within his own community and his own home. She rested a hand atop his arm and smiled up at the man. "Someone else's anger is not your fault."

"But if my choice led someone to kill, I am to blame."

She considered his words, the meaning behind them making it difficult to breathe let alone think. "You can't really believe Mose killed Harley, can you? Your dat is *Amish.*"

"That did not stop him from hating for sixteen years."

It was a simple statement and one she couldn't dispute no matter how much she wished she could — for Isaac's sake and for

Jakob's. Abandoned beliefs often had a domino effect.

"You have to know that the last thing your brother wants to see is Mose convicted of any crime, much less murder."

"Dat will not speak to him."

"He might not have a choice."

"Dat will not speak to him," Isaac repeated, the force of his statement softened somewhat by the worry that tugged at his broad shoulders.

"Jakob will figure this out, Isaac. I'm confident of that." And she was. Jakob Fisher was a smart man. He also maintained a fierce and undying loyalty to the family who'd long since turned their backs on him. "If Jakob needs me to step in and help by talking with Mose, I'll do that. He just has to ask."

She felt Isaac's worried gaze turn to one of a more studying variety and she looked down, unsure of his thoughts. "For so many years I worried about Jakob. I wondered if he was well. If he was happy. If he was lonely. I would lie in my bed at night trying to picture his new life. Even though I did not know much of life outside, I would picture only good. Like you. You are good for Jakob. You make him happy. Martha sees it, too."

She pushed off the support beam, her face warm. "It's not like that with Jakob and me. We're just . . . friends. Please make sure your sister knows that."

"Friends, yah. But there will be more. Esther tells of the smile Jakob has for you."

Torn between the desire to set Isaac and his family straight, and the flutter the man's conviction caused inside her stomach, Claire merely looked away, desperate for a way to steer the conversation into safer territory.

"I'm going to miss your niece when she gets married."

"Esther will still make things for your shop the way Martha does." Isaac stepped around Claire to get a closer look at a simple wooden chest. "She will slow down a little once children are born, but she will still do some, I am sure."

So much for safer territory . . .

She tried again, taking the conversation back to Harley. "I'm sorry about your friend . . . and your job. Perhaps you could take over with a fix-it business of your own once the dust settles."

His brows furrowed. "Dust?"

"With the investigation." She wandered over to the window and peered outside, the gathering storm clouds she spied in the distance an obvious player in the decreasing foot traffic along Lighted Way. "If there was a market for Harley's woodworking know-how, surely there will be a market for yours, too."

Isaac's momentary hesitation gave way to a nod and the faintest hint of a smile. "Perhaps you are right. Perhaps I could even give someone work the way Zook gave me work."

"You'd already have an apprentice in place in Patrick Duggan . . ." she reminded.

"If that Englisher were to work with me, he would have to do his own work. I would not have time to fix his mistakes."

She stared at Isaac. "Are you saying Patrick wasn't a hard worker?"

"Yah. He did not want to work."

"Then why did Harley keep him on?"

Isaac's shoulders hitched upward beneath his suspenders. "I do not know."

CHAPTER 9

"Good heavens, Claire, how many times are you going to read that same page before you either *turn* it or put the whole thing down?"

Surprised, Claire glanced up from the paperback mystery novel in her lap to find Diane eyeing her curiously from across the dimly lit parlor. "Oh. Aunt Diane. I didn't hear you come in just now."

"I've been sitting here for nearly ten minutes, dear." Diane maneuvered her knitting needles in, out, and around the royal blue scarf taking shape in her hands. "Is everything okay? You were unusually subdued with the guests this evening."

She bolted upright. "I'm so sorry. Did someone complain?"

"No, of course not. I think everyone was so hungry after their day they didn't even notice. But I did." The needles stilled along with Diane's hand. "You seemed a million miles away when you got home from work, but I let it go because of timing. However, dinner is over now and our guests have retired to their rooms. So tell me, what's on your mind? Did something happen with Jakob this morning?"

She couldn't help but smile at the obvious hope in her aunt's voice at the mere mention of Detective Fisher. In fact, if the sixty-something woman had her say, Claire would give in to the feelings Diane was convinced she had regarding Jakob, and another Heavenly wedding would soon be in the works.

No. As tempting as it was to vent the disappointment she felt over her abbreviated morning with Jakob at Zook's farm, to do so would only encourage the woman. Besides, Diane was sharp. She could spot a shift in Claire's feelings a mile away. Especially if those feelings were starting to shift in a direction Diane had been championing for months.

Instead, Claire let her head drift back against the cushioned chair while her mouth gave voice to one of the other topics derailing her pitiful attempt to read. "I know it was sixteen years ago, but do you remember much about John Zook's murder?"

"Of course I do," Diane said as her hands returned to the scarf in her lap. "I remember all of it like it was yesterday."

Before Claire could formulate her next question, Diane continued. "There'd never been a murder in Heavenly before Harley's brother. And, until two months ago, there hadn't been one since. People only forget when something is commonplace."

"The forgetting would be nice, but I sure wouldn't want something like that becoming commonplace around here." And it was true. Heavenly was supposed to be about peace and serenity, not murder.

"Amen."

She allowed the flicker of candlelight across bookshelves and framed photographs to guide her eyes around the room until they were, once again, trained on the woman she loved like a mother. "Tell me everything about his murder."

"It was a crime that never should have happened. And it wouldn't have if it weren't for pure, unadulterated ignorance."

"Ignorance?" she echoed.

Diane nodded as the knitting needles in her hand continued to zip in and out of impossibly small loops. "The murder was classified as a hate crime."

"Go on . . ."

"While one could argue that Harley Zook pushed the Amish envelope on occasion and let compassion rule when it came to things

106

like shunnings, his brother towed the line perfectly. He followed the Ordnung to the letter, so to speak."

"But the Ordnung itself is really an unwritten code of order, isn't it? Doesn't that, by its very nature, leave a little wiggle room?"

"If by wiggle room you mean smiling at someone like Jakob when no one else is looking, I suppose . . . but it's rare." Diane laid her needles down in her lap and stretched her arms over her head. "The Ordnung might be unwritten, but it's been handed down over the generations. It's those expectations for social and spiritual behavior that are ingrained in the Amish from birth. They really don't know any other way. They've thrived under their beliefs. It's why they don't hide cars in their barn and take them out for a spin when no one is looking. They don't want to do that. They embrace their world with both arms."

Claire processed her aunt's comments then tucked them away in favor of the question she really wanted answered. "So how does all of this figure into John's murder?"

"The Amish, by their very nature, live a quiet life. Yes, they live among the rest of us, but they do it as quietly as possible."

"Meaning?"

"Meaning they keep their buggies to the side of the road whenever possible. At Lighted Way business meetings they have a presence but rarely interject comments unless asked . . . and even then, it's done in a very unassuming way." Diane set her scarf and needles to the side and stood, the nine thirty chime of the grandfather clock in the hallway signaling her final task of the night. Crossing to the window that overlooked the darkened fields of the Amish countryside, she took one more look at her beloved town then drew the thick velvet curtains closed.

"They are passive people, Claire," the woman continued en route back to her spot on the sofa. "They don't believe in engaging in arguments, and they don't force their lifestyle down anyone's throats. As a result, there are an awful lot of misperceptions about the Amish that are born from a place of ignorance and allowed to go unchecked by a group of people who separate themselves from the ills of the world."

Claire leaned forward, intrigued by her aunt's words. "Okay, I'm following you . . ."

"The night John Zook was murdered, he'd gone out to his barn in the middle of the night to check on a cow who was getting ready to give birth. The next morning, Harley found him slumped alongside the new calf. He'd been shot in the back of the head."

"Oh my gosh, how awful!"

"Harley was devastated, as was the entire town — Amish and English alike. Especially once it was determined he'd been killed by a hunting rifle from within a range that eliminated all possibility of it having been a stray shot."

The scarf and needles remained untouched as Diane slipped sixteen years into the past. "We'd had an accident or two, of course, but, before that night, the extent of *crime* in Heavenly was confined to a rare teenage prank — a knocked-down mailbox on prom weekend, an occasional tire mark on someone's yard on the last day of school, that sort of thing. When they were caught, they were always English. The Amish kids just didn't conduct themselves like that."

"How long did it take for the police to figure out who killed John?" she asked.

"Too long." Diane ran her fingers along the tasteful pattern on the arm of the couch and sighed. "That's why Jakob left. He'd already had a fascination with the police — one he'd fed during his very brief Rumspringa. For him, his experimentation with the English world didn't have him buying a CD player for his buggy or sneaking a cigarette out at the covered bridge on Route 50. He simply spent his very short Rumspringa talking to the police officers in town and riding along with them whenever he could."

Everything she was hearing fit so well with the man she'd come to know over the past few months. Jakob's sense of honor, as well as the unwavering respect he had for his former community and its lifestyle, made his desire to solve John Zook's murder easy to understand. She said as much to Diane, who offered a slow but definitive nod of agreement in return.

"It hurt him deeply to watch Harley suffer the loss of his brother. The fact that the police couldn't seem to finger a killer only compounded that hurt. So while the rest of his brethren waited for news of an arrest, Jakob made the ultimate sacrifice in the hopes he could help deliver that news faster."

"But he'd have to test into the academy and then go through months of training before he could even secure a job as a police officer . . ."

"Yes, however, it was still an *action* as opposed to an inaction."

Claire of all people understood that notion. Sometimes doing something was better than doing nothing. "But then they solved it just as he left, right?" This was a part of the story she had heard before, the nugget that made the severing of ties with Jakob's family even harder to digest.

Again, Diane nodded. "Yes, that's right. But by then it was too late. He was already cut off and there was no going back even if he'd wanted to. But for Jakob the calling that had convinced him to leave the Amish didn't go away just because John's killer was found. So he kept his plan to become a police officer and he did so in New York."

There was so much about Jakob's life in New York she wanted to hear, but now was not the time. Besides, the questions she had weren't ones Diane could answer. No, those would be for a future date with Jakob.

A future date . . .

Shaking the part-frightening, part-intriguing thought from her head, Claire forced herself to focus on the details her aunt remembered about the senseless crime they'd been discussing.

"So the police apprehended Carl Duggan for John's murder, yes?"

"Yes."

"Did he know John personally?"

"No. John's death was a hate crime against the Amish as a group. Carl Duggan simply picked a random barn and waited."

"But why? What did the Amish do to him?"

"Carl was struggling financially. He'd lost his job, he was behind in his taxes, and he was in danger of losing the home he shared with his wife and young son."

Claire shifted her feet off the ottoman and onto the floor, leaning forward as she did. "That's this Patrick fellow, right?"

"That's right." Diane stilled her finger atop the arm of the sofa and closed her eyes briefly. "So, rather than try to change his situation somehow, Carl lashed out against the Amish, convinced of the often-spread yet completely wrong allegation that they don't pay taxes."

She felt her jaw slack. "What?"

"Carl, like so many other ignorant people, believed the Amish don't pay taxes. That, of course, isn't true. They pay taxes just like the rest of us with the exception of social security since they don't partake in that program. Mind you, the bulk of the taxes they pay go to services they don't utilize, but they pay them anyway. Just like everyone else."

"So this man killed John in retaliation against a myth?" she said, the gasp in her voice making them both look toward the front hallway and the stairs just beyond. When no guest doors opened on the second floor in response, she breathed a sigh of relief. "Sorry about that, Aunt Diane. I . . . I just can't imagine someone losing their life in such a tragic way to begin with, only to find out it all happened because of *a lie.*"

"That's why I always make a point of sharing as many facts about the Amish with our guests as possible. So much of what people think they know about them is wrong." Diane plucked her canvas knitting bag from the floor and set it on her lap. Then, with loving hands, she put her scarf, yarn, and knitting needles inside. "Harley was robbed of a brother that fateful night. But instead of becoming bitter the way so many of us English would, he turned the other cheek the way he was taught. He tried to reach out to Carl's wife and son, and let them know he did not hold them accountable for his brother's death. He cast aside his own interest in woodworking to run John's dairy farm. And he tried, unsuccessfully, to champion Jakob in the eyes of his own community."

"So that's why Harley had Patrick working as his apprentice? Because of the whole turning the other cheek thing?"

Diane met Claire's eyes across the top of

113

the knitting bag. "Patrick was almost ten, I believe, when his father went off to jail, sending him into quite a tailspin from what I've heard here and there over the past sixteen years. His acting out certainly compounded the strain on his mother, I would imagine.

"Harley heard of the trouble Rita was having with Patrick and decided to try and help. He told me he understood Patrick's aimless wandering because he'd felt that way, too, since John's death. He felt that by continuing to devote his life to John's dairy farm, he was remaining stuck in the past. That's why he decided to heed my advice and start his mobile carpentry business."

She listened to all that Diane was saying, the gaps her aunt was helping to fill in invaluable. "And bringing Patrick on was Harley's attempt at pulling Carl's son out of the past, too?"

"That and the fact they shared a common loss."

"A common loss?"

"Of course. Carl Duggan may still be alive, but his actions made it so Patrick grew up without a father just as those same actions made it so Harley no longer had a brother." Diane grasped the handles of her knitting bag and scooted forward on the couch. "He was hoping the lift that he got from working with his hands would be shared by Patrick."

"Only it wasn't, was it?" Claire glanced at the small clock on the bookshelf to her left and knew her time with Diane was nearly over. Like everything else in the woman's day, bedtime followed a schedule.

Diane pushed off the couch but remained in the room. "If what I witnessed the few times Patrick accompanied Harley here to the inn was any indication, I'd have to say no."

At the confirmation of Isaac's words, Claire pressed on, a last round of questions firing from between her lips in rapid succession. "Then why did he stick with it? Why didn't he just quit?"

For a long moment, Diane said nothing, the pensive expression on her face the only indication Claire's inquiries were still on the table. Then, finally, "I can't answer that, dear. All I can really say is that I found myself wondering the same thing."

"And?"

Diane's diminutive shoulders hitched upward. "Maybe he did it for his mother? Maybe it gave him somewhere to go, something to do? Maybe it was just being around Harley's positive outlook and forgiving heart? I don't really know. I suspect the only person who can truly answer that would be Patrick, himself."

There were so many other things she wanted to ask — things about Harley and Patrick and even Jakob. But Diane needed her sleep. The shadows of a long day spent fawning over guests were darkening beneath her aunt's otherwise comforting eyes. To keep her there past her bedtime would be wrong. Morning would come soon enough for both of them. And with the start of a new day came new opportunities for talks while they worked at their various tasks.

"You get your rest now, okay? I'll meet you in the kitchen first thing in the morning for French toast prep."

"Sounds good." Diane crossed to Claire's chair and planted a kiss on the top of her niece's head. "Now try to put all of this out of your head for the night and get some sleep."

She smiled up at her father's oldest sister, the deep love she felt for the woman forming a lump inside her throat. "I love you, Aunt Diane."

"I love you, too, dear."

CHAPTER 10

She was halfway down Sleep Heavenly's driveway when she heard her name being called. Turning, she spotted Megan Reilly descending the steps of the inn's front porch, her hand waving wildly in the air.

"Claire! Claire! Can you hold up a second? I'd like to ask you a question before Kyle and I set off for the day."

Claire retraced her steps until they met in the middle. "Sure thing, Megan, how can I help?"

Pushing a strand of blonde hair behind her ear, Megan laughed, the happy yet slightly high-strung personality she'd exhibited thus far during her stay on full display. "House hunting has got me going a little mad. Which, in turn, has Kyle going a little mad."

Claire smiled. "I'm sure it's a stressful time . . ."

"It is," the woman agreed, "but I tend to

make everything more stressful than it needs to be. It's that Irish worrywart in me."

"Trust me, I've been there a time or two myself." And she had. Though, now that the end to Heavenly Treasures was no more than three months away, she couldn't help but see all the times she'd borrowed trouble she didn't need.

Lifting her face to the warmth of the morning sun, Megan sighed. "I just want to find the perfect house for us, you know?"

"Nothing yet, I take it?"

"Oh, I've found a lot of my must-haves and even some of my wish-I-hads, only I've yet to find them all in the same place." Megan shielded her eyes with her hand and peered out at the farmland in the distance. "But this town is so — so quaint, so peaceful, so *perfect* for raising the kids, that I don't really want to look at any other communities, you know?"

Claire did know. In fact, when she let herself dream about giving marriage another try and the children she'd have as a result, she always envisioned it happening in Heavenly. Like somehow the kindness and goodwill that was ever present in the town via people like Aunt Diane and Claire's soon-to-be-former fellow shopkeepers would aid in the raising process.

She opened her mouth to voice her agreement but shut it again as Megan continued. "I think we'll probably end up building in the second development the Realtor took us to on Saturday. The floor plans are nice, the location good, and they're even going to have a swimming pool for those warm summer months when it's all done."

"That sounds nice."

"It is. Only my continued harping on that development we saw on Friday has Kyle in desperate need of a break from house hunting."

"Which development was that again?" she asked.

"Serenity Falls — the one on the Amish side that Diane mentioned over breakfast on Saturday. The location is second to none in my opinion. It's like it is over here on the English side . . . only better. Because instead of just moments of peacefulness when a buggy happens to go by, you're right there with the buggies and the simplicity *all* the time."

"So why don't you just build there, then?"

Megan shook her head, scrunching her nose as she did. "I like to open my windows on all but the coldest days of the year. I couldn't do that if we —"

"Megan? Are you coming?"

Together, they turned toward the inn and Megan's very impatient-looking husband.

"Uh-oh. I'm talking about exactly what I promised him I wouldn't talk about today." Megan smacked a gentle hand against her forehead and groaned. "I really am a hopeless cause, aren't I?"

Claire laughed. She liked Megan Reilly, liked her honesty. "You're a mom. You want to find the right home for your kids. I think that's pretty commendable."

Megan's eyes widened just before she reached out to rest a hand on Claire's forearm. "Thank you for saying that. Truly."

"You do realize the poor woman is trying to get to work, right, Megan?"

Waving her free hand toward her husband, Megan leaned closer to Claire. "If you had a day to do whatever you wanted in Heavenly, what would you do?"

"What would I do?" she repeated with a grin. "I'd sleep in until eleven, I'd grab a biscuit or whatever yummy breakfast leftover I could find in my aunt's kitchen, and then I'd head toward the Amish side of town with a book in my hand."

Megan considered Claire's words. "But you see, if Kyle sat down to read, I'd start yacking in his ear all over again. So what we need is something that can distract *me* from talking about the whole house-hunting thing."

"Ahhh, I get it." She reconsidered her answer and tweaked accordingly. "Then, in that case, I'd spend the day on Lighted Way, just meandering in and out of the shops. Intersperse that with some coffee at Heavenly Brews, some lunch at Tastes of Heaven(ly), and then cap it off with a piece of Ruth Miller's Shoo Fly Pie at the bake shop next to my place and you'll have your relaxing day."

"Mmm . . . Sounds perfect."

"Stop into my shop when you're wrapping up and let me know what you thought, okay?" Then, with a glance down at her watch for the confirmation she knew she'd find, she turned back toward the street, the pre-opening tasks she'd hoped to complete at Heavenly Treasures no longer a possibility. "Enjoy your day, Megan."

"Thanks, Claire. I owe you one."

On one hand she was thrilled to have Esther at the shop all day. The girl's presence and rapport with the customers made getting to the mountain of things on Claire's daily to-do list easier. The fact that she could do the bulk of those while smiling and laughing with one of her favorite people made it even sweeter.

Yet as wonderful as it was to have Esther there, the girl's keen eyes and familiarity with the inner workings of the shop made things like phone calls with the bank and any crying jags that might ensue impossible to accommodate. There was no doubt she'd like to unburden some of the stress she'd kept to herself thus far, but to do so with Esther was unfair. Especially when the bride-to-be's happy news had been marred enough already by Harley's murder and her grandfather's potential ties to the crime.

"You have to come," Esther said, breaking through Claire's woolgathering with her hope-filled voice. "Mamm said so."

She looked up from the handmade baby bibs she was stacking on a shelf for the upcoming Thanksgiving holiday. "That's okay? For an English person to be at an Amish wedding?"

"You are my friend, yah?"

"Of course I am." She moved on to the pile of handsewn onesies, checking their count against the printout on her clipboard. "I guess I assumed it would just be for your family and others in your community."

"They will be there, too." Esther wandered over to the side window that overlooked the alley between Heavenly Treasures and Shoo

Fly Bake Shoppe. The slump of her shoulders as she reached her destination let Claire know that Eli's buggy had not yet arrived for the young man's afternoon check on his twin sister, Ruth. "Talk of the wedding brings a smile to Mamm's face." Esther cleared her throat quickly, the sound breaking through Claire's concentration once and for all. "She says you are to bring someone with you."

She gave up on counting. "You mean like a guest?"

Esther turned around yet remained by the window. "Yah."

"There's no one to bring, Esther, you know that." Then, nudging her chin toward the window, she addressed the subject of another noticeable absence. "I haven't seen Benjamin around the bakery since Saturday. Is everything okay?"

Oh, how she hoped her question sounded natural, like that of any other shopkeeper on Lighted Way who'd come to know the routines of her fellow shopkeepers. "I mean, I know he hasn't been around much to begin with, but after he came by on Saturday I figured that was changing."

Esther smoothed her hands down the sides of her lavender dress just before taking a second and still unrewarded peek out the window. "Eli says Benjamin has said little since Mr. Zook was found. When Eli has tried to speak with him, Benjamin says only that he is busy."

"Benjamin thinks highly of your grandfather, doesn't he?" Claire tugged the clipboard to her chest, her mind no longer on her inventory.

"Yah. Dawdy thinks well of Benjamin, too."

Pushing the instant image of Jakob from her thoughts, she forced herself to focus on Benjamin and his state of mind, instead. "Do you know if they've talked since Harley's death?"

"Yah. Last night, when everyone was leaving after a day of visiting, I saw Benjamin speak with Dawdy. I do not know what was said, only that they spoke. Dawdy moved his hands often and I saw Benjamin walk off for a spell, but I do not know more than that." Esther bowed her head until her chin nearly touched the top of her chest. "Eli says Benjamin is one of the only ones who does not think Dawdy hurt Mr. Zook."

Claire sucked in a breath. "You don't think your grandfather had something to do with Harley's murder, do you?"

"I do not know what to say," Esther said once she'd finally reengaged eye contact with Claire. "I do not want to believe such things. It is God's will when a person's life is to end, not man's. That is what we believe."

"As does your grandfather."

A weighted silence that hung in the air to the point of suffocation finally gave way to a choked whisper. "But Dawdy had such *anger* for Mr. Zook. It was an anger he did not hide in front of anyone. Not even the bishop."

"But you said he was shunned for that, didn't you?"

"Many times. But, Dawdy believed it was Mr. Zook who should be shunned and that he should be the one to lead that."

"Why did he think Harley should be shunned?" she asked, quickly.

"Because Harley spoke well of my uncle."

"Jakob?"

"Yah." Esther nibbled her lower lip then released it along with a quiet sigh. "Benjamin always made things right. He helped people to see Dawdy's ways were born from the grief of losing Jakob."

"But Jakob is still very much alive, Esther." She tightened her grip on the clipboard. "And he's right here . . . in Heavenly!"

Esther merely shook her head. Sadly. "He

is lost to Dawdy."

"And to you?" Claire heard the rise in her voice, knew it was unfair in light of Esther's upbringing, but she could do little to stop it. Jakob was a good man. A decent man. He simply didn't deserve to be excommunicated for choosing a noble profession like police work. "What is Jakob to you, Esther?"

The *clip-clop* of Eli's horse through the open window saved Esther from having to answer and Claire from having to digest that answer. "Eli is here!"

She couldn't help but manage the faintest hint of a smile for her friend. How could she not when the presence of another human being could make Esther so happy? Without so much as a glance toward the window, Esther's pleading gaze sought and received permission to head out into the alley for a quick visit with her betrothed.

But two minutes later, Esther was back behind the counter, the breathtaking smile that had met Eli's arrival gone as quick as it had come.

"Esther? Is everything okay?"

Esther nodded but said nothing.

"You could have stayed out there and visited a little longer. I've got everything under control in here."

"It was Benjamin, not Eli." Esther's shoulders lurched forward in obvious disappointment only to resume their normally stoic pose in short order. "Eli is finishing with the harvest. He asked Benjamin to say hello."

"Oh." She looked toward the rear of the shop and the offshoot hallway that linked to the back door. "Did he say if he was going to stop in after he looked in on Ruth?"

Esther removed the tray of plain sales tags from the shelf beneath the register and began to fill in prices for the candles she'd brought in that morning. "He did not say, but he asked after you."

Claire set the clipboard down on the blankets that were next on her inventory list and shifted from foot to foot, waiting. When Esther said nothing else, Claire asked the only question she could and hoped her reason wasn't as transparent as it felt. "And? What did you say?"

"I said you were inside taking inventory. He did not say anything else."

She looked toward the hallway once again, but, still, there was no sign of Benjamin. "Oh, well I'm sure he is busy, too." But she knew better. Benjamin was always busy. Yet, since they'd met shortly after she opened Heavenly Treasures, he'd always found time to step inside and say hello, to ask if she needed anything before he left. Despite the fact that she always said she was fine, he had a way of finding something to do to make her day a little easier — taking out the trash, reaching something on a top shelf, or moving a bulky item to a new location. His failure to stop in and say hello, if nothing else, spoke volumes.

She'd questioned his friend's innocence in regards to Harley Zook's murder. That, coupled with the uncertain ground they'd found themselves on since he admitted his feelings for her, had added up to this.

"You do not look happy, Claire."

Esther's quiet words snapped Claire back to the moment and the basic realities that could not be changed.

Mose Fisher was a likely suspect in Harley's murder. Sixteen years of anger had hit a breaking point the moment the victim offered a job to Isaac. Everyone knew it, including Mose's only family. Of course she hoped he wasn't responsible, but considering the possibility didn't make her a bad person.

And as for a future with Benjamin, it simply couldn't happen. Not if she didn't want to see such a wonderful person face the pain and rejection Jakob lived with on a daily basis.

To Esther, she said only, "I'm okay. Just tired, I guess. I've got a lot on my mind these days."

"I am a good listener." Esther paused her pen above her latest sales tag and waited.

"Yes, you are, Esther. Yes, you are."

"I am listening now . . ."

Claire laughed. "Point taken."

At Esther's expectant stare, Claire relented with the only worry she could share aloud. "I'm worried about your uncle. This crime is going to stir up a lot of hurt for him. And while I understand the Amish are different, I will never understand how the decision Jakob made should have him missing out on the lives of the people he loves more than anything else in this world."

At Esther's stunned silence, Claire worked to soften her tone while still being true to her feelings. "Do you know how much he misses having a relationship with your mother? How much he'd like to get to know you and your siblings? Do you know how much his heart aches not to be able to hug his own mother? *I* know. It eats away at him every single day. It's why he walks by this store every afternoon in the hopes you might look outside the window at the exact moment he passes. It's why I see him driving in the opposite direction of his home when he gets off work. He yearns to be close to all of you, to be a part of your lives, to witness the important milestones like your upcoming wedding to Eli."

Esther's gaze dropped back down to the blank sales tags and the pen poised tightly between her long, slender fingers. Slowly she began to write, the prices they'd agreed on being recorded with careful precision. "You must bring a guest when you come to the wedding. Mamm would like that."

CHAPTER 11

There was something about the lazy, rhythmic creak of the porch swing beneath her body that called to her at the end of a long day. It was as if the staccato-like sound slowly sucked away the busyness while the panoramic view of the Amish countryside ushered in the sense of peace and tranquility that was Heavenly, Pennsylvania.

The trees that only a week earlier had exploded in a final brilliant bouquet of crimson, orange, and gold were beginning to show their yearly bow to a season that demanded a different, starker beauty. Even the lush green of the crops was gone, the land turned over in preparation for spring.

Yet despite the duller colors synonymous with the start of November, there was still something magical, almost awe-inspiring about the sight of so much uncompromised land. Suddenly it made sense why the Amish were so quiet and calm, why they were able to resist the often too-fast pace of the English world.

"Penny for your thoughts?"

Startled, Claire stopped the foot-powered sway of the swing and turned toward the familiar voice coming from the bottom step of the front porch. "Jakob, hi . . . I . . . I didn't hear you drive up."

"That's because I walked." The broad-shouldered detective made short work of the steps and the distance between them. When he reached the swing, he pointed toward the empty space beside Claire. "May I?"

Nodding, she scooted to the left, the warmth of his shoulder as it grazed hers quickly changing the tempo of her heart-beat. "It's nice to see you," she said in the best matter-of-fact voice she could muster.

The question she saw behind his large hazel eyes made its way past his lips in short order. "So where were you just now when I walked up?"

She looked again at the fields in the distance, shrugging as she did. "I wasn't really anywhere. Just enjoying the view and finding it immensely relaxing."

"Long day?"

She felt him studying the side of her face as she contemplated her answer. Did she tell him she was disappointed in the way he bailed out of their time together the day before with nary an explanation? Or did she move on, coming to terms with the fact that she'd put far more importance on their fence-fixing mission than she'd allowed herself to believe?

Move on . . .

Lifting her hand from her lap, she waved it toward the Amish countryside now slowly disappearing in the gathering dusk. "I wish it could be like that around here all the time. There's more than enough real world everywhere else."

She didn't need to look at him to know his gaze had left her face. She could feel its absence like a tangible thing. "Claire, I'd be lying if I didn't say I'm terrified of where this case might take me, because I am. I got into police work because I wanted to help people — both Amish and English, alike. But if this case plays out in the way I'm dreading it might, that work will lead me to hurt the people I love in ways I can't ever erase."

"But Jakob, if, by chance, your father *did* kill Harley, the consequences will be on *his* actions, not yours." Hiking her bent leg onto the swing, she pivoted her body so as to face him. "Please, Jakob, tell me you know this.

Tell me you believe this."

"But Mose is my dat, Claire. My *dat*. No one wants to arrest their dat and see him locked away for the rest of his life for murdering a good and decent man."

She grabbed hold of his hand and held it tight, the coolness of his skin surprising. "If that happens, Jakob, it's not because you told him to do it. He will have made that decision all on his own."

"A decision he was led to by me."

She stopped the swing with her opposite foot. "Led to by you?" she gasped. "How on earth could you even *think* that let alone say it?"

"Because it would be true?" Gently, he disengaged his hand and ran it down his face in despair. "C'mon, Claire, think about it. Mose's hatred of Harley began sixteen years ago when I broke the vow I made at baptism in order to help solve his brother's murder. If I hadn't done that, Mose never would have become so bitter, so" — he stopped, swallowed — "so *hateful.*"

"Mose is bitter because he chose to be bitter," she protested. "Look, you know I have the utmost respect for the Amish. I love so many things about the way they live, their respect for God and the land. But you have to know that I think the way they treat you is awful. You didn't leave to become some sort of drug dealer. You didn't leave because you wanted to get into a business that would bilk innocent people of their hard-earned money. You got out so you could become a police officer." She hooked her finger underneath his chin and guided his focus until it was squarely on her face. "A *police officer,* Jakob. You have absolutely nothing to be ashamed of or feel guilty about. If anything, *they* do. For turning their backs on such an honorable man."

For just a split second she saw it — the kind of raw emotion and heartfelt appreciation that no words could ever do justice. Yet, as quick as it came, it was gone, hidden behind a set of beliefs no amount of time in the English world could ever stamp from his makeup. "I knew the consequences of my decision, Claire. And I left, anyway. The repercussions are mine alone."

"Fine. But Mose's decision to kill another man is not one of them." At Jakob's noticeable slump, she altered her words to include the subordinating conjunction she knew he needed to hear. "*If* Mose is even the one responsible at all."

Wrapping his hand around hers, he lowered it from his face to the limited space between them, his grip never wavering. "I need you to know that it's only because of this case that I ended our time together so quickly yesterday. I hated doing it, especially when I'd been looking forward to it all night long . . . but I had to. I had to spend a little time with the first potential non-Mose thread to cross my path since you stumbled across Harley's body in the middle of my father's maze."

"Non-Mose thread? I don't understand." She heard the hope in her voice, knew his explanation meant way more than it should in light of the way she tried so hard to convince herself and everyone else they were just friends.

"It's what you said yesterday out at Zook's farm. About Carl Duggan's kid working with Harley. I had no idea."

"Okay . . ."

"Don't you see? There's potential baggage there. Baggage that could lead to a motive for murder for some."

For the first time since he took her hand, the thumping in her chest ceased. "What are you talking about?"

Releasing her hand, he rose from the swing and wandered over to the porch railing, his focus somewhere other than her aunt's front porch. "Sixteen years ago, Patrick Duggan was robbed of his father.

And, from the little I've been able to piece together over the past twenty-four-plus hours, his life hasn't been terribly easy since that time. Money struggles set in motion by attorney fees and the loss of an income made things more than a little difficult for Carl's wife and son over the years. Those money struggles made it so Rita Duggan had to take on a second job just to keep their heads above water. Her increasing time out of the home each day to work those jobs left young Patrick alone for long stretches of time — stretches of time that some kids might use to be productive, while others use it to get in trouble."

"They say negative attention is often better than no attention, don't they?" she offered.

"Exactly. Then, suddenly, in his mid-twenties, Patrick wants to get his life in order? By signing on as an apprentice to the man who could be seen, by a troubled kid, as the person ultimately responsible for the loss of his father?"

"And thus you have revenge . . ." She, too, abandoned the swing in favor of the same railing where Jakob was now perched. "So it was me mentioning Patrick's apprenticeship that got you researching his life post murder trial?"

He ran a hand through his sandy blond hair, flashing a quick dimple-laden smile as he did. "Trust me, Claire. That's the *only* thing that could have made me skip out on a breakfast date with you."

She felt the warmth rising in her cheeks and was instantly glad for the increasing shadows engulfing the porch. "But why wait sixteen years for revenge? I mean, I get a ten-year-old boy not being capable of murder. But he's been a grown man for some time now, right? So why now?"

"Which brings me to the first big sticking point" — Jakob slid his hands down the railing on either side of his body — "and keeps my father still very much on the top of the list. Isaac *just* took the job with Harley. That's a far more recent wound."

"Have you questioned your father yet?"

"One of my other officers did. Mose refused to talk to me. But either way, they were the basic 'where were you when the body was found' kind of questions."

"And Patrick? Have you questioned him? Do you think there's a chance he's responsible?"

"No, I haven't questioned Patrick yet. I'm trying to piece together a timeline for the past sixteen years for the Duggan family before I even talk to him. I'm almost there, but there's still a few more things I want to nail down. I don't want to stir up any more grief for Rita Duggan than absolutely necessary, especially considering the word around town that her health may be starting to fail."

"His mother's health is failing?" she repeated.

At Jakob's noncommittal nod, she posed another theory. "Let's assume Rita is all Patrick has left. Couldn't grief and fear make the loss of his father rise to the surface in an all-new wave of anger?"

He didn't say anything for a minute, his gaze dropping to the wood-planked porch floor.

Feeling suddenly foolish, she walked around Jakob and took a seat on the top step. "I'm sorry. I imagine the last thing you need right now is me trying to play Nancy Drew."

"No!" He shifted his view upward to the porch roof. "Actually, there could be some merit to what you said. If nothing else, it could be used to address that first big sticking point where Duggan's son is concerned."

"Which, in turn, adds someone other than your father to the list of suspects."

Jakob puffed his cheeks with air only to let it diffuse slowly through pursed lips.

"Claire, I want nothing more than to get my father's name off the suspect list. For him, for Mamm, for Martha, for Isaac, for Esther — oh my gosh, Esther!" He pushed off the railing with a sudden urgency. "Esther shouldn't have something like this shadowing her wedding plans!"

"No, she shouldn't." It was a simple reply, yet no less accurate.

"Claire, I've got to fix this. I've got to find out who murdered Harley, and I'm praying with everything I am that Mose isn't that person," Jakob murmured, his frustration-laced desperation palpable. "He just *can't* be responsible."

"But what if he is?"

CHAPTER 12

Claire wasn't sure who jumped farther, her or Jakob, but if there was a difference in either direction, it was negligible. They'd been so wrapped up in their discussion that neither had noticed Isaac standing in the shadow of the weeping willow tree for an undetermined amount of time.

"I am sorry. I did not mean to frighten you." Isaac Schrock, the young man Jakob's family had raised since the age of four, approached the front porch with humble steps. If Jakob's presence caused any hesitation for the man, it did not show. "But I cannot stay silent."

Claire looked from Isaac to Jakob and back again, the slack of the detective's jaw spearheading a smile across her face. "It's okay, Isaac. We're glad you're here. We just didn't know you were out there until you spoke." Rising to her feet, she backed up the steps and gestured for Isaac to follow.

"Please, come sit."

Isaac waited at the bottom, his gaze inventorying his brother's face in a way that felt as if he was trying to memorize it. "I know I should go. I know that is what is expected of me. But I cannot. I have tried to honor the Amish way these past few months, but it is hard. I miss you, Jakob." Lowering his hatted head ever so slightly, he cleared his throat of the emotion that was fusing into his voice and then looked up once again. "I miss my brother."

For a moment, she wasn't sure if Jakob had heard, his feet seemingly rooted to the floor of the porch, his eyes closed tightly. But just as she was about to touch his arm to bring him back from wherever he'd gone, he brushed a quick hand across his now open eyes and stepped forward, clapping a hand atop Isaac's shoulder. "As I have missed you."

She saw Isaac swallow as he worked to reclaim his normal stoicism. "I know it was not right to listen to your words. But what you said . . . I am worried it is not true." Slowly, Isaac climbed the steps to stand beside Jakob and Claire. "I do not want Dat to be reason behind Zook's death. Yet I fear that he is."

Grabbing hold of a pair of wicker chairs

grouped together on a far side of the porch, Jakob pulled them over to the swing and invited Claire and Isaac to sit down. Then, when they were settled, Jakob began asking the very questions firing away inside Claire's head. "Why? Why are you so certain that Dat may have done this? Mose Fisher, of all people, believes in living life by the Ordnung. So why would he snap and kill another man?"

"He did not like Zook."

Jakob gently thumbed the underside of his chin. "I know that he held Harley responsible on some level for my leaving. And I know that Harley's quiet yet persistent support of me didn't help the situation. But really, that was sixteen years ago. If Dat was to snap and kill because of *that,* he'd have done it a long time ago."

"When I told Dat of new job, he hit table with fist. His face became purple with anger in a way I have not seen. I told him it was a good job. That I would not always fix things and build things in same place as Zook. That we would work together in business but not always side by side. But he did not listen."

"What *did* he do?"

"He made house shake when he shut the door. He took the buggy to Zook's house and Mamm begged me to follow. When I got to Zook's farm, Dat was yelling, telling Zook to find someone else. But I told him I had accepted and would not go back on my word," Isaac said. "Zook told him I was a man and could make my own decisions just as my brother did."

Jakob and Claire winced at the same time.

"I imagine that didn't help things . . ." Then, realizing she'd spoken aloud, she clamped her mouth shut for fear she'd derail Jakob from procuring the information he needed.

"It did not. Dat believed Zook cost him one son; he did not want Zook to cost him another. He said there would be consequences. I was glad Mamm was not there to see the anger in Dat's eyes when he said those words. She would have been frightened." Isaac leaned forward and lowered his hatted head in shame. "It is wrong that I am here, that I am saying these things of Dat. Benjamin would be furious."

Claire didn't need the light that streamed onto the porch from the inn's front windows to see the way Jakob's face darkened at the mention of Benjamin. Nor did she need the sight of the detective's clenched fists to know he was angry. His words, delivered through tight lips, only served to underscore the emotion. "Dat is not any of Benjamin Miller's concern. Mose is not his dat. And Benjamin is not Dat's son. *You* are. And" — he inhaled sharply — "*I* am."

"Today, Benjamin acts more like Dat's son than I. For he believes Dat is innocent of this crime while I believe . . ." Isaac's sentence petered off just before he shook his head in disgust. "I am no son with such thoughts."

Jakob teed his hands in the air. "Wait just a minute. You have been a wonderful son to Dat. You did your chores faithfully and without complaint from the moment you moved in with us. You never caused a moment of grief for Mamm or Dat during the next five years I was living at home. And you are still there while I am not."

Claire reached across the arm of the swing to capture one of Jakob's hands in hers. "You are a wonderful son, too, Jakob, whether your father sees that or not."

"Thank you." He flashed a tender smile in her direction then turned his focus back on his brother. "Please. Finish what you were going to say."

Isaac's brow furrowed. "I do not know what you mean."

"You were starting to say something about the difference between Benjamin and you in relation to Zook's murder, yet you didn't complete your sentence."

Isaac's head sunk lower only to lift enough to pin Jakob with a helpless stare. "Benjamin is certain Dat could not kill Zook. Yet, I am his son and I do not know."

"Okay, so he was angry you took the job with Harley. Lots of people get angry, Isaac," Claire said before realizing she'd weighed in on a discussion where she wasn't meant to be anything more than a spectator. "I'm sorry. This isn't any of my business."

Jakob waved her apology away. "Isaac came here, to your house. I believe he wants it to be your business." He looked at his brother for confirmation. At Isaac's nod, Jakob resumed the conversation. "Claire is right. So maybe Dat wasn't happy about your working alongside someone whom he saw as being partly responsible for my choice to leave. Maybe he even unleashed a little anger when he raced out to Harley's farm that day. But to snap and kill so quickly? I just can't wrap my mind around that one."

"It was not quickly. It has been building for long time."

"Building? As in getting worse?"

Isaac nodded.

"But why?" Jakob insisted, clearly perplexed. "It's been *sixteen* years, Isaac. Surely Dat has put me out of his mind the way he's expected you and Martha and Mamm to do."

"We tried but it was not possible for any of us. I do not believe it was possible for Dat." Isaac covered the lower half of his face with a splayed palm and released a burst of air against his skin. "Zook did not believe it was possible."

Claire glanced at Jakob to see if he was following his brother's words. The blank look she found there confirmed he was as lost as she was. "Harley didn't believe *what* was possible, Isaac?"

Slowly, Isaac let his hand fall to his lap. "That Dat no longer considered Jakob his son the way he said."

The pain from Isaac's words skittered across Jakob's eyes only to be dulled away by whatever wall the detective had erected around his heart in the years he'd been living with his family's disgrace. "Did Harley say or do something that makes you so sure he saw a crack in Dat's resolve?"

"Each day that he passed Dat, Zook would make mention of you. He would tell of how hard you must be working in the big city. He would wonder if you were married

147

and if you were a father yourself. When you came back to Heavenly this summer, he said it was good you had come back home where Dat could see the man you had become." Isaac straightened his back against the wicker chair and shrugged. "His words reminded Dat each day of your choice and of your absence."

"Wow." Jakob stood, took a step or two in the direction of the railing, then doubled back toward his chair, the reality of Isaac's words clearly affecting him on a deeper level. "I had no idea Harley lobbied for me so hard."

"Lobbied?" Isaac repeated. "I do not know what that means."

"Spoke out in my defense, supported me, championed me, that sort of thing." Jakob sat once again, this time turning his entire body in his brother's direction "So you're saying that the constant reminder of my choice by the man Dat saw as partly responsible *for* that choice not only kept Dat's anger fresh, it also allowed it to build?"

"Yah. That is right."

"Were there indications it was building? I mean, real signs?"

"Yah. Signs I did not see until I took job with Zook."

"I'm not talking about Dat yelling at

Harley when he learned you took the job, Isaac," Jakob implored. "I'm talking about signs before that final straw."

"I speak of the same thing."

"Tell us about these signs," Claire interjected in an effort to ward off Jakob's budding frustration. "Help us to understand why you believe Mose's anger has been building to an unhealthy level all these years."

"I do not know how he did it. I do not remember him leaving the fields during the day to do such things, but perhaps when I am with Lapp making toys, he leaves. It is the only way I can see it happening. Zook worked long hours and was gone much of the day." Claire met Jakob's troubled gaze and followed it back to Isaac, the weight of the man's rambling answer clearly weighing on his mind and body. "But I suppose it could have happened at night when Zook was sleeping and Mamm was not awake to notice Dat leave . . ."

"What could have happened at night, Isaac?" Jakob pleaded. "What do you think Dat has been doing at Zook's farm?"

As if some unseen switch had been flipped off, Isaac stood. "I have said too much. I cannot say any more. I cannot be one to hurt Mamm in this way."

Jakob jumped to his feet and grabbed hold of his brother's arm. "Isaac, wait. You can't say this much and then walk away. Finish what you started."

"I have spoken against Dat. He would never forgive me if he knew I was here . . . with you . . . saying such things about him. I have said enough. Now, you must see signs on your own."

"What signs?" Releasing Isaac's arm from his grasp, Jakob threw his hands up. "How can I help if you don't talk to me? You have to know that I don't want Dat to be responsible for Harley's murder any more than you do, Isaac."

"You do not need my help. You must only go to Zook's farm to see what I will not say. If you do, you will see signs of Dat's anger with your own eyes and I will not be forced to betray him more than I already have. I, in turn, will pray that I am wrong."

CHAPTER 13

The line was five deep at the counter when Claire arrived at Heavenly Brews, the faces in front of her all familiar and all desperate for a little help in shaking off the same morning fog that had her hiding more than a few yawns behind her hand. If any of her fellow shopkeepers noticed her arrival, they didn't let on, their collective focus on the barista tasked with providing the jolt of energy that would get them through the first half of their workday.

At the front of the line was Howard Glick, the round-faced man who owned Glick's Tools 'n More. The popular hardware store served as Heavenly Treasures' opposing bookend alongside Shoo Fly Bake Shoppe. Glick's store was a popular tourist stop for both men and women alike. The men liked the hands-on Try-Me sections Howard had set up around his showroom. The women liked the extended shopping windows those

Try-Me sections afforded them in return. It was truly a win-win for everyone.

Behind Howard and waiting expectantly for his turn to order was Al Gussman, the proprietor of Gussman's General Store and the landlord for most of the buildings along Lighted Way, including Claire's. He'd always been a nice man, yet she couldn't help but wonder if she'd see a different side when she told him she needed to break her lease nearly six months early.

Next in line was Sandra Moffit, the owner of Tastes of Heaven(ly), the quaint eatery on the far side of the street. Like its sister eatery, Shoo Fly Bake Shoppe, the café was a popular spot for tourists craving authentic Amish dishes. For Ruth, the pies and treats she baked were made from simple recipes she'd tasted and helped make her whole life. For Sandra, the restaurant-style food she served in her café was based on years of research and trial and error about a facet of the American population that had intrigued her since childhood.

Directly in front of Claire was Drew Styles, the mostly absent owner of Glorious Books, the new bookstore that had opened next to Yoder's Fine Furniture the previous month. The shop had been an instant draw much to the delight of both Drew and his fellow Lighted Way business owners who'd been around long enough to recognize the fact that the success of one had a positive effect on all. Assuming, of course, their shops weren't so far gone any benefit was swallowed up whole . . .

She tapped Drew on the back, raising his answering smile with one of her own. "Good morning, Drew, it's nice to see you. How are things going?"

"Hi, Claire. They're going quite well, thank you." Drew jerked his left hand upward to call her attention to the briefcase he held. "Now that it's wedding season around here, you'll be seeing me on this line every Tuesday and Thursday morning. My wife, Jolene, calls my morning cup of joe my sunshine maker. In fact, if you listen to her, the United States Coast Guard should send out storm warnings to all sailors in the vicinity of *anywhere* if I miss a day."

"I'd be just as bad if it weren't for the smells I wake up to every morning. It's hard to wake up in anything other than a happy mood when there's such amazing food at the ready one floor down."

"Did your aunt take the morning off?"

She laughed. "Why? Do I look that grumpy?"

He waved away her lighthearted concern with a flick of his free hand. "Nah, just tired is all. Like the rest of us."

It wasn't a surprise, really. Especially in light of the way she'd tossed and turned throughout the night thinking about Isaac and Jakob's shared anguish. To Drew, she merely offered a shrugged agreement before taking the conversation back a step to the first glimmer of hope she'd had for a turn-around in weeks. "Are we expecting a bigger rush in conjunction with wedding season? Is that why you'll be coming in on those days?"

Sandra turned. "The Amish tend not to work on Tuesdays and Thursdays during this time of year. Which is why, I suspect, both Samuel and Ruth will not open today. Those of us who employ Amish help simply know we'll be short staffed on those days."

"Esther never said anything about not coming in today," Claire offered while trying not to let her shoulders sag too noticeably. So much for a glimmer of hope . . . "In fact, she made a point of telling me she'd be in today."

"Then she must not have a wedding to attend." Sandra let out a happy sigh as Howard took his coffee, instantly moving her to second in line. "Sometimes that happens, though it's rare."

"There are that many weddings in Heavenly each week?"

"No. Sometimes they're in other Amish communities in other parts of the state. If it's not too far, they take their buggies. If it is, they hire drivers." Sandra split her focus between Claire and Drew behind her, and Al in front of her — her words tossed over her shoulder in their direction when necessary. "You should drive past an Amish home when there's a wedding sometime. The line of buggies goes on and on and on. Then again, you'll be seeing what might be an even longer line when that man's body is finally released and they hold his funeral."

"Man?" she echoed before answering her own question. "Wait, you mean Harley Zook?"

"Crying shame what happened to that fella," Drew murmured. "You don't expect something like that to happen in these parts. The two images just don't go together, do they?"

Indeed they didn't.

As Al's order was filled and Sandra stepped forward, Claire found herself slipping into her own thoughts only to be snapped out of them by the jangle of bells over her shoulder. Turning around, she smiled at the face that had been absent from the dinner table the night before. "Megan, hi! How was your day with Kyle yesterday? Did you guys have fun?"

The young mother took her spot in line behind Claire. "Oh, Claire, it was perfect. We spent hours poking in and out of the stores. We tried that bakery you mentioned and it was out of this world. Then, before dinner, we took a walk out toward the Amish farms. When we were done, we came back and had dinner at" — Megan pointed at the front of the line — "that woman's café. It was delicious. Everything we did, everything we tried, was perfect. Including the coffee from this place."

"I'm glad. I kind of knew you'd have a good day here." Claire kept her focus on Megan even as she stepped forward in line to accommodate Sandra's successful coffee purchase. "So" — she looked around — "where's Kyle this morning?"

Megan hoisted her cavernous purse higher on her shoulder. "His new boss called him into the office today to go over some upcoming project. It's not the end of the world, though, because it means I have a little window for exploring."

"There are great outlet stores in Breeze Point," Claire offered. "It's no more than maybe a thirty-minute drive and they have basically every store you could want there. It's a favorite day trip for many of Diane's guests throughout the year."

"Kyle suggested the same thing after breakfast this morning but . . . well, I have different plans."

She felt her eyebrows rise. "Oh?"

Megan nodded and lowered her voice. "If I mention those Amish lots one more time to Kyle, I think he's going to have me fit for a muzzle. But, since he's not here today, I can give them one more look and see if maybe we could make it work."

Drew pulled out his wallet and placed a five-dollar bill on the counter signaling the completion of his purchase and Claire's turn to order. She glanced back at Megan. "A second look is always good, right?"

"That's what I think. Kyle, however, doesn't agree. Not for these lots, anyway. But maybe it'll be different today. Maybe Friday was a fluke."

Claire tried to focus on Megan's words, tried to nod accordingly, but as soon as Drew's lid was in place, her attention needed to be on the barista. "Maybe . . ."

"If you have a little time later today, do you think you could meet me out there and tell me what *you* think?" Megan asked, her bright blue eyes wide with unrestrained hope. "Another opinion would really help get this place out of my head once and for all. Which, in turn, would make Kyle happy."

"Uh, I guess. If you think that would help." Claire stepped back to give Drew exit room and then slid into his spot, the promise of coffee making her mouth water. Within seconds her request was being poured into a waiting to-go cup. "What time are you thinking about meeting? I could probably do something in the neighborhood of three, maybe four o'clock?"

The woman did a slight hop of pleasure, instantly chasing away any reservation Claire was feeling about the added task for her day. "Four would be great. Do you know where it is?"

"I don't think so."

Megan angled her body toward the coffee shop's front window and motioned with her hand toward the main thoroughfare that was Lighted Way. "Take this road all the way out past the Amish farms until you get to the end. Make a left and the entrance to the development will be right there. It's just a dirt road right now as there aren't any homes yet, but that's where I'll be at four o'clock."

"Then that's where I'll meet you." Claire turned back to the counter, swapping her money and a thank-you for the now-ready cup of coffee. Then, nodding back at Megan, she headed toward the tiny seating area in the front of the shop to check the phone she'd felt vibrating inside her purse while paying.

Setting her coffee down momentarily, Claire retrieved her phone and flipped it open, the missed call icon leading her to Jakob's name and number. A quick check of her voice mail box showed he didn't leave a message.

She called his number and waited as the phone rang, once, twice, three times.

He picked up. "Detective Fisher."

"Hi, Jakob, it's me, Claire." She did her best to ignore the butterflies that flapped in her stomach in reaction to his voice. She was hopeless, utterly and completely hope-less . . . "I noticed you tried to call. Is everything okay?"

"I just wanted to check in and say thanks for the talk last night. Aside from the prevailing subject of that talk, it was nice spending time together."

She swallowed.

"Anyway, I'd hoped to get out to Zook's place and follow up on everything Isaac said last night, but my morning has turned into a bit of a juggling act."

She seized the safe ground of Jakob's words and reined in the odd emotions coursing through her body — emotions she wasn't ready to try and analyze. "What's going on?"

"For starters, Harley's body will be released later today, which means the viewing will start either at his farm or that of one of the other members of his district probably as soon as this evening."

"Will you attend?" she asked.

"I doubt that would go over all that well." Then, moving on quickly, he switched gears toward a subject with far fewer personal ties. "Then, on top of that, we got a call last night from Rita Duggan. Seems Patrick was acting up. By the time our officers got out there, he had fallen asleep. I need to get some more information on what happened to make her call us. See if it might lead back to the investigation in any way."

She waved as Megan exited the coffee shop, the mere sight of the woman giving way to a plan. "I have to head out past Harley's farm later this afternoon to meet one of Diane's guests. I could stop there first to make sure no more cows have escaped, and, while I'm there, maybe see if

I spy one of those signs your brother was talking about last night." She lifted her cup to her lips and took a quick sip, the bold flavor, coupled with her suggestion, chasing away the last of her morning fog. "I mean, if it's okay with you, of course."

CHAPTER 14

For the second time in as many days, Claire found herself staring at the run-down farmhouse that had been home to Harley Zook. Even now, she was still shocked by its appearance. She supposed there could be something to the notion of a person in a particular field of work not wanting to have anything to do with that same kind of work off the clock, but still. How hard could it have been to tack down a few roof shingles, or tighten an ill-fitting door?

Especially when it was obvious he'd taken such good care of the dairy barn and just about everything else pertaining to the cows who shared his address.

A soft tap at the driver's side window made her nearly jump out of her skin. Jerking her head to the left, she willed her heart rate to slow as she took in the teenaged Amish boy standing just outside her door. She stepped from the car, scrunching her nose and extending her hand as she did. "Hi. I'm Claire. Claire Weatherly."

"Yah."

If the pervasive smell of spoiled milk bothered the young man, he kept it to himself. She, however, switched to a mouth-only breath that required its fair share of concentration. "And you are?"

"Luke Hochstetler. I live on the other side of Lapp." It was such a simple reply yet told her everything she needed to know. The young boy bowed his head ever so slightly, a grim set to his mouth visible beneath the brim of his hat. "Mr. Zook is not here, Ms. Weatherly. He has passed."

She glanced at the farmhouse and then back at Luke. "I know. I'm the one who found him in the corn maze." At his widened eyes, she continued. "So what brings you out here, Luke? Are you looking after Harley's place?"

"I'm looking after his cows. Dat is hoping we may get some of them." Luke looped the fingers of his left hand around one of his suspenders and nudged his chin in the direction of the barn. "One of my sisters wants Mary, the other one wants Molly. Dat just wants fresh milk."

She laughed, the sound diffusing the last of the tension ushered in by the teenager's surprise appearance. The wants and needs of the Amish were so humble, so straightforward. "So how are they holding up?" At the uncertain rise to his brow, she swept her hand toward the barn. "The cows. Are they doing okay?"

"It is easy for them to be okay." Luke grinned. "Dat brought my brothers here when they had finished with their morning chores. He wanted to show them how a mucked stall should look. I do not think they will complain again."

"They're that clean?"

"Yah. Even now, four days later, they are cleaner than most. And Dat said Mr. Zook did that with no sons to help. My brothers felt shame for their efforts." Luke rubbed his hand along his jaw, a motion he'd probably seen his father make countless times. "Dat said we could chase cows, though."

"Chase cows?" she repeated. "I'm sorry, I'm not following."

"If we get some of Mr. Zook's cows, we will not have such a fence as that." Luke's hand left his jaw to guide her eyes toward the pasture. "Dat has sons who can fetch a loose cow."

"That's probably smart considering the fact that a fence like that still couldn't keep Harley's cows where they belonged." Then, at Luke's knowing smile, she said, "I met Mary on Friday night. She was hoping to be milked."

"I milked her and brought her home."

She tried not to think about that night — a night that had started out so light and fun yet ended as far from those two adjectives as one could get. "It's almost as if Mary was searching for Harley."

Luke shook his head. "Nah. Cows do not know such things. Mr. Zook took care of his cows like children, Mamm said. But they are not. They are cows . . . with fancy names."

She hadn't really considered the fact that Harley lived alone until that moment, the loss of his brother sixteen years earlier coming a decade after the death of his wife — a woman unable to have children, according to Diane. Yet, according to Jakob and her aunt, Harley had been a cheerful man, offering forgiveness and work to his brother's killer's son and relentlessly trying to open Mose Fisher's closed mind in regards to Jakob. It was a sad twist of irony to think that one of those kindnesses may have ultimately led to the man's demise . . .

"Will your family sell the milk for cheese, too?" she asked.

"Dat will purchase a bulk cooling tank

with an agitator. That way we can sell for a higher price."

She allowed herself one quick nose breath, realizing her error almost immediately. "I'm sure your neighbors will be grateful."

"I must go. Dat will be looking for me if I do not get back. There is much work to do at our own farm before sunset." Then, with a nod of his head, Luke was gone, his pale blue shirt and black pants the last two things Claire could see before the teenager disappeared around a bend in the driveway.

Suddenly, she was all too aware of being alone, the knowledge that Harley's beloved cows were mere steps away doing little to soothe the sense of unease Luke's departure had set in motion. Yet, as little comfort as their presence provided, she found herself moving in the direction of the barn, none-theless.

Once inside the large doors, she was able to breathe a little easier thanks to the thick walls of the well-constructed barn and a potpourri of new smells including cows, lots of cows. A quick mental count showed that there were two dozen bright-eyed Holsteins, all looking at her as if she could solve the many mysteries of the world, or at least the only one they cared to truly know.

It was an answer she wished she didn't

have to give.

Squaring her shoulders, she approached the first cow she came to, a large black-and-white animal with the kind of thick eyelashes most women would envy. She checked the small wooden sign above the cow and addressed her accordingly. "Well, hello there, Mavis. Did Luke take good care of you just now?" Mavis's mouth moved round and round, her focus never leaving Claire's face. "I wish I could tell you Harley will be back, sweetie, but I can't. All I can do is tell you that Jakob won't rest until he figures out who did this to him and why."

Slowly, she reached out, stroked a hand down the side of the animal's face, her touch unable to alter the rhythm of its mouth. She wished Mavis could understand her words, perhaps even give voice to whatever the animal was thinking behind those big, soulful eyes.

"Have a good day, okay?" she whispered in farewell as she moved down the line, passing Molly, Mindy, and Mandy before finally reaching the latest escapee, Mary. "Remember me? I met you on the side of the road a few days ago."

Like Mavis, Mary worked her mouth round and round in response, giving Claire a few moments to look around at the rest of the barn. Like its other Amish counterparts, the dairy barn was simple, yet spacious, the walls and doors constructed by those to whom hard labor was second nature. Here, though, things were even tidier than normal, as if the care and comfort of the animals not only claimed the top spot on the daily to-do list but every other spot as well.

She swatted a pesky fly off Mary's ear then wandered across the barn to inspect an odd swath of white paint to the left of the door. As she approached, she spied a second, bigger swath no more than ten feet from the first — the similar stroke pattern making her wonder whether Harley had been testing a paint color and found that he needed better light with which to make his final decision.

Part of her found it curious that someone would entertain the notion of painting the interior of a barn, but the other part — the part that had just seen the carefully etched names of each cow inscribed above their pen and heard the details of Harley's meticulous care from Luke — knew it wasn't out of the realm of possibility. Harley Zook had cared for his cows as if they were his children. Perhaps he'd wanted to give them something more than just a standard barn in which to live . . .

A wave of sadness rushed in and forced her back outside into the rancid-smelling sunshine. Everything she'd heard about Harley thus far had come together to create an image of a happy-go-lucky Amish man whose contagious smile and unfailing kindness allowed him to get away with being a little eccentric.

She picked her way across a hoofprint-strewn path to the empty pasture and leaned against the sturdy fence. Her gaze moved from hay roll to hay roll as she imagined Harley looking after his herd through the long winter months, covering them with handmade quilts to keep them warm as they ate. It was a ludicrous thought yet one she couldn't quite shake loose even if she'd wanted to.

Yes, picturing Harley tending his beloved cows was far more appealing than remembering him as he'd looked in the corn maze. She ran her hand along the top rail of the fence as she walked, her feet stopping only when she reached the now-secured gate. Now that Harley was gone, she wondered if it would be Luke and his siblings who would fetch Mary and the girls if they headed off campus in search of greener pastures. Yet standing there, studying the gate's intricate-locking mechanism, she couldn't help but wonder how they got out in the first place. Or rather, why.

It was obvious Harley had invested time and money in securing his cows. In fact, now that she thought about it, all the other Amish farms between Harley's place and Lighted Way boasted a simple handmade fence if they had one at all. So why go to the added expense and effort only to be careless in the end?

"What a waste," Claire mumbled before turning back toward the farmhouse and her waiting car. Step-by-step, she made her way back to her starting point, her progress thwarted only by a poorly discarded can of spray paint that preyed on her inner neatness.

"Claire?"

She stilled her hand atop the dented can and listened.

"Claire? Is that you?"

Retrieving the trash from its spot beneath a row of overgrown hedges, she straightened at the vaguely familiar voice that didn't fit with her current surroundings. "Hello? Who's there?"

"Woo-hoo, Claire, it's me . . . over here! You turned too soon!"

Scrunching her eyes in what she imagined was a mirror image of her nose, Claire looked past the farmhouse and her car to the line of trees that separated Harley's property from that of his neighbor's. And there, just inside a miniscule break in the natural border, was the face that went with the voice.

CHAPTER 15

Clutching the empty can to her chest, Claire navigated her way around a series of deep tire ruts before stepping through the opening in the trees that denoted the end of Harley's property and the start of the next. "Megan, hi! Is everything okay?"

Megan waved aside Claire's question with an air of distraction. "You just turned too soon is all."

"Turned too soon?"

"You were supposed to take the road all the way to the end before you turned but that's okay. I can't imagine the Amish would mind you parking in their driveway."

She tried to follow what her aunt's guest was saying but came up short. "I'm sorry, I'm not sure what you're talking about."

Megan's face paled. "Oh. I'm sorry. I . . . I thought you'd made a wrong turn on your way out to meet me . . ." Her voice petered off as she looked down at the stapled sheaf of papers in her hand. "I guess it was silly of me to ask in the first place on account of you having an actual life and all, huh? Kyle keeps saying we need to just make a decision and make the best out of whichever one we choose, but sometimes that's harder to do than it sounds."

Something about Megan's demeanor, coupled with the tidbits Claire was actually able to follow, began to put things in focus. A glance at her wrist watch merely acted as confirmation.

"No, no, no . . . I wanted to come and help with the house thing, I really did — I mean, do. It's just that" — she gestured over her shoulder with the spray can — "I guess I lost track of time. I would have remembered as soon as I got back in the car, though."

She tried not to wince at the suggestion she'd forgotten their meeting, and focused, instead, on the smile that lifted at least one side of Megan's mouth.

"So you didn't make a wrong turn?"

"A wrong turn?" Claire echoed before putting two and two together in the conversation department. "Oh no, I meant to stop here first. That's Harley's farm right there, the man who —" She stopped mid-sentence and shook her head. No, there was no reason to rake Heavenly's latest blemish back up to the surface. That, her aunt's guest could read about in the paper. Instead, Claire nudged her chin in the direction of Megan's car. "So what brings you here?"

Megan hoisted the papers into the air with one hand and waved to the area around her car with the other. "This is it."

Claire's gaze played follow the leader with Megan's hand as it swept to the left and then the right. "It?"

"Yes. This is Serenity Falls — the development I was telling you about this morning. The one with the spectacular location."

Finally on board with what was going on, Claire allowed herself to really take in her surroundings, the bits and pieces she'd managed to make out through the treeline from the passenger seat of Jakob's car over the weekend finally assembling themselves into some sort of sense. The rusting metal boxes she'd caught only glimpses of were utility hook ups for the homes that would eventually be built on the land, the gravel pathways a precursor for the blacktopped roads that would surely follow. "Oh. Wow. You weren't kidding about being able to live on the Amish side of town, were you?"

Megan's smile crept all the way across her face. "See? Isn't it perfect for people like you and me? People who love the same peace and tranquility the Amish enjoy twenty-four/seven?"

"Any chance they'll erect a small cottage or two out here, too?" she quipped only to rescind her words at the mental knock of reality that was her financial situation. "You know what? Ignore me. I'm not ready to leave the inn just yet. Diane's cooking is way too good."

"That's what Kyle said last night," Megan replied, wide-eyed. "He said he wished we could buy the inn and hire Diane to dote on our whole family the way she's doted on the two of us these past few days."

"I'll have to share that with Diane. She'll be tickled to hear it." Claire left the area where they'd been standing to walk around, imagining a handful of large homes scattered about the land, further blurring the invisible yet very real line between the Amish and English sides of town. Suddenly, she couldn't help but wonder what such a blurring would mean for the Amish. Would the English who built there embrace the slower pace of its neighbors? Or would the slow-moving buggies and simple farming lifestyle eventually start to scratch at the nerves of the very people who chose to eliminate the line in the first place?

She hoped for the former but knew the latter was the more likely scenario. Right or wrong, it was the way things seemed to work in life. "So what's the issue?" she asked, swatting at a fly with the paint can as she did. "If you like the lifestyle of the Amish and the location of this development, why don't you just build here? They're a custom-home development aren't they?"

Megan looked down at the papers in her hand and nodded. "They are. They've got a number of existing plans they'll build from if you find one you like, or, if you want to do your own thing, you can bring in your own plans. But the lots are expensive. And with the rules and regulations the builder has in place for this development, the homes won't be cheap, either."

"Oh." Claire didn't know what else to say. Megan and her husband's financial capabilities really weren't any of Claire's concern. "Then maybe you really should consider the English side if they have homes that are more within your parameters."

With several long strides, Megan closed the gap between them and offered the folder for Claire to see. "No, we can afford them. Kyle's taking a nice pay bump to move here."

Claire took the folder and flipped it open

against her can-holding hand. The artist's rendering of the proposed development along with the starting price of its homes caught her breath and held it tight. "Wow. This — this is *gorgeous.*"

"Isn't it?" Megan's eyes sparkled long enough to make their subsequent dullness all the more noticeable. "But Kyle said there is absolutely no way he's going to spend that kind of money to never be able to open his windows."

"Excuse me?"

Megan sniffed, her nose crinkling instantly. "Don't you smell that? It's awful!"

For the first time since stepping into Harley's barn, she had to consciously think about the smell that wafted across the tree line along with a few handfuls of bothersome flies. "Oh, that?"

"Yes, that."

She thought back to the last time she'd noticed the smell and said the first thing that came to her mind. "Honestly, if it helps any, you almost get used to it after a while." And it was true. Though, now that Megan had called it to her attention again, she couldn't help but wish for a nose plug.

"I tried to say that to Kyle when we came out here on Friday, but he said he isn't going to pay Serenity Falls' prices to have to get used to anything." Megan reached across Claire's arm and flipped the welcome page over to reveal the first of many renderings that walked prospective buyers through what could eventually be their neighborhood if they signed on the dotted line. In one picture there was a playground for the kids. In another, a fitness trail and workout stations for the adults. The next page showed families coming together under a pavilion to enjoy a potluck dinner and a series of old-fashioned family games. It was, in a word, the epitome of the American dream for a mom like Megan.

"I can see why you can't put this place out of your mind." And it was true. Then again, Megan's answering flip of the next page brought Kyle's position into perspective with an underscore or two to boot. "Oh. Wow. Yeah, those are kind of expensive, aren't they?"

She tried to imagine making the kind of money that would allow her to even consider building a home like those pictured in the folder, but she couldn't. Not when running a specialty gift shop in the middle of Heavenly, Pennsylvania, was her one and only source of income, anyway.

Then again, adding a detective's salary to the mix wouldn't get her a whole lot closer . . .

Her mouth grew dry at the thought.

Where on earth had *that* come from? Especially now, when her only thought should be on the income she was months away from losing altogether . . .

To Megan, she said, "I can see why you like it out here so much. I would, too. It's like you'd truly leave the hustle and bustle of life behind every time you turned your car toward home. And when you *got* home, the atmosphere would be so different I'm not sure you'd even remember work or school or wherever it is you came from."

Megan's eyes glowed. "Yes! That's exactly what I think every time I revisit this place in my head at night. I mean, can't you just see two kids growing up here? The fun they'd have on that playground? The physical activity they'd get looking for frogs in the pond instead of trying to whack them over the head on some television screen? And out here, I wouldn't have to worry about the next-door neighbor cursing as he worked on his hot rod in the driveway or having to pick up empty beer cans along the side of the road."

Claire couldn't help but laugh at the picture Megan painted. Yet, at the same time, she understood. Those were the kind of images Claire had, too, whenever she dared to let herself dream of having children one day.

Feeling the heaviness of her thoughts, she searched for a way to lighten the mood and seized on the can still wrapped in her hand. "If it's any consolation, being out here doesn't entirely negate the possibility of a litter bug." She lifted the can into the air long enough to bring home her point, then handed the folder back to Megan. "I don't know what to tell you, Megan. It's beautiful out here, no doubt. And the pictures in that packet make it hard to resist. But Kyle has a point. Can you really justify spending that kind of money when there's a very real possibility your kids won't want to be outside long enough to chase frogs?"

A beat or two of silence was followed by Megan's two hands — and the folder — being raised into the air in complete surrender. "You're right. You're absolutely right. Kyle and I are getting ready to uproot our children from the only home they've ever known. They're trusting us to give them a new home they can love and embrace every bit as much as we do. I don't need a mailing address on a certain side of town to make my home peaceful. That part is up to Kyle and me and no one else."

Claire reached out and gently squeezed Megan's free hand with her own. "I think you've made the right choice, Megan. I really do. I mean, I'd like to tell you things will change soon, but who knows; it could get worse. Either way, there's no guarantee. And for that kind of money, I can't imagine taking a gamble."

"Thanks, Claire. I think, deep down inside, I knew this all along, but I guess I just needed a little added reinforcement to quiet the pesky what-ifs." Megan crossed to her rental car and tossed the folder into the backseat. "Are you okay out here alone? Because I can drive you around to your car if you want."

"No, I'm fine. My car's literally on the other side of those trees." Claire pointed toward the break in the over-grown tree line that had allowed her to join Megan in the first place then reached into her pocket for her vibrating phone. The name she saw displayed on the screen sent an instant and undeniable crackle of excitement down her spine. "Besides, I've got a call coming in so I'll be fine."

She flipped open her phone and held it to her ear. "Hello."

"Hi, Claire, it's Jakob. Are you still out at Zook's place?"

"I was and now I'm heading back there after a slight detour to meet one of Diane's guests on the empty lot next door." At the silence in her ear, she filled in the gaps. "The Reillys are in town house hunting. Megan Reilly, the wife, was interested in the development going in behind Harley's property and wanted my thoughts. Now I'm heading back to my car."

"Any idea what these signs Isaac was talking about might be?"

"No, I didn't see anything. Just a herd of very sad cows."

Jakob's laugh traveled through the phone and warmed her ear. "Sad cows, eh? Hmmm . . . Spoken like a true city girl."

"Hey!"

"Hey, yourself," he joked. "Now, any interest in taking a drive out to Rita Duggan's house with me? Maybe your presence will make her more comfortable."

She stopped midway to her car. "You want to take me on an official call? Are you even allowed to do that?"

"Technically it's not official because I promised Rita it wouldn't be. I told her I just wanted to stop by and see how things are going after Patrick's little meltdown last night. Maybe chat with him, too, and see if there's anything I can do to help. It's the only way she'd agree to talk, and until I have a reason to question her son in relation to Harley's murder, I think the unofficial visit is the best way to go."

"Okay, sure. Esther is in charge of the shop this afternoon, and she already told me she'd be happy to close up on her own at six. So, yes, I'll drive out there with you." She resumed her pace, suddenly aware of the can she still touted in her hand. "Shall I meet you at the police station in ten minutes?"

"Ten minutes is perfect. I'll see you then."

When the line disconnected, she closed the phone inside her free hand and dropped it in her pocket, her gaze gravitating toward the one side of the farmhouse she'd yet to see from the driveway or the pasture.

There, on the scrap of foundation visible between the ground and the faded clapboard exterior, were five words spray-painted in bright white paint — five words that froze her in place as they came together to form a single, solitary, chilling sentence . . .

One more and you're dead.

CHAPTER 16

She slid into the passenger seat of Jakob's car and tried to narrow in on the best way to tell him Isaac's accusations about Mose were correct. It wasn't easy to find the words, especially when she knew they would only serve to increase the detective's stress level.

"So you really didn't see anything to back up what Isaac was saying the other night, huh?" he said as he shifted into drive and pulled out onto Lighted Way. "I mean, I guess that's good. The less incriminating evidence aimed at my father, the better."

Oh, how she wished her answer hadn't changed the moment she hung up the phone outside Harley's farmhouse. But it had. Now the only thing Claire had to decide was whether she should ask him to pull off at the park so she could break it to him gently or take the chance that he could handle the news while driving. "Um, actually . . . after we hung up earlier, I —"

The squawk of Jakob's radio provided the momentary reprieve she hadn't realized she'd been praying for until it happened. Yet, now that it had, she couldn't help but breathe a sigh of relief as he excused himself to check in with the dispatcher, their subsequent back-and-forth quickly claiming her attention.

"The coroner's office called, Detective. Mr. Zook's body has been released. It was claimed for viewing and burial by his bishop, Atlee Hershberger, about an hour ago. The viewing, from what I was just told in the same phone call, has already started."

Jakob nodded along as the dispatcher wrapped up her report. "I wasn't sure I should bother you with this, but the chief said you'd want to know."

"No, Sue, you did the right thing."

"Also, Officer McKenzie is asking if you'd like him to sit outside the viewing and keep an eye on things for the next few hours?"

He drummed his fingers on the steering wheel as they headed into the English side of town, Rita and Patrick Duggan's home their intended destination. "You know, that might not be such a bad idea. Let him know I'll be there to cover that spot by nine o'clock."

Claire noted the time on the dashboard and the four-hour buffer he'd given himself.

"You got it, Detective. Should he raise you on the radio or your cell if something comes up?"

"Have him call my cell." They passed four streets to their left and five streets to their right before the car began to slow and he shifted his focus from the road in front of them to the note he'd affixed to the center console between them. There, in his unusually neat handwriting, was an address that had them turning right at the next stop sign. "And Sue? Thanks for letting me know."

"My pleasure."

And then Sue was gone, the background noises on the radio disappearing along with her voice. "Sorry about that, Claire. But it was a tidbit of information I needed to know."

She smiled at him across the seat and followed it up with a tiny shrug. "No, that's okay, I understand. But . . ." Hesitating just a moment, she finally gave in to the question she'd found herself wanting to ask since nearly the beginning of the radio transmission. "Is that really the way they do their viewings? In the bishop's *home*?"

"No. Usually the deceased is viewed in their own home. I suspect the bishop is hosting simply because Harley has no other living family in Heavenly."

"But in a home?" she repeated.

"Sure. It's like everything else the Amish do. They don't rely on the outside world for anything, really. A funeral isn't any different." He slowed the car still further as they wound their way around parked cars on the first of two side streets that would take them to the Duggans'. "And because it's in their home, as opposed to a funeral parlor, the viewing isn't confined to two separate two-hour sessions. An Amish viewing lasts for twenty-four hours or more, with members of the community here in Lancaster County and beyond stopping by to pay their respects at all hours of the day and night."

"Seriously?" At Jakob's nod, she glanced out the window and tried to visualize such a viewing. "And the actual funeral? Is it any different than ours?"

"It's simpler. The tombstones are far simpler, too. Harley's will just contain his name and the dates he was alive. There are no statues, no mausoleums. The Amish don't elevate themselves in life or death."

"Can only the Amish attend an Amish viewing?" she asked.

"If a person wishes to pay their respects, they are welcome to do so." He turned his gaze toward her long enough to ask a follow-up question of his own. "Why? Are you thinking about going?"

"I kind of think I should. I mean, I'm the one who found him, you know?" She shook off the reappearing image she'd managed to hold at bay for much of the day and answered his question with one of her own. "You're going to go, too, aren't you?"

He grew silent beside her as he pulled to a stop in front of a simple ranch-style home with tan siding and fading burgundy shutters. The mailbox at the end of the driveway confirmed they were in the right place. "I'd like to," he finally said, his voice so hushed she had to lean closer to hear his response. "I mean, Harley championed me for sixteen years. The least I can do is repay the favor for five minutes, right?"

"But . . ." she prompted in light of the audible hesitation that dotted his words.

"But I'm quite sure my presence will not be welcomed by Bishop Hershberger."

"Can he keep you out?"

"I don't think so, but he'll certainly make it as uncomfortable for me as possible."

She felt the familiar anger that always accompanied the subject of Jakob's excommunication rising up in her throat and did her best to keep it in check. Instead, she

188

settled on the simple facts. "That's okay, right? Because you're not there for him. You're there for Harley. The rest really doesn't matter."

"If only that were true," he mumbled before flashing the momentary smile she needed to see. "But yes, deep down inside, I know you're right. And I appreciate the encouragement and support more than you can realize. So thank you for that, Claire."

Then, jerking his chin in the direction of the Duggan house, he guided her focus back to the reason she was sitting in his car at all. "Are you ready to go inside?"

If it meant another temporary reprieve from sharing news of the spray-painted threat on the side of Harley's house, she was more than ready to go inside. To Jakob, though, she simply nodded. "Is there a certain role you'd like me to play in all this?"

He considered her words for a few moments. "Well, I guess I want this to seem as casual and nonthreatening as possible in the hopes Rita will talk freely."

"And as for why I'm here with you?"

"I was kind of hoping maybe I could say we're headed out on a date, if that's okay with you?" She heard the slight stumble in his request but opted not to make a big deal of it, aloud. The increased thumping in her chest took care of that all alone. "I'll just say something about it being my first chance to stop by or something like that. Sound good?"

"Uh, yeah, sure." She resisted the urge to cool her flushed face with her hands and opted, instead, to turn her head toward the Duggans' front porch and the hint of light that streamed through the open front door. "Do you want me to say anything? Ask anything?"

"If you come up with a question or comment you think will help facilitate the talking process, by all means, yes. But no pressure if you don't, okay?" At her slow nod, he put his hand on the door handle and pulled. "Let's do this."

The range of emotions across Rita Duggan's heavily lined face ran the gamut from pure, unadulterated exhaustion to an intermittent hostility that seemed to lack a discernible target. One minute, Claire was sure it was aimed at Patrick's inability to sit still and focus. The next, it seemed as if it was directed at the two of them and their presence in her home.

But still, the wife of convicted murderer Carl Duggan offered them cookies and lemonade and a spot on her tattered sofa.

"How's it going, Patrick?" Jakob asked, waving off the snack to focus his undivided attention on the burly, brown-eyed man pacing around the room. "I understand you had a little bit of a rough night last night."

The twenty-six-year-old stopped mid-step to rake a hand through his greasy hair, the gesture one of not-so-quiet irritation. "I was tired is all. That ain't a crime, is it?"

"No. But most folks don't throw things across a room because they're tired."

"I was looking for a video game."

Jakob looked to the diminutive woman seated across from Claire for confirmation. At her angry nod, he addressed Patrick once again. "Is that really a reason to throw things and yell at your mother, man?"

"I wanted to play. Wanted to shoot some stuff up."

"And I didn't want to listen to those noises all night long," Rita hissed through clenched teeth. "Sometimes I need to think, Patrick."

"Why? Nothing ever changes in there from what I can see, so why bother?"

Rita propped her hands on her hips and narrowed her eyes on her son. "How dare you question the kind of mother I've been. Have you had a roof over your head these past sixteen years, Patrick? Have you had food in your stomach?"

Patrick's head dropped in shame, yet Rita continued on, her tirade just getting started. "You're not the only one who's suffered all this time. And me? I've done my suffering while working two jobs and trying to keep you out of trouble. No one says I have to make your life easier. You're an adult now, Patrick. Part of being an adult is learning when to show restraint and how to exercise patience. I've given you all the rest."

"Your mom is right," Jakob said. "If she didn't want you playing games last night, there was a reason. You'll play them again another day. You can't go flying off the handle because you don't want to wait."

A quiet rage flashed behind Patrick's eyes as he pinned Jakob with a near-death stare then turned and disappeared down a hallway that led to the back of the house. Seconds later a door slammed.

"He's an angry young man," Jakob stated to no one in particular.

And, just like that, all of the anger Rita had displayed toward her son only seconds earlier was now aimed squarely at Jakob. "He has every reason to be angry if you ask me."

Jakob's brow raised, but he said nothing.

"For nearly a year after the murder, all

the papers talked about was the Zook family. The" — Rita lifted both hands into the air and wiggled her fingers up and down to simulate air quotes — "other victims, they called them. But when Carl was arrested, on trial, and then locked away, no one said a thing about Patrick and me. It was as if everyone thought our loss, our life upheaval was different. But I didn't ask to raise a young boy on my own and that young boy didn't ask to be fatherless any more than Harley Zook asked to live without his brother or their parents without a son."

"I can only imagine how hard it's been on the two of you," Claire finally said. "You're right. As a society we rarely seem to notice the pain of the people standing on the other side of a tragedy. Unless they were holding the gun or knife or whatever else, the bystanders on that side are victims, too."

Anger morphed into anguish as a stifled cry emerged from between Rita's tightened lips. "Had Patrick been a teenager when everything happened, maybe he could have rationalized everything better in his head and seen it for what it was. But a ten-year-old who worshipped the ground his father walked on? Losing Carl from his life like that was traumatizing. One minute he'd be crying inconsolably and the next he'd be tearing through the house breaking everything in sight."

"Did you get him a counselor?" Jakob asked.

"I couldn't *afford* a counselor, Detective. I was raising a child by myself and trying to keep our heads above water from a typhoon of someone else's making. I worked a job that had him cooking dinners for himself most nights, and a second job that had him heading off to school in the morning by himself. Looking back, I guess in his head my working was about rejecting him. That's the only reason I can figure he'd proceed to make my life hell over the last decade or so. When I wasn't working, I was sitting in the principal's office at Patrick's school trying to plead with them not to suspend him yet again. When he was a little older, I took my pleading to the office of many a store manager, offering to pay for whatever stupid little thing he'd tried to shoplift out of the store. At home, it was more of the same; only here, he didn't shoplift or punch a classmate, he just yelled and screamed and broke things every time I tried to lie down and take a well-earned nap."

Claire scooted forward on the sofa until Rita's focus was back on her. "Did it ever get better with Patrick? Did he work through the hurt and anger?"

"He'd hit these patches from time to time when he was almost quiet. I wish I could say those were the good times. And in the beginning, I could. But I began to realize that's what he did right before his latest trick. It wasn't long before I started dreading his quiet times more than his acting out. At least with the latter, I knew what I was dealing with." Rita sagged against the back of the wing chair. "But then Dave Riddler came along. Dave was Patrick's high school shop teacher his senior year. He came into my son's life and recognized him for the damaged soul he was. Dave took Patrick under his wing and gave me a real glimpse of the boy my son might have been had Carl never been shipped off to jail." The woman's voice took on a faraway quality matched only by the look in her eyes. "Things were better for a while. Dave even kept in touch with Patrick after graduation . . . calling him on the phone and meeting him for a soda every few weeks or so until he ended up moving to the West Coast with his wife about six months ago. That's when things got bad again."

Jakob claimed a spot on the sofa beside Claire. "Bad how?"

"The anger was back. The restless energy

was back. The depression was back." Rita shook her head slowly. "Then that man showed up and offered to help. I didn't like it. I didn't like the two of them being together at all. But after thinking about a few things, I decided to let them do it."

"By that man, do you mean Harley?" Claire clarified.

"I sure do." Rita rose to her feet and wandered around the room, stopping every few feet to look at something on the wall or on a shelf, yet touching nothing. "That man was always stopping by, asking how we were doing. I stopped answering the door when I heard his horse comin' down the road. But I wasn't home that last time and so he got hold of Patrick on his own. He mentioned the work he was doing and asked if Patrick wanted to earn some money helping him. When I got home later that night, Patrick dumped that on me and wouldn't let go until I finally gave him permission."

Jakob braced his hands atop his thighs. "Why do you think he wanted to work with Harley so bad?"

"Near as I can figure, it's 'cause he's been hearing things about them people his whole life and wanted to see it with his own eyes."

"Did he talk about his day when he got home each night? Did he tell you whether he liked Harley or not?"

Rita's gaze moved to Claire. "Patrick isn't one to talk about his feelings. He prefers to act them out. If he's not yelling and swearing or breaking things, he tends to stay to himself as he did when he was working with that man."

"When he's staying to himself, would you say he's happy?"

"Like I said before, I think it's merely the calm before the next storm."

She broke eye contact with Rita long enough to make a mental note of the way Jakob leaned forward on the heels of the woman's assessment. "When did this most recent storm start?"

"I don't know, maybe a week or so ago."

CHAPTER 17

If she weren't so hyperaware of everything about him at that exact moment, Claire might have reached across the table and tried to smooth the worry from Jakob's face. But when her heart started racing at the image of touching him, she knew it would be a bad move.

It wasn't all that long ago that her heart had reacted the same way whenever Benjamin Miller was near, as well. And while she knew her feelings for Jakob were growing with leaps and bounds, she was also well aware of the way her thoughts still meandered toward Benjamin and the life he'd proposed every now and again.

"I'm not being the best company, am I?" Jakob finally asked as he pushed his half-eaten hamburger off to the side and propped his elbows on the edge of the table.

She took a bite of her chicken sandwich and tried to think of the best way to address his comment without sounding patronizing. "You have a lot on your plate. I think it would be odd if you weren't distracted." That said, she couldn't help but wish for a do-over of that moment without the cloud of Harley Zook's murder investigation hanging over their time together.

Jakob rubbed at his chin, shaking his head as he did. "Is it just me or don't you find it ironic that the one person who continued to reach out to Rita and Patrick more than a decade after John's murder was Harley Zook, himself? I mean, of everyone on the fringes of what happened back then, Harley was the one who had a right to be angry, to resent a man who robbed him of his brother based on reprehensible ignorance. Yet, there Harley was, offering to expose Patrick to the one thing he'd finally allowed himself to have after sixteen long years of trying to maintain a connection with his dead brother through a herd of cows."

She peered at Jakob over her water glass. "You lost me."

"Harley. He always loved building things. When a barn burned, he was the first one there, leading the charge to raise a new one. When repairs needed to be made at the school down the road, he made them despite not having any children of his own. It was his passion the way police work was mine and dairy farming was John's."

"Oh, I get it now. He abandoned his own intended career path to follow John's in his absence, right?"

Jakob nodded, once, twice. "From what — um, I *gather,* Harley jumped into the dairy business with both feet for the first thirteen or fourteen years. Then, around that time, he got wind of the fact your aunt was looking for a fix-it man and he did a few odd jobs for her here and there over the next year or so. Something about doing that kind of work again really spoke to him and he started devoting more time to that and less to the dairy farming."

She considered calling him on the details Diane hadn't provided but decided to let it go. If Jakob wanted to keep the occasional clandestine meeting with his sister a secret, it wasn't her place to out him. Instead, she kept the conversation on topic and hoped he'd trust her enough one day to actually come clean on his own. "I suppose that explains a lot about the farm being the way we found it."

"There's not a lot of room for pursuing passions in the Amish community. People who have a special affinity for painting like my sister, Martha, can paint . . . if it's on a stool or something useful that will make money. But Harley? He liked working with his hands. He truly liked it for what it was. The fact that it also happens to be a field that fits well with the Amish made it a no-brainer. But then John died and Harley pushed his own interests to the side. He finally allows himself the chance to live his own life instead of the one left to him, and someone decides to take it from him." He filled his cheeks with air only to let them deflate slowly, audibly. "Would you mind if I try and talk through some of my thoughts with you? See if they make sense to someone other than a guy who wants to find anyone but his father to blame for Harley's murder?"

She set down her glass and pushed her plate to the side, too. "Of course. Go ahead."

"Okay, so Patrick was around ten when his dad shot and killed John. Carl stays under the radar for nearly six months. When he's fingered for the crime, he essentially confesses . . . proudly. He ends up in jail where he remains to this day."

"Go on . . ."

"So Carl is hauled off to prison and his kid is left behind, angry at the world. He's lost his dad, he's probably taunted in school for being the son of a murderer, his mother takes a second job to make ends meet, and he suddenly finds himself alone in more ways than one. He starts acting out. You know, the whole negative attention is better than no attention you mentioned earlier . . ."

"That's what they say. And it certainly sounded as if that was the case listening to Rita a little while ago."

"The rare times he quieted down, it was in preparation for the next major meltdown. Which, if you think about that, could point to a period of plotting."

"Plotting?"

"Yeah. Because if you think about everything Rita said, the times that he was quiet were probably when he was plotting his next move."

She traced her finger along the outer rim of her glass and tried to imagine what the past sixteen years had been like for Rita Duggan, the accidental single mom of an angry little boy. "That had to be a tough way to live, you know?"

"My only question now is this: what was he plotting during the quiet period that ended a mere day or so before Harley Zook's murder?"

Her mouth gaped. "Wait. You think Patrick may have been plotting Harley's murder during that time?"

"Sure. Why not? It could fit."

"I suppose. But what would his motive be?" she asked.

"Anger. Revenge. Take your pick."

"But sixteen years later?"

"Sixteen years later . . . when the man who gained the most from Carl's incarceration became a daily part of Patrick's life."

She pulled her hand from the top of her cup and ran it through her hair, the dull but lingering scent of spoiled milk still clinging to its ends nearly two hours later.

The Zook farm . . .

Closing her eyes against the image of the spray-painted threat she'd managed to forget temporarily, she sighed. Nothing in the world would please her more than to see Jakob's despair over his father's potential role in Harley's murder disappear once and for all. Patrick as the killer would make that happen.

But to stay silent and let Jakob close in on that target without full disclosure would be unthinkable.

"Did I say something wrong, Claire?"

She inhaled the courage she needed to answer and prayed she was doing the right thing at the right time. "Jakob? I have something I have to tell you. Something I found after we hung up the phone earlier. You know, while I was still out at Harley's farm . . ."

Something about the tone in her voice made him pale. "Tell me."

"I . . . I . . ." She stopped, swallowed, then made herself start again. "I think I found one of the signs Isaac was talking about the other day. The ones he said prove Mose's anger was gathering to a breaking point."

"Just one?"

She thought back over the patches of paint she'd found in the barn earlier in her visit and shook her head. "When I first saw the swaths of paint in the barn, I figured Harley had been testing colors or something. But now, in light of what I found at the end, I think they were probably there to cover more of the same."

"I don't understand. What did you find?"

"I found a threat spray-painted across the foundation on one side of Harley's house."

"A threat? What kind of threat?"

"The worst kind." She knew she was being a little evasive, but knowing her words were going to send Jakob right back to where he'd been in the investigation prior to their stop at Rita Duggan's house made sharing them all the more difficult.

He pushed back his chair and stood. "Tell

me, Claire. What did it say?"

" 'One more and you're dead,' " she whispered.

He staggered backward only to drop into his chair once again. " 'One more and you're dead?' " he repeated.

"Isaac could be wrong, Jakob." This time, she reached across the table and patted his arm, any racing of her heart be damned. "It might not mean anything at all."

"Or it could mean everything."

At the crack in his voice, her pat turned into a squeeze and her report into a plea for caution. "Anyone could have written that, Jakob! Maybe it was a — a group of crazy English teenagers who dared one another to write on an Amish house instead of the usual overpass or playground wall."

"Or maybe it was a warning from one Amish man to another," Jakob whispered, his pain so raw, so real she found it difficult to catch her breath.

"C'mon, Jakob. The sentence doesn't really even make any sense. One more? One more what?"

For a moment she didn't think he was going to answer. Then, when he finally did, she couldn't help but wish he hadn't.

"One more son out from under my father's day-to-day scrutiny?"

CHAPTER 18

So far she'd counted ten buggies that had come and gone from Bishop Hershberger's house in the thirty minutes they'd been sitting there. Each had pulled to a stop on the side of Route 100 to usher in the latest group of Amish wishing to pay their respects to Harley Zook.

It wasn't what Claire had thought they were going to do when Jakob first suggested they go together while walking out of Tastes of Heaven(ly). She'd almost declined in light of the funk she'd singlehandedly foisted on him with news of the threatening graffiti, but she decided to go in the end as her way of trying to make amends. Besides, paying her respects to the man she'd found strangled in a corn maze four days earlier seemed the proper thing to do.

So far, though, they hadn't moved from the car. Instead, they just sat there, watching and waiting. What, exactly, they were waiting for, though, was the part she didn't quite get.

"Jakob?" she finally asked. "Is everything okay?"

Slowly, he turned in his seat to make eye contact for the first time since he'd shifted into park and cut the engine. "I'm sorry, Claire. Every time I want to spend time with you . . . and maybe even show you I'm a pretty nice guy . . . it seems something happens to prove otherwise."

"Wait a minute. I know you're a nice guy. I knew that from the first day I met you and you actually liked the welcome to Heavenly gift I gave you."

The smile she loved crept across his face and set off the dimples she loved even more. "Liked that gift? Are you kidding me? I'll never forget the sight of you standing in the lobby of the police department, holding that blue-and-green-striped gift bag." He shook his head at the memory, the smile he wore as bright as ever. "I still have that, you know."

"Have what?" she asked.

"The bag. It's in the box where I keep special things."

She felt her cheeks warm and was glad the lack of streetlights on this side of Heavenly provided a cloak of privacy to the feelings she didn't want on display. "It was just a bag, Jakob."

"But it came from you." He stretched his arms above the steering wheel only to bring them back down to his lap once again. "I refuse to light any of the candles because I don't want them to go away. I like the way they look around my otherwise stark home. And the framed photograph of Lighted Way in the snow? That holds a place of honor smack-dab in the middle of my mantel. I look at it every night when I find myself wondering why I ever bought a television set."

She opened her mouth to speak but closed it just as quickly when she realized the lump in her throat would call out the rush of emotions she wasn't ready to share.

"Sometimes, I let myself believe you had me at that blue-and-green-striped bag. But other times, I know it happened even before that, when I first stepped out into that lobby and saw you standing there, waiting."

At a loss for what to say, she dropped her gaze to her own lap and worked to steady her breathing instead. She'd always suspected Jakob had some interest in her, but now, there was little doubt.

"I'm sorry I had to dump that graffiti thing on you at the restaurant." She knew it wasn't what he probably wanted to hear at that exact moment, but she wasn't ready to acknowledge his feelings aloud yet. That would have to wait until she could examine the reason behind the tears that were no more than a blink or two away.

She felt him studying her and instantly knew he was trying to decide whether or not to challenge her on the abrupt change in topic. Finally, though, his focus left her face and returned to the modest home on the other side of the street. "I needed to know it was there, Claire, even if I'd rather it wasn't. Wishing away reality isn't an option in my profession. And, whether I like it or not, the cold, hard reality I can't get around is the fact that, for my father, my decision to leave the Amish will forever be linked to the murder of Harley's brother. The fact that Harley then spoke out in favor of my decision — and continued to do so for the next sixteen years — only added salt to the wound. Isaac agreeing to work with him may very well have been the powder keg that made my father finally blow."

The resignation in his voice tugged at her heart, bringing with it an overpowering need to make things right. "You also have a twenty-six-year-old man with all sorts of anger issues and a whole lot of resentment toward Harley for being the roundabout reason he hasn't had a father the past sixteen years of his life. Then, all of a sudden, that reason is *in* his life on a near-daily basis, telling him what to do and how to do it and giving you another potential powder keg to consider."

"Is it wrong of me to hope that's the one that actually blew . . ." Jakob's question petered off as a buggy approached from the opposite direction and slowed to a stop directly across from their car. Suddenly, the lack of streetlights that had saved Claire mere moments earlier and done a decent job of shrouding mourners' faces thus far was no match for a brother when it came to his beloved sister.

Instantly, he shifted forward in his seat, ducking his head back and forth between the windshield and the driver's side window in an effort to gain the most unobstructed view. As they watched, a second buggy — an open top — pulled in behind the first.

"I think that's Esther and Eli," she whispered, nodding confirmation of her own words as she, too, leaned forward in her seat. "They really are good together, aren't they?"

"Eli will be a fine husband for Esther," Jakob agreed. "He is smitten with her, that's for sure."

"As she is with him." She followed both couples all the way to the door then leaned back in her seat when they disappeared inside. "I can't think of two people I'd rather see get married. They're going to have a beautiful life together."

"I'd give just about anything to be able to be there at the celebration." The wistful quality of his voice was impossible to miss. "I've missed so much of Esther's life these past sixteen or so years. When I left, she was turning three and chasing barn kittens around the yard in her bare feet. Now, she's nineteen and weeks away from getting married and starting a family of her own. And all I can do is watch from a polite distance."

She sucked in her own breath and counted to ten in her head, savoring the one bright, shiny bit of news she could offer against an otherwise bleak backdrop. It was a tidbit she'd wanted to share with him several times over the past few hours but kept to herself for fear she'd put a hidden meaning where there had been none.

Yet no matter how many times she replayed her last wedding-related conversation with Esther in her head, the same instinct kicked in and it was time to finally share it with Jakob. "The other day we talked about the wedding and Esther told me all about the food that would be prepared and the people that would come from far and wide to celebrate with them."

Jakob nodded. "They will build a temporary addition to the house just to hold the guests who will come."

"She mentioned that." Claire took a second, longer breath and held it a beat. "But she also said she wanted me to come. That she and Eli are counting on it."

"That's wonderful. But how will you handle the store that day? Will you be able to find someone to fill in for you or will you close for the day the way the Amish do?"

Claire resisted the urge to tell him what was happening with the store. Now was not the time. Jakob had far more important things on his plate than the fate of her gift shop. Besides, she'd talked it through in her head a million times already. The subject didn't need any more talking. "I'll welcome that worry when it comes and enjoy Esther's wedding, either way."

His smile stopped just shy of his eyes. "You'll have to tell me all about it. How she looked, how he looked, what they said, how the celebration went . . . all of it."

"Actually, I won't have to tell you anything. Esther wants me to bring you as my guest!"

Whatever reaction she'd imagined in her head every time she thought of that moment, it didn't come. Instead, he met her proclamation with a tiny shrug and an "I know."

"You know?" she echoed. "But how?"

She didn't need anything more than the touch of moonlight that finally peeked through the trees to see the way his face turned crimson. And at that very moment, she had her answer. The same answer that now made its way through her mouth in the form of a rhetorical question. "Martha?"

"She thinks if I go with you, it would raise fewer eyebrows," he said. "But I will never know for sure because all I'd see if I went with you would be the backs of heads."

"Maybe. But at least you'd be there to see Esther and Eli marry." She used the approaching lights of an oncoming car to take advantage of a little eye contact, using the tip of her finger beneath his chin to insure that it held until she was done. "Come to the wedding with me, Jakob. Backs or not, Esther wants you there. Martha wants you there. In the grand scheme of things, does anyone else really matter?"

"That depends. Do you *want* me to go as

your guest?"

She heard the slight rasp in his voice and knew he'd finally backed her into a corner with no alternate escape route possible. "Yes." It was all she could trust herself to say at that moment.

"Then you're right. Backs or not, no one else matters."

The headlights that, only moments earlier, had allowed her to see Jakob's face clearly disappeared into darkness and guided their attention to a nondescript four-door sedan parked behind Eli's wagon. "Hmmm," Jakob mumbled beneath his breath, "who do we have here?"

Two figures stepped from the front seat of the car, one small and round, the other tall and lean. But it was the flannel shirt worn by the man on the passenger side of the car that confirmed her initial guess. "That's Howard and Al. I guess they've come to pay their respects." Then, taking hold of Jakob's hand, she motioned her head in the direction of the bishop's house. "Maybe this would be a good time for us to go in, too. Maybe you'll blend in better if there are more English around when we arrive."

"There will be no blending in with Bishop Hershberger, but we can't sit out here all night. I'm supposed to relieve McKenzie over there in less than an hour." She followed his gaze to the patrol car parked farther up the road, only to return with his, to the home across the street. "I think I should warn you, though."

"Warn me?"

This time, when he looked at her, there was no tenderness, only concern. "While the state of Pennsylvania mandates that all bodies be embalmed, the simple fact that the Amish wake their deceased in their homes removes the mortician from the equation in terms of" — he stopped and inhaled — "*prettying* up the body."

"I don't understand."

He lifted his chin as if he was looking for something above her head then lowered it in time to offer an explanation. "Harley's eyes won't be open, but any bruising he sustained during the murder will be in plain view. The Amish don't use makeup in life; they're most certainly not going to use it in death, either."

"Oh." For the first time since he mentioned driving out to the viewing together, she wished she'd said no. If she had, she'd be sitting in Diane's parlor, happily reading away the remaining hour or so before bed.

No, you wouldn't. You'd be wearing out the numbers on the calculator trying to find money you don't have . . .

"Would you rather wait here?"

She took a deep breath and held it to a count of ten then squared her shoulders and reached for the door handle. "Considering I'm the one who found Harley after he was strangled to death, the way he looks really shouldn't come as any big surprise, right?"

The warmth of his hand on her wrist made her gasp. "If you need to turn away, that's okay. Either way, I'm right there next to you and we don't have to stay long."

She felt the lump returning to her throat and knew it was one of fear this go-round. "Is it really going to be that bad?"

"I don't know. I just know it'll be different than anything you might be used to." He tightened his grip a hair-breadth then nodded at her door while simultaneously opening his own. "C'mon. Let's go."

She crossed around the car and met him on the approach to the house. "Martha is still inside, you know," she whispered as they passed his sister's horse.

His only answer came by way of a pace that quickened, then slowed, and then quickened again. Step-by-step they made their way to the bishop's front door. Inside, candles glowed in the window, bathing the traditional front room in muted light.

When they reached the door, Jakob placed his hand on the small of her back and guided her inside to the waiting casket. There, just as she'd been warned, was Harley Zook as he looked in death, his clothes no different than he wore every day of his life. Yet instead of the smile both Diane and Jakob remembered him for, his mouth was open in a way that suggested a last gasp rather than a final breath of peace. Angry blue veins, dulled slightly by the passage of time, claimed the skin around his neck and face, reminding all who saw him that his death had been traumatic. She looked away and swallowed.

"You doing okay?"

She startled at the warm breath against her ear then found the closest thing to a smile she could muster. "The warning helped. Thank you."

Jakob bowed his head slightly then returned to the silent prayer he was undoubtedly offering for a man who'd been able to see Jakob's choice as the honorable road it truly was rather than the disgrace so many others believed it to be.

She, too, said a prayer — a prayer of thanks for a man who not only lived life with an open heart but also lived it with a forgiving one, as well.

"Ready?" he whispered.

At her nod, he tucked his hand beneath her elbow and guided her back toward the door, his desire to make it out of the bishop's house without incident palpable.

"Claire! It's good to see — oh, I didn't see you there, Jakob." Howard Glick stepped through the open doorway connecting the front room from the kitchen and planted a kiss on Claire's cheek. Then, extending his hand to Jakob, he pulled the detective into the kitchen and motioned for Claire to follow. "Everyone is in here."

In an instant, the hushed voices she'd been vaguely aware of while praying over Harley's body grew eerily silent as six pairs of eyes narrowed in on Jakob's face only to turn away in true domino style . . .

The bishop . . .

His wife . . .

Abram . . .

Eli . . .

Martha . . .

And, finally, reluctantly, Esther . . .

She heard herself gasp, felt the momentary confusion that blanketed her own heart give way to a slow boiling anger she was hard-pressed to contain. "Wait a minute," she protested. "I don't —"

"I should not have come, Claire. I don't

belong here." Jakob grabbed hold of her upper arm and escorted her to the door. She considered yanking free of his grasp and saying her piece but opted, instead, to leave with Jakob.

He needed her more at that very moment than she needed to rail against an injustice that would never change, anyway.

"I'm sorry, Jakob." It was such a lame statement in light of what had just transpired, but it was all she could think of as they stepped onto the sidewalk and made their way toward the car. "I . . . I have to believe the only reason Martha and Esther turned away like that was because of the bishop."

"They did as they should under the circumstances," Jakob said in an emotion-chocked voice. "I had no right to expect anything different."

She broke into a jog to keep up with him, capturing his hand and turning him to face her as they reached the car. "But you have to know it killed them to do that. Did you see Martha's face? Did you see the way Esther hesitated? They love you, Jakob."

He tilted his head upward, seemingly taking in the stars that had exploded in the sky during the short time they were inside the bishop's house. A hand on his chest was the only hint he was also trying to catch his breath and rein in the pain he was unable to keep from his face. "I know they do. And that is why I can't go to Esther's wedding with you."

"Can't go?" she echoed. "But you agreed that the only thing that matters that day is seeing Esther and Eli marry."

"That was before I saw the pain on my niece's face just now."

"But —"

Slowly, he lowered his gaze until it mingled with hers. "No, Claire. I refuse to see that look on Esther's face on her wedding day. I can't, and I won't."

CHAPTER 19

For the first time since opening the shop over the summer, Claire bypassed her office and went straight to the main room. There were only so many times she could look at the numbers. She was spending money faster than it was coming in, and at the rate she was going, Heavenly Treasures would be closed inside ten weeks, twelve at best.

The one and only saving grace was the knowledge that Esther's wedding would happen first. Somehow, knowing she wouldn't have to let Esther go lessened the sting of packing up her dream and calling it a day.

But then there was Aunt Diane . . .

No, there was no getting around the pain Claire's inevitable exit from Heavenly was going to cause the innkeeper.

"You look as if the weight of the world is on your shoulders right now."

Startled from her thoughts, Claire grabbed

hold of the counter for support and jerked her head in the direction of the front door. There, just inside the entryway of Heavenly Treasures, stood Martha, quietly clasping her hands while glancing over her shoulder toward the sidewalk. "The bishop says God will provide. He will make all things right."

"I think God is looking after those with far bigger problems than mine." Claire forced herself to focus on the here and now, or, at the very least, the here and the previous night. "Do you always listen to everything Bishop Hershberger says, Martha?"

"Yah."

"Seems to me you might do better to listen to your heart once in a while, too."

"I do not know what you speak of."

Warning bells began to clang in her head, the sound, she assumed, designed to keep her from saying something she'd regret. Yet, despite the mental reminder that Martha was Esther's mother, she continued on, undeterred, the connection between Martha and Jakob every bit as important. "I respect your way of life. I have since I was a little girl. I think the way you rely on one another over technology is to be commended. I admire the way you all work so hard, making your own way in life. I admire your large families and the respect you have for one another. And I admire your ability to turn the other cheek when you are wronged . . . but I will never understand how the Amish can offer forgiveness to a stranger for something like *murder,* yet refuse to give it to one of their own for becoming a *police officer.*"

Martha met Claire's gaze with one that was hooded, maybe even a little sad. "Jakob knew what would happen if he left."

"Do you really think that makes it better somehow? Do you really think that knowing what would happen and actually living it is the same thing? Because I don't. I've only known your brother a few months now and even I can see how much his decision has cost him." She brushed a shaking hand through her auburn hair and began to pace, the frustration over her financial situation and her anger over Jakob's treatment the previous night propelling her back and forth across the room. "He gets that he will never have a real relationship with you and your husband, or with Esther and the rest of your children. But is it so wrong for him to get a smile? To get a quick wave? To squeeze his hand as you go by? Because from where I'm standing . . . and where I was standing *last night,* I don't see why such tiny courtesies could be so wrong."

"That is how it must be in front of the bishop."

Claire wanted to argue, to tell Martha to be proud of the fact she and Jakob were rebuilding their foundation one clandestine meeting at a time, but to do so would be to potentially harm the progress they'd made so far. Besides, Jakob had never come out and said he was still meeting his sister by the pond. Claire only assumed and Jakob neither confirmed nor denied.

Like it or not, Martha was not only Jakob's sister but Esther's mother, as well. To continue bemoaning an injustice that wasn't going to change no matter what she said was futile. Instead, she gave up and steered all further conversation toward safer territory.

"If you give me a second, I'll step out to your buggy with you and help you bring in whatever creations you have for me this week." Any hope she had for keeping the store going until mid to late January was due, in no small part, to Martha's hand-painted milk cans and footstools. Positioning the Amish woman's work in the front window virtually guaranteed Claire'd make a sale by the end of the day. Unfortunately, the kind of detail Martha put into each item took time, and even two or three footstools a week wasn't enough to keep Claire's head above water any longer. Still, some time was better than no time.

Especially when that time would enable her to see Esther married and happily embarking on her new life with Eli before Claire was forced to take down the Heavenly Treasures' shingle.

"I do not have any items for you today. There is much to do these next few weeks to prepare for Esther's wedding. There will be many guests. My painting must wait until her wedding day is over."

"You — you don't have *anything* with you today?" she stammered above the sudden roar in her ears. "No spoons? No milk cans? No *stools*?"

Martha's left brow raised ever so slightly beneath her kapp. "That is right. I have nothing. Is there something wrong, Claire?"

Yes, she wanted to shout. I'm months — perhaps now, *weeks* away from losing the only dream that's ever truly been my own.

But she couldn't say that aloud. Not yet, anyway. Not until she could say it without crying. Not until she was able to figure out her next plan. Instead, she hitched her shoulders upward in what she hoped was a casual shrug and turned back to the empty pad of paper and the day's to-do list she'd planned to write. "So how can I help with Esther's wedding? May I host the shower? I'm sure my aunt would let us have it at the inn. It's big enough to accommodate a nice number of ladies."

"What is a shower?"

The question took her by surprise for a moment and she looked up. She'd grown so used to the Amish dress code and the sight of their buggies that she'd almost forgotten there were more differences — vast differences.

"I'm sorry. I wasn't thinking." She came around the counter once again, this time patting one cushioned stool while claiming the other. "Please. Come sit. Instead of me babbling on about the way the English prepare for a wedding, I'd much rather hear how things will be done for Esther in the days leading up to her big day."

Slowly, Martha crossed to the stool and sat. "I would like to hear of this shower. That is an English custom I do not know."

"Okay . . ." Claire scooted her stool back a smidge and did her best to describe the age-old tradition that was slowly falling by the wayside in favor of the more raucous bachelorette party preferred by a growing number of brides-to-be. "Well, a shower is essentially a big party that is thrown — usually by the bride's friends or family — in honor of the bride-to-be. Only women are invited to the party and it's given as a way to celebrate the new role she'll soon have as a wife. The guests bring gifts — things she'll use in her new home. Perhaps a toaster or a mixer . . . or sheets and a blanket for the couple's bed . . . that sort of thing. Useful things that help them start off in their new life together."

"The Amish give gifts, too, but they give them after the wedding," Martha explained. "On the day they are to be married, people come from many places to celebrate the day. There is much food and happiness. But it is later, over the next few days and weeks, that the man and wife drive to their guests' homes to collect the gifts."

For the first time since she'd arrived at work that morning, Claire felt the knots of tension in her neck and shoulders dissipating, her fascination with the Amish way of life and the chance to learn yet another interesting facet of their existence providing a brief but welcome reprieve from reality. "You mean Esther and Eli will go to people's houses *after* the wedding in order to get their gifts?"

At Martha's nod, Claire took full stock of the answer and the subsequent questions that found their way past her lips. "Esther told me there can be as many as three hundred people at a wedding. If even a third of those are adults and married, that's still fifty-odd homes they have to visit."

"It is done to encourage Esther and Eli to visit. We do not telephone as the English do. We talk on the porch or in the kitchen. It is what we do on non-church Sundays. It is what we do when the work is done."

"It is a part of your life I truly envy. People spend so much of their time these days looking down at their contraptions instead of looking up and saying hello to one another." Claire lifted the pen from the top of her to-do list and lazily twirled it between her fingers. "Being able to connect with people again is one of the things I will treasure most about my time here in Heavenly. It has been such a blessing."

"Are you leaving?"

Uh-oh . . .

Dropping the pen onto the pad of paper, Claire slid off her stool and clapped her hands together in what she hoped was an award-worthy attempt at changing the subject. "Do you know what sorts of things would help Esther and Eli as they go off on their own? Any particular items they need for their kitchen?"

"Esther thinks fondly of you, Claire. She would be saddened if you left."

She blinked against the prick of tears that burned at the corners of her eyes. Should she tell Martha? Impress upon the woman how badly she needed new items if the shop was to last through the holiday season?

No. When the time came to share the news of her closing, Esther should be the one she told. Not Martha. "I am so happy Esther has Eli. He will look after her and give her a good life."

"Eli will be a good husband for my daughter. When God sees fit to give them children, he will be a good father, too. But you, Claire, are a good friend. To Esther, to Eli, and to me."

She swallowed in a futile attempt to clear the lump Martha's words lodged in her throat, the tears she worked valiantly to thwart ready to spill down her cheeks at a moment's notice. "Esther is the first real friend I've had in a very long time and I treasure every moment I get to spend with her. Through her, I have met so many wonderful people — people like you and Eli."

"You will come to the wedding, won't you?"

"I wouldn't miss it for anything in the

world." And it was true. Wild horses couldn't drag her from Esther's wedding. "It will be my honor to be there to celebrate her special day with all of you."

Martha stilled her fidgeting hands atop her lap and eyed Claire closely. "Perhaps, one day, we can all share your day with you."

Confused, she drew back. "*My* day?"

"Yah. The day you will marry my brother."

CHAPTER 20

For more years than Claire cared to admit, cooking had been a source of pain. Night after night she'd spend an hour or more in the kitchen in the hopes that a good meal and any accompanying conversation might save her failing marriage. More times than not, though, she ate alone, the candles she'd lit burning down to nothing as she watched the hands of the clock rob her of her latest round of hope and slowly seal the fate of a union entered into by two, yet nurtured by one.

Yet, somehow, in ways she couldn't quite pinpoint, cooking had undergone a rebirth in her heart since moving in to her aunt's inn. Suddenly, the act of experimenting with flavors and spices was no longer done out of desperation but, rather, served as a way to unwind after a busy day at work.

And the conversation she'd longed to have with Peter all those nights was hers for the taking now every time she sat down across the kitchen counter from Diane for a post-guest meal or took a place at the dining room table with new and interesting people eager to share tidbits about their lives while learning everything they could about life in Amish country.

Perhaps the best part of cooking these days, though, was doing it alongside her aunt. Some nights they'd chatter nonstop while they prepared the various parts of the evening's menu. Other nights, they relished the peace and quiet while knowing the other was there beside them, softly humming or singing a favorite tune.

It was a nightly routine Claire'd come to treasure along with so many other aspects of life in Heavenly the past nine months, and it was a nightly routine she'd looked forward to enjoying for many more to come. Unfortunately, her bank account had other ideas . . .

Shaking her head free from the kind of thoughts destined to put her in a funk for the rest of the night, Claire looked up from the potatoes she was mashing to find her aunt studying her closely. "Do I have potatoes on my nose or something?" she joked before ducking her head to check her reflection against the side of the pot. "Because if

I do, you could just say so, you know."

"And if there's something bothering you, you could just say so rather than make me guess." Diane crossed to the refrigerator, removed the butter dish from the upper shelf, and then handed it to Claire along with a knife. "The McCormicks like lots of butter in their potatoes."

She traded the masher for the knife and sliced several pats of butter into the pot, watching with minimal interest as they hit the warm potatoes and began to melt almost immediately. "Nothing is bothering me. Really."

Diane's left eyebrow rose upward. "Nothing? Then why have I heard you pacing in your room until the wee hours of the morning virtually every night for the past week?"

She paused mid-stir and contemplated her response. If she admitted the problems at the gift shop, Diane would try to step in and help despite her own financial responsibilities at the inn. And while her aunt was in better shape than Claire was in that department, Diane wasn't made of cash, either. Besides, the whole point of opening Heavenly Treasures in the first place was so Claire could realize a dream on her own.

Realize or sink, that is . . .

"There! *That's* the look you've had on

233

your face more times than not these past few days."

She consulted the side of the pot once again, the tired eyes and worry lines she saw reflected back forcing her to come up with a response, fast.

"There's been a lot going on with the murder and everything. I mean, finding a body the way I did doesn't exactly make for a restful night's sleep."

The same worry she'd seen just moments earlier in the pot crept its way across Diane's face. "Would it help to talk to someone, dear? Because I could arrange for that."

"You mean like a counselor or something?" At Diane's nod, Claire shook her head. "I'll be fine."

Diane sidled up to the stove and peered at the beef stew that was a favorite among each round of guests that passed through the inn. "I'm glad to hear that, of course. Stumbling across something like that must eat away at you. But the pacing I'm talking about started *before* you found Harley's body."

It was time to play dumb, and play dumb she did. "Maybe you heard one of the guests? Or someone's television? I just know the only things on my mind right now pertain to Harley's murder in one way or the other."

"Such as?" Diane grabbed a stack of stew bowls from the cabinet beside the stove, set them on the counter beside her favorite ladle, then turned to Claire for the answer she sought.

"Well, I'm worried about Jakob for starters."

This time it was Diane's right eyebrow that lifted in surprise. "Jakob? Why?"

Claire gave the potatoes one final stir then covered them with a lid to keep them warm. "Having his father in the mix of suspects in Harley's murder is weighing on him heavily. And then, last night, I went with him to Harley's wake and the treatment he got from Martha and Esther while he was there cut him to the core."

She allowed the words that left her mouth to transport her back to the shop and the odd way her conversation with Martha had ended that morning. "But let's forget that for a minute and let me ask you something, instead. Jakob's sister said something really strange today."

Diane folded her arms across her apron front. "Go on, dear . . ."

"If I understood correctly, it almost sounded as if Martha could have a relationship with Jakob's wife if he got married. Is that true?"

"Yes, that's true. *Jakob* has been excommunicated, not his future wife and any children they might have."

She stared at the woman standing just on the other side of the counter while she tried to make sense of the nonsensical. "Wait. So if I'm hearing correctly, you're saying that Jakob's wife and kids could share Christmas dinner with his family but he could not?"

"He could be there, they just wouldn't talk to him. They'd speak only to one another and to his wife and children."

Abandoning her watch over the potatoes, Claire walked around the counter, scooped up the stew bowls, and headed toward the dining room and the table that was virtually set save for a few last-minute additions. "I couldn't do that. I couldn't sit there and socialize with people who opted not to speak with my husband."

Diane followed with the bread basket and the guests' butter dish. "You mean if you were Jakob's wife?"

Claire stopped short at her mistake. Nothing like drawing herself into the picture her aunt was painting for Claire's life. "Hypothetically, of course."

"Yes, of course, dear . . ."

She heard the strangled laugh as it slipped between her lips and let it propel her around the table, her fingers depositing stew bowls at each spot as she passed. "How can one Amish man take such good care of his cows, treating them as though they were his children, while another mandates his family cut off one of their own forever?" She headed back toward the kitchen and the last few remaining jobs that needed to be done before the guests arrived at the table for dinner. "There are so many things about the Amish I adore, but that's not one of them."

"The repercussions for leaving after baptism are known by all. They may not be something we understand, but the person who considers leaving does." Diane retrieved her oven mitts from the center of the counter and used them to lift the stew pot from the stove while Claire gathered up the water pitcher and the ladle. "As for Harley and his cows, they were all he really had. And while none of them were alive when his brother was, they are all descendants of ones who were. I think, in some ways, he cared for and protected them in a way he could no longer do for his brother."

She spun around. "Oh my gosh, that's it!'

Diane walked carefully through the kitchen and into the hallway that linked it with the dining room. "What's it, dear?"

"Ever since Jakob and I went out to Harley's farm to make sure his pasture gate was closed, something has been eating at me that I couldn't quite put my finger on until now." She heard the sound of guests approaching and did her best to share her revelation as quickly as possible. "You said, the other day, that Harley was always chasing down one cow or the other, right? That he joked about his little ladies missing him when he went off to work?"

"I did."

"Why would a man who put in a state-of-the-art latch for his pasture gate leave it open when he left for work?" When Diane said nothing, Claire continued on, putting two and two together and actually having it add up to something that made sense for the first time in days. "I mean, if he was as protective of his cows as you say, and he looked after them the way that Luke Hochstetler said and I saw with my own two eyes when I visited the farm yesterday, the whole careless thing doesn't make sense."

Diane lowered the stew pot to the waiting buffet table and turned to face Claire. "I've always attributed it to someone playing a prank. After a few instances, Harley began to think so, too."

"A prank would be to do it once. But this

happened multiple times, didn't it?" She lowered her voice as the parade of footsteps grew closer. "Why didn't Harley tell someone? Why didn't he report it to the police?"

"The Amish are wary around the police."

"Wary?"

"First of all, the Amish are pacifists, as you know. They believe that things will work out on their own. A loose cow, or even a dozen loose cows, certainly doesn't warrant bringing in the police as far as the Amish are concerned."

Kyle Reilly was the first into the room, followed by his wife, Megan, and the McCormicks. "Good evening," Diane said, smiling at each of her guests as they took their place at the table. "How was everyone's day?"

"It was good but it's even better now," Will said as he beamed at his wife and then Diane. "Why, I smelled that beef stew the second we came in from a walk and I knew what it was right away. My grandma used to make a stew that smelled just like that when I was no higher than her knee."

Ten minutes later, when everyone was settled in with a heaping bowl of stew and a large piece of still-warm bread alongside a hefty helping of homemade potatoes, Kyle brought Claire back to the conversation that had been cut short by the dinner hour. "I hope you don't mind me asking, but I heard you talking a little while ago about the way the Amish don't seek out the police. I've heard that before and I've always wondered if that belief makes them an easy target for would-be thieves who see the Amish as vulnerable. They don't have phones to call for help, and even if they do, it seems as if the police are some of the last folks they'd call, on account of their beliefs and all."

She knew Will responded, even made out bits and pieces of what he said, but, for the most part, her mind was off and running. Kyle was right. If someone was even semi-versed in the Amish culture, they'd know that a certain level of mischief would go unanswered simply because of the whole turn-the-other-cheek way of life they embodied.

If someone monkeyed with their pasture gate and a few cows got out, the Amish would simply round them up, secure the gate, and proceed on with their day.

If someone wrote nasty things across a wall inside their barn, they'd merely paint over it and go on with their day.

"The cows . . . They were a sign, too!" She smacked her hand over top of her mouth as five sets of eyes turned in her direction and let her know with absolute certainty that she'd shared her little revelation aloud.

"Claire?"

She grabbed the pitcher from the buffet table and made herself loop around the table, topping off everyone's glasses as she went, a smile she knew Diane wasn't buying plastered across her face. "I'm sorry, everyone. Don't mind me. I was thinking about a book I was reading last night. I've been having a hard time figuring who did it."

"And did you finally figure it out?" Megan said, grinning.

"Not yet, but I'm getting a little closer." She pulled the near-empty pitcher to her chest and backed away from the table. "Is there anything else you need at the moment?" At the collective shake of their heads, she carried the pitcher back to the kitchen, anxious to have a few moments of privacy to pick Diane's brain.

"I don't think Harley's loose cows were a prank, Diane." She set the pitcher on the counter closest to the sink and turned to face her aunt. "Not the kind done by someone on a lark, anyway."

Diane pulled the dishrag from her apron string and began tidying up, her nightly routine making the larger cleanup job after dinner far less daunting. "You think there was malice behind it?"

"When you couple the loose cows with the graffiti he was forced to cover in his barn and the graffiti he hadn't yet gotten to on the side of his house, I can't help but see a picture that isn't very nice."

"I didn't know about the graffiti," Diane offered between swipes with her rag. "I did know about the milk and the cows, but not the graffiti."

"The milk? What about the milk?"

Diane swapped the rag for a sponge and cleaned around the sink and the stovetop before stopping to wash and dry her hands for the inevitable second check on the guests. "Periodically, milk cans would disappear from Harley's property."

"He had a service come in and collect them, didn't he?"

"Not on as regular a basis as he once did." Diane checked her hair in the mirror to the left of the sink then filled the pitcher with fresh water and ice. "The more work he found with his hands, the less interested he became in the business side of having dairy cows. So even though he noticed cans disappearing from time to time, it didn't seem to bother him all that much. He'd mention it offhand if he was talking about his day, but he shrugged it off in a manner that suggested it wasn't a big deal."

"I'm afraid it was a very big deal." Claire heard the rasp to her voice and saw Diane stop midway across the kitchen with the pitcher between her hands.

"What are you saying?"

"Isaac said his father's anger toward Harley had been escalating the past few months. He said there were signs of it all over the Zook farm." Her mind began to race as it worked to tie up all the realizations she now had in one perfect package. Unfortunately, it wasn't the package she wanted to give Jakob. "I think he was talking about those things — the cows, the milk, the graffiti threats . . . all of it."

Diane completed her trip to the kitchen door and leaned partway into the hallway, the sound of happy chatter from the table buying her a little time to stay. "Even if Mose did those things, Harley would be the first person to brush it off as frustration."

"Frustration?"

"You said this was escalating over the past few months, right?"

Claire nodded.

"Then it would match up perfectly, wouldn't it?"

She stared at her aunt. "I'm not following what you're saying . . ."

"Think about what happened in Mose's life a few months ago."

She started to shrug, to repeat her previous statement, but stopped as reality took center stage and brought clarity to Diane's words. "Jakob. He came back to Heavenly." And, suddenly, everything she'd been dancing around in her head made perfect sense. Right down to the chill-inducing timing.

"For someone like Mose who took Jakob's departure as a blemish on himself, he probably saw Jakob's return as a reminder to his community that he'd failed as a parent."

"And he couldn't lash out at Jakob, so he lashed out at a man who wasn't shy about singing Jakob's praises . . ." She whispered the last few pieces of the puzzle into place and groaned, loudly. "Oh, Diane, don't you see what this means?"

"I see a man releasing his anger in the only direction he felt was safe."

"Safe?"

Diane scanned the kitchen looking, no doubt, for anything else her guests might need. When she came up empty, she smiled at Claire. "In the grand scheme of things, letting a few cows wander the Amish countryside so Harley had to run around fetching them isn't that bad."

"And the stolen milk?"

"Also not a big deal when you consider the fact Harley was only playing at the dairy business the past year or so."

"And the graffiti?"

"That's what paint is for."

"It wasn't just random words, Diane. The graffiti I saw threatened death."

Diane's face paled. "Death? Well, that's certainly not right, but sometimes a person has to release their anger. The rest of us, we can scream and shout. For the Amish, it's different. Harley knew that. And, I believe, he understood that where Mose was concerned."

"You think he knew Mose was behind the mischief at his farm?"

Diane paused, then nodded. "I can't say for certain that he did, but I wouldn't be surprised."

Claire took in everything she was hearing and held it against her common sense. "If you're right, how could he let it continue, unchecked?"

"Harley Zook was a very tolerant man, dear. He was always happy, always smiling despite the heaviness he carried in his heart at the loss of his brother." Diane took a step toward the door once again, her duty to her guests bringing a rapid end to their talk. "How many other people would seek out the son of their brother's killer to help him find his way? Not many, if at all. But he recognized the fact that Patrick had been through a lot without his dad, and Harley was determined to make a difference in the young man's life if he could. Fortunately, he was meeting with some success in that regard."

Claire pushed off the counter in surprise. "Wait a minute, Aunt Diane. I thought Patrick hated working with his hands. That he did very little as Harley's apprentice . . ."

"I suppose that's true, but Patrick loved *being* with Harley. He loved listening to Harley's stories and his little tidbits about life and hard work." Diane turned her ear toward the door once again. "Sometimes, if I happened by the room where they were working, I'd stop and simply watch them together. Harley would be working on the door frame or the step or whatever I had him doing that particular day and there Patrick would be . . . handing him an occasional tool and listening with wide eyes to whatever Harley was saying. It was a beautiful sight to see, and it's one I'll always treasure from that last day."

"Last day? What last day?"

"The day Harley was murdered."

She froze in place as her head tried to make sense of what her ears had just heard. "Are you saying that Harley and Patrick did a job for you the day Harley was murdered?"

Again, Diane nodded. "I told you that. I told you he was here, working on the back step that Friday morning."

"Have you told Jakob they were here that day?"

"He was here when I said it. He must not have thought it was all that important." Diane gestured toward the pitcher with her chin and then stepped into the hall. "I really must check on the guests again, dear."

"That's fine, Diane, but I'm betting Jakob didn't make the connection, either. So will you tell him again? Please? Maybe, just maybe, Harley and Patrick said something that day that could help in the investigation somehow."

Diane stopped. "Perhaps Patrick might be able to shed light on the time after they left here, too."

"What do you mean?"

"Harley drove Patrick home in the buggy that day."

CHAPTER 21

She repositioned her pillow against the headboard and flipped the page of her latest book of choice, the twists and turns of the story a welcome tonic for a brain that had been unable to stop processing various aspects of her talk with Diane. So much of what Claire'd learned while standing in the kitchen that evening had left her reeling.

Sure, she could see how her aunt might think the loose cows and stolen milk cans might be harmless in nature if considered on their own merits. But when considered in the context of Isaac taking a job with Harley, they could also be seen as the buildup to the final explosion that was an innocent man's murder.

And then there was the reality that had Harley driving Patrick home just before he was murdered. Coincidence? Maybe. Then again, maybe not.

But if it was Patrick, what made him snap

in an instant? Or, was it as Jakob had hypothesized and the violence was being hatched all along?

She read her way down the page, only to realize she hadn't absorbed anything in the past few paragraphs. Yes, she'd done it again. She'd allowed her brain to roam off on its very own whodunit. The fact that the whodunit was one she'd rather not figure out if it meant watching Jakob suffer, made it even worse.

Jakob . . .

There was no doubt she had feelings for the detective. He was fun to be with, a great conversationalist when he wasn't tortured by an investigation, and he opened his heart to her in countless ways.

He was, in a nutshell, everything she'd always wanted Peter to be and nothing he'd ever been. But still, she wasn't sure. Not entirely, anyway. She had, after all, thought Peter was a good fit once, too.

A rustling sound outside her partially open window made her sit up tall, the absence of any discernible breeze through the trees only heightening her radar further. But when she set the book on her lap and listened closely, she heard nothing except the sound of a passing car as it made its way through the streets of Heavenly.

She inhaled slowly, silently laughing at herself as she released the same breath of air. Her plate was full enough with real problems. The last thing in the world she needed to do was add to it with phantom sounds and an overactive imagination.

Still, the book had lost its ability to hold her attention despite the fact she'd hit a pivotal point in the story. Instead, she let the book close on its own as she turned her attention to the only other subject that had a prayer of settling her down for the sleep she knew she needed.

Her talk with Martha earlier that day had squashed any thoughts she'd had about throwing Esther a shower. Which meant she had to come up with something else, something special that would let Esther know just how much Claire treasured their friendship.

Somehow a set of sheets fell short in that endeavor.

The unmistakable snap of a twig outside the same window brought her to her feet while the answering thump in her chest made her reach for her phone. Quickly, she scrolled through her contact list until she came to Jakob's number and hit dial.

Two rings later, the sound of his voice in her ear settled her nerves enough to allow her to think clearly.

The sound had stopped — a sound that easily could have been made by one of the three or four cats who lived next door . . .

Feeling suddenly foolish, she covered her late night phone call with the only explanation she could find at the ready. "Hi, Jakob, I hope you don't mind me calling so late but I was lying here, thinking about what happened at Harley's wake, and, well, I guess I want to make sure you're doing okay."

The lame excuse was barely out of her mouth before she smacked herself in the forehead. Why, oh, why did caller ID have to be the norm these days?

"Uh . . . I'm hanging in, I guess . . . thanks." He cleared his throat of any signs of sleep and turned the conversation back in her direction. "Is everything okay with you?"

"Yes. Yes, of course." Immediately she knew she'd answered too quickly. Her rapid response negated any believability her just-called-to-say-hi-and-see-how-you-are phone call may have otherwise held. She groaned inwardly.

"Now, don't get me wrong here, because I'd welcome a call from you anytime — day or night. But, that said, are you in the habit of checking in on folks at midnight?"

"Is it that late? I . . . I didn't —" She stopped, mid-lie, and leaned toward the open window, the lack of any odd noises making her feel all the more ridiculous. Instead, she changed topics. "I was talking to Diane tonight about some different things and I had a thought."

"Okay . . ."

"Maybe Isaac is wrong. Maybe those signs he was talking about had nothing to do with your father and everything to do with Patrick. Maybe it was *his* bubbling anger that finally exploded."

If he responded, she didn't hear, because at that exact moment a string of nonsensical mutterings seeped their way through the screen, churning her stomach with fear in the process.

"Claire?"

"Shhhh," she whispered. "This time I'm sure . . ."

"Sure? Sure of what?"

"Someone is outside my window."

Instantly, any and all sleep that had been detectable in Jakob's voice was gone, in its place the sound of someone on full alert. "Are you sure?"

"Yes."

"Do you think it's just one of your aunt's

guests?"

She slid off the bed and tiptoed to the window, a quick inventory of the parking lot and the lack of light reflecting on the lawn enabling her to give a confident no. "Everyone was in their room by nine o'clock tonight," she said. "I've been hearing odd noises for a while now but kept thinking it was something else."

"And now you don't think it is?"

She stood to the right of her room's creakiest floorboard and squinted into the darkness below, her first sweep of the ground outside her window revealing nothing of consequence. "I don't know. I think I just heard someone mumbling . . ." She shifted slightly to the left and bobbed her head still further in the same direction. "I guess I was — no!" She cupped her hand around her mouth to quiet her words even more as she gave a play–by-play of the shadowy figure that emerged from behind a tree and slinked along the outer edge of the front porch.

"Can you tell anything about this person? Is it a male or female?"

She dropped into a squat and leaned closer to the screen. "It's definitely a male. He's broad shouldered . . . maybe a little stocky. Could you send a patrol car, please?"

"I'm already on my way, Claire. But stay on the line with me until I get there."

She continued to follow the stranger as he crept around the corner of the porch and into a narrow patch of moonlight just bright enough to send a shiver of awareness and fear down her spine.

"Jakob," she hissed into the phone, "it's Patrick. Patrick Duggan! Please, please hurry!"

She glanced over Jakob's shoulder at the inn's still-dark second-floor windows and allowed herself a moment to breathe. The detective's arrival and subsequent collaring of Patrick Duggan had been surprisingly quiet, and for that she was grateful. The last thing Diane or any of the guests needed was to have their sleep disrupted by news of a would-be prowler.

"Seems a little late for a walk, don't you think, Patrick?"

Patrick's shoulders rose and fell against the side of Jakob's car, yet he remained silent, the agitation he wore in his eyes and across his face speaking volumes all on its own.

"It's your prerogative, of course, not to answer, Patrick . . . but it's also mine to put you in the back of my car and bring you in for trespassing."

"Last I checked, taking a walk wasn't a crime." Patrick, too, crossed his arms in front of his chest. "Has that changed?"

"If you were walking down there" — Jakob pointed down the driveway and toward the main road — "it wouldn't be an issue. But you weren't. You were walking here . . . on *private* property."

"The lady that owns this place knows me. She invites me onto her property all the time."

Jakob's gaze shifted to Claire. "Is that true?"

Before she could answer, Patrick did some pointing of his own. "See them steps over there? The ones that go to that back door? I helped fix them just the other day. And that window to the right of the front porch? I helped caulk that just last week. Both times, I was *asked* to be here."

"Did you make both those repairs at midnight?" Jakob asked as he looked, again, at Patrick.

"Nope."

"Did Diane Weatherly call you this evening and ask you to come fix something out here this late?"

Patrick narrowed his eyes. "Nope."

"Then you're trespassing, Patrick. And if

Ms. Weatherly, here, wants to press charges, I can haul you into the station right now." He nodded at Claire, yet kept his gaze firmly on Patrick. "Claire? Do you want me to take him in?"

"Hey now, there's no reason for this." Patrick let his arms drop to his sides. "Look, I realized I left something the last time I was out here, and I just figured I'd come out and get it. No big deal, you know?"

"What did you leave behind?"

Again, the arms crossed. Again, the touchy demeanor was back. "What business is it of yours?"

"When you're slinking around on private property at midnight, it becomes my business, Patrick."

"A hammer. I left a hammer." He threw his hands up in the air and pushed off the car only to lean against it once again when Jakob blocked his path. "Can I go now?"

"Did you find your hammer?"

"No."

"You use this hammer while you were working for Harley Zook?"

Something Claire couldn't quite identify passed across Patrick's face, and she wondered if Jakob had caught it, too.

"Yeah. So what?"

"What did you think of working for Harley?"

The look was back, but, once again, it was fleeting. "It got me away from my mother."

"And?" Jakob prodded.

"It was a job. Period."

Whatever Jakob was looking for in Patrick's response, he wasn't getting it. Long seconds passed as he seemed to wait for a different, more acceptable answer.

But none came.

He tried a different approach. "Did you *like* Harley?"

"Does it matter?"

"That doesn't answer my question."

"I realize that." Patrick parted company with the side of Jakob's car for the second time, this time leaving the space he created despite Jakob's unyielding presence. "So? Can I go now? I'll check with Diane about the hammer tomorrow."

"*I'll* check with Ms. Weatherly about this hammer of yours tomorrow. If she has it, I'll let you know." Then, as Patrick made a move to leave, Jakob blocked his path once more. "Tell me something, Patrick . . . Have you ever been out to Harley's farm?"

Patrick's head jerked up, his gaze skirting between Jakob and Claire. "To his farm?"

"Yes, to your employer's farm. You ever

been there?"

She held her breath in anticipation of the answer to a question she'd been dying to ask for the past several minutes. In her mind, his answer would remove Mose from the list of suspects in Harley's murder and relieve Jakob of the incredible burden he'd been carrying the past few days on top of his already broken heart.

Reality, however, had a very different feel as Patrick brought his eyes level with Jakob's. "I might not be the brightest bulb in the box, but I know the big business these Amish folks are in this town. People come from all over just so they can gawk at people riding around in a buggy instead of a car. They buy postcards by the dozens of folks who never agreed to have their picture taken in the first place because they think it's being boastful or something like that." He flicked his left hand toward the inn and clenched his teeth around his words. "Heck, that place right there probably wouldn't even exist if it wasn't for all those people who want to experience a more peaceful way of living for a few days. They sign up for tours, drive their cars past Amish schools, and point at the farmers as they work in their fields from one end of the day until the other.

"And stores like yours," he said, acknowledging Claire, "enjoy a booming business because people like that want to bring stuff the Amish make home with them at the end of their trip. If they didn't, why else would they spend hundreds and hundreds of dollars on a quilt?"

At any other time and in any other place, she might have considered challenging him on the "booming business" part, but to do so would derail the conversation and bring unwanted scrutiny her way.

"I'm not sure how any of this is answering my question, Patrick. Have you or haven't you ever been to Harley Zook's farm. It's a simple yes or no."

This time, the look on Patrick's face was easy to decipher. Even in the dark.

"Those folks come here out of curiosity. Either they read about the Amish in a book or watched a movie about the Amish or had parents who talked about the Amish in a way that made them want to learn more . . . see the way they live up close and personal." Patrick took another step forward, his clenched fists and restless demeanor bringing Jakob's hand to rest on the top of his gun belt. "Then there's me. I was raised right here in Heavenly. I've seen thousands of buggies out my window since I was a little boy. I've crossed paths with Amish kids my own age along the way, some of whom I even wished I could be friends with back then. Yet, in all that time they were practically living in my backyard, I'd never stepped foot on an Amish farm no matter how close I may have been."

"Never?" Jakob challenged.

Slowly, Patrick raised his field of vision upward, to the stars that dotted the night sky above. "You seem to forget who my dad is, Detective."

"I know who your father is, Patrick."

"Then you have a pretty good window into how I was raised."

She looked at Jakob to see if he was following everything that was being said, but what she saw in his face only shored up her own confusion.

"I'm listening."

"Despite my grandparents' best efforts, I was raised around hatred. The kind of hatred that makes a person kill because of a difference — a different look, a different belief, a different way of living." Patrick took one more look at the stars then angled his body toward the driveway and the deserted road that would eventually lead him back home. "When a kid is raised around that kind of hatred, Detective, it's awful hard to shirk it off all by yourself. It's like being taught to tie your shoe. You're taught it often enough, it sticks. And if the teaching stays the same, the learning will, too."

CHAPTER 22

Despite her bleary eyes and sleep-deprived brain, Claire knew something was off with Esther the second she reported for work Thursday morning.

The first glance at her Amish friend told Claire the basics — no discernible smile, fidgety fingers, and red-rimmed eyes that hinted at recently shed tears. The second glance revealed nothing additional except a general sense of foreboding deep inside Claire's heart.

"Good morning, Esther." She stepped through the doorway between the back hall and the shop and hung her keys on a hook underneath the register. "You can certainly tell the colder weather is coming. I actually had to button up on the way here just now."

Button by button she worked her way out of her autumn jacket and then draped it over her arm. "Did Eli bring you by this morning?"

It was a simple question. One she asked virtually every morning Esther arrived at Heavenly Treasures. But something about the way she asked it or, perhaps, the morning itself, netted a far different reaction than the usual face-splitting smile and emphatic head nod that was the norm.

"No."

Claire waited for her normally chatty friend to say more, but nothing else came. Just the one no, followed by a sinking of Esther's narrow shoulders and two distinct sniffles.

But it was enough for Claire to go on even if she didn't like the direction in which her thoughts were already beginning to travel.

"Esther? Are you okay, sweetie?" She transferred her coat from her arm to the counter and then patted the pair of stools with her hand.

When Esther shook her head and remained standing, Claire bypassed the stools completely and came around the counter to stand beside Esther near the front window. "Talk to me, Esther. What's wrong? Did you and Eli have a fight?"

"Eli and I, we do not fight." Esther reached up and carefully adjusted her white head cap. "But he is not happy with my suggestion."

"Do you want to talk about it?"

Slowly, Esther shifted her focus outside, to the cars and buggies that passed the shop on their way to wherever it was they were going at that particular moment. Seconds turned to minutes, yet still Claire's question went unanswered.

At least in a verbal way, anyway.

"I think it's best if I leave you alone for a while." She reached out, squeezed Esther's shoulder quickly, and then retraced her steps back to the counter and the coat that needed to be stowed in her office for the duration of the workday. "I'm here, though, if you want to talk, okay? Just say the word and —"

Esther spun around on the soles of her simple black lace-up boots and held up her hands. "It is not that I don't want to marry Eli! I do! But to do it now . . . at a time when so much is wrong . . . would only make things worse on everyone."

"You called off the wedding?" Claire heard the shock in her voice and saw the pain it stirred on Esther's face just before being covered from view by two trembling hands.

"I did not call the wedding off. I will marry Eli. I . . . I" — Esther gulped for air between sobs — "just said maybe we should w-wait. Until there is n-not so much s-sadness and worry."

"You mean with Harley Zook's murder and the possible connection to your grandfather?"

Esther sniffled, nodded, then sniffled some more. "Y-yes. We do not want to burden my mamm and dat at a time when their hearts are heavy with worry. Eli tried to ask Benjamin his thoughts, but Benjamin, too, thinks of other things."

Benjamin.

Just the mere mention of Eli's older brother brought an ache to Claire's heart. She missed Benjamin. Missed their talks. Missed his smile. Missed the way he listened. Missed the hope he'd helped bring back to her life . . .

"Hope . . ." Yes, she needed to find some more hope. Hope that she could find a new job after the shop, something to fill the void she knew would forever be in her heart in the wake of her failure.

"Claire?"

Esther's voice, shaky and confused, broke through Claire's woolgathering and brought her back to the moment — a moment that included Esther, not Benjamin or Heavenly Treasures' impending demise. Claire forced herself to focus.

Esther's wedding . . .

"So what's the worst that would happen if you postpone the wedding?" she finally asked. "You wait, what? Three, maybe four months? Maybe that wouldn't be such a bad thing in light of everything that's going on."

"It would be a year. There is far too much to do in the fields once spring comes. There would be no time for a wedding until November. It is this that upsets Eli."

"And you?" It was a rhetorical question, really, because she already knew the answer. All she had to do was look at her friend's tear-swollen eyes to know how the notion of waiting even a day longer than they'd planned hurt Esther deeply.

"I do not want to wait, but there would be some good, too."

"Like what?"

"I could stay here and work with you even longer."

Claire closed her eyes and allowed herself a moment to imagine twelve more months working alongside her best friend. But just as she felt the smile creeping across her mouth, reality came knocking.

Pretty soon there would be no shop for Esther to work in, no shop for Claire to own. No, it was better for Esther to marry as previously planned.

Better for Esther.

Better for Eli.

And better for Claire in the long run, too . . .

Squaring her shoulders, Claire reached out, tucked a stray strand of hair back into place beneath Esther's kapp, and then nudged the young woman's chin upward until their eyes met. "One way or the other, you and Eli will be married this month just as you planned. You have my word on that."

By the time six o'clock rolled around, all Claire wanted to do was go back to the inn, grab a pair of headache relievers, and disappear under her covers until morning. Yet when she pulled onto Lighted Way and turned east instead of west, she knew Esther's words from earlier that morning had taken control of her evening.

Sure, on some level, she'd been keenly aware of Benjamin's absence over the past few days, but she'd managed to stuff it to the side in lieu of things like helping Diane and worrying about Jakob. All legitimate concerns on their own, but none big enough to remove the handsome Amish man from her thoughts completely.

They needed to talk. Or, at the very least, *she* needed to talk to *him.*

Her destination suddenly clear, she drove

into the quiet countryside, passing one farm and then another before turning left, the midsize sedan making the winding climb with ease. The covered bridge at the top of the hill vibrated beneath her wheels as she entered and then exited out the other side. When she reached the point where the road narrowed and wound into the woods, she pulled off to the side and parked beside the familiar horse and buggy.

Instinct had told her he'd be there.

Need had made her come.

Yet, as she unlocked the door and stepped from the car, a wariness settled around her like a formfitting coat, rooting her feet to the ground and making her scrutinize everything about her decision to come to a place that was his and his alone.

Less than a month earlier, he'd proposed leaving the only life he'd ever known in favor of a life with her, and she'd turned him down. Her reasons had been far more noble than she truly was, and she still stood by them, her heart be damned, but she'd hurt him, nonetheless.

Did she really have a right to be there? To fight for a friendship she wasn't sure he even wanted?

She took in a breath only to release it into the air as she spied him through the waist-high prairie grass that shielded their special rock from the virtually nonexistent passerby. Even in the gathering dusk, she could make out some of the features that took her breath away every time she saw Benjamin Miller — the erect posture, the hint of the high cheekbones visible in his side profile, the dark brown hair that escaped from underneath the black hat he proudly wore. What she couldn't see, her mind filled in via the memory of his piercing blue eyes and the sensation of his strong, callused hand on hers.

"I can leave if you need time alone with your thoughts." He slid to the edge of the rock and stood, turning to face her as he did.

She wondered if he heard her gasp but decided it didn't matter. Instead, she let her mind wander back to the late summer night when they'd sat together on that very rock and looked up at the stars. It was an evening she'd never forget, with a man she didn't ever want to lose from her life. "No. Please. I came here to find you."

He stood ramrod straight as she picked her way across the prairie grass to the very rock where she'd first begun to realize there was hope for a future after Peter. Looking back, there wasn't one specific thing Benjamin said that first night that gave her back that hope. In fact, it wasn't anything he'd said at all. Rather, it had been the fact that he had listened to her dreams and made her feel as if they were interesting and exciting in a way her ex-husband had never done.

When she reached him, she rose up on her tiptoes and planted a friendly kiss on his cheek then followed it up with what she hoped was a friendly smile. "It's good to see you, Benjamin. I've missed you around the shop these last few days."

She found a spot on the top of the rock and positioned her body so as to afford the best view of his face. "I know you are upset with me over the things I said about Mose the other day, but I also think things have been strained between us since that day behind my shop earlier in the month."

"It is for the best. I know that now." Benjamin's gaze dropped to his feet only to lift to meet hers once again. "But I would have left. For you."

She could feel the tears forming and did her best to hold them off. What they needed now more than anything was dialogue, not emotion. Dialogue would move them forward; emotion would hold them back. "Knowing that means more than you could ever know, Benjamin. And I will always treasure you for that. But I treasure you for so much more, too."

"Yah?"

"Your friendship — the way you listen, the way you encourage me, the way we laugh — that has made such a difference in my life. I don't want that to ever stop, Benjamin. Not ever." She glanced upward and pointed just over his head and to the right. "It's not dark enough to see just yet, but right there? That's where I saw that star I wished on with you the first time you brought me here."

"Yah. And you wished for a simple life surrounded by love and family."

Her mouth gaped open as she stared at him. "You remember that?"

"It is that wish I tried to give you." The huskiness in his voice tugged at her heart and almost made her hope that things could be different — that her convictions hadn't been so strong and that her feelings could have been stronger. But they had been and they weren't.

"I could not enjoy that wish if it was at the expense of someone else. You would not be whole without Eli and Ruth and your family. It would have affected that love in the end." She forced herself to look back at the sky, to remember that first night and the conversation that had led to her wish. "That's the thing about wishes, Benjamin. Sometimes they come true just as you wished them, sometimes they don't. Sometimes they take a better, different form than you thought and sometimes they come true only to slip right out of your hands" — she took a deep breath in an effort to soften the emotion she heard building in her voice — "while you're not really paying attention."

She felt him studying her and made a point of averting his gaze. Benjamin was sharp. If she looked at him now, he'd see the tears in her eyes.

Finally, he spoke, his words bringing an instant lump to her throat. "You told me you wished for your store. That is one wish that came true."

"For a while." She swallowed once, twice. "Until I messed it up."

She shivered at the feel of his hand as he lowered the angle of her head until she was looking at him. "I do not understand. You enjoy your shop, no?"

"I love my shop, Benjamin. It's everything I ever wanted and a million times more." Just like that, the affection she felt for her job came rushing through her mouth. "I love talking to people who come into the shop asking about the Amish. I love helping them select a special memento of their trip to Heavenly. I love sitting in the craft room Diane has set aside for me behind the kitchen. Some days, when I'm not working, I lose myself in that room as I make my candles and experiment with new frames and wall hangings. I love coming to work and seeing the gorgeous items Martha brings in for me to sell. I love working beside Esther most days . . ." She stopped talking, the pain too strong to get through without crying.

"It is as I said before. Esther will still be your friend even after she marries Eli. You do not need a shop to be friends."

Her laugh caught in her throat and emerged as more of a half laugh, half sob. "That's good, because I won't have my shop for much longer."

He dropped his hand to his lap but kept his focus trained on her face. "I do not understand. What is wrong with your store?"

Suddenly, she couldn't hold it in anymore. In a rush of tears that wouldn't stay hidden this time, she unburdened herself of the secret she'd been carrying around for far longer than she cared to admit. "I'm running out of money."

"Running out of money?"

Pulling her knees to her chest, she

wrapped her arms around her legs and fixed her gaze on the faint outline of a windmill she could still make out on Benjamin's property at the base of the hill. "When I moved here, I had a certain amount of money in my savings account. In hindsight, I realize it wasn't enough. I should have saved more before I opened the shop. But I really thought what I had saved, plus the money I'd make on the inventory, would be enough to keep it going."

"It was not enough?"

She shook her head, slowly, sadly. "That nest egg has dwindled to almost nothing."

"But people bring bags out each day. I see them when I drive by or stop to check on Ruth . . ."

"They buy bibs and Amish dolls and even some of my candles, sure. But the money I make after I pay Martha or Esther isn't enough to cover my expenses let alone make a profit." She released her legs and reclined back until the only thing she saw was the night sky. "On the rare occasion I have something like a high chair to sell, I make a little more money. But I don't have enough of those large handmade items at any given time to really make a difference to the bottom line."

"How soon?"

She turned her head just enough to see his face. "How soon what?"

"Before you must close your shop?"

"I had thought I could make it to the end of January, but now, with Martha unable to paint any stools or milk cans for me until after Esther's wedding, I'm not sure I can make it that long, anymore." She willed the stars to hurry up and come out yet knew even they couldn't make a difference. "So, I don't know . . . maybe the second week of January if I'm lucky?"

"Will you stay in Heavenly?"

That was the million-dollar question. The one that kept her up late at night, pacing. "I won't live off my aunt for the rest of my life, Benjamin. I can't."

"Does Esther know?"

She bolted upright. "No! And she can't! Please! She has much too much to worry about right now without that being added to the list. Especially when there's nothing she can do to change things where the store is concerned." She swung her body around to face Benjamin. "Please. Promise me you won't tell her."

"If that is what you want, I will not tell Esther."

Slumping forward, she grazed his shoulder with her head before she realized her mistake and pulled back. "I'm sorry, Benjamin. I didn't come here wanting to dump all of my problems on you." She stopped, considered her words, and decided to recant. "Actually, maybe, on some level, I did want to tell you all of this simply because I knew you'd listen and not race around trying to fix the unfixable the way Aunt Diane or Esther would try to do. But I also came because I want to see how you are. To apologize for not seeing how Harley's murder and talk of Mose's suspected involvement might affect you. I hope you can forgive me for that."

It was his turn to shrug. "You are not the only one who thinks Mose is guilty. Everyone in the district thinks there is a good chance he murdered. Even his family — Martha and Abram, and even Isaac — seem to think there is a chance. But I do not. I do not believe Mose could take a man's life. Life ends when it is *God's* will, not man's."

"You're close to Mose, aren't you?"

"Yah."

"Was that from when you and Jakob were friends as young boys?" She drew her knees to her chest a second time and rested her chin there as she watched Benjamin.

"Yah. Jakob's dat helped us catch frogs. One day, I showed him a small bridge I had built over Miller's Creek." He pointed toward the other side of the hill. "He said I did good work. I showed him more things I had made and he said it was good work. He taught me things I did not know, and I showed him new ideas. Mose Fisher is a good man even if you do not hear such things from his son."

She listened as he talked about his relationship with another boy's father, the reason for the true son's hurt and anguish over that relationship suddenly crystal clear and even a little heartbreaking.

There were so many things she wanted to say — explanations for Jakob, understandings to foster along, pleas for two old friends to find each other again — but when she finally spoke aloud, her heart settled on the only one that mattered at that moment. "I wish I could tell you that everything with Mose will work out okay, Benjamin. But I can't. What I can tell you is that the last person on the face of this earth who wants to see Mose charged with murder is his son . . . Jakob."

"I do not know if I can believe that."

"Do you believe in me?" she whispered.

The brim of his hat tilted upward as he took a brief glimpse of the sky. "Yah."

"Then believe me when I tell you Jakob is

tortured over what's going on." She swung her legs over the edge of the rock and jumped to her feet. "I better head out now, Benjamin. It's getting late. Diane gave me the night off, but she'll still worry if I don't check in with her soon."

He lingered in his spot for a moment, his eyes never leaving her face. Then, just as she started to move toward her car, he, too, got to his feet, his voice thick with emotion. "You would make a good couple."

"Excuse me?"

"You. And Jakob. I see the way you smile with him. I see the way he smiles back. He would give you a good home and look after you."

She wanted to shake her head, to dispute the words she knew were responsible for the pain on his face at that very moment, but she didn't. She couldn't. Because, deep down inside, she suspected Benjamin was right.

CHAPTER 23

It was a beautiful night whether sitting on a rock high atop the Amish countryside or swaying back and forth in a swing the way she was at that very moment. There was so much about her day, her week, her future that would have been better dissected with pen and paper while sitting at the desk in her room, but something about the night air and the peace and quiet of her aunt's porch had won out for Claire in the end.

So what if she couldn't pore over a black-and-white version of yet another pro-and-con list comparing a future in Heavenly to a future somewhere else? So what if she couldn't doodle Mose's and Patrick's names in another part of her notebook in the hopes she'd crack the murder case wide open? Sometimes it was okay to feel instead of think.

Diane had taught her that the past nine months.

And as she herself had learned over the span of her life thus far, Diane was most always right.

There was no getting around the fact that on paper and pen, her best course of action was to start looking for a job in a place where jobs were easier to come by than Heavenly, Pennsylvania. She was fairly good with a computer, she had a good work ethic, and she got along with just about everyone she met. What, exactly, that qualified her to do, though, was anyone's guess.

Besides, she didn't want to leave Heavenly. She didn't want to leave Diane and the new friends who'd unknowingly helped to make her whole again. And whether she was ready to explore the reason or not, she didn't want to leave Jakob, either.

Heavenly was her home . . .

She turned at the faint sound of a click and blinked against the sudden burst of light that seeped onto the porch. "Diane? Is that you?"

"No, it's me. Megan." The pretty blonde stepped onto the porch with a folder in her hands and closed the door behind her as she did. "I was hoping that maybe I could borrow you for a second?"

Claire straightened her foot against the slats of the porch floor and brought the swing to a stop long enough for Megan to sit down. "Of course. Is everything okay?"

"I think so. But as I'm fairly sure you know by now, I like to talk things to death. I'd like to think it's just because I'm a mom who wants to make sure she does everything right where her kids are concerned, but that's not all of it. The rest is that I'm just type A and it's how I handle everything in life. I go-go-go and I obsess over each and every go along the way." Megan set the folder on her lap and shrugged. "And before you ask . . . yes, I exhaust myself sometimes, too."

It was hard not to laugh. Megan was definitely high-strung, but she was also endearingly honest when it came to admitting her faults.

"You're still thinking about Serenity Falls, aren't you?"

Claire didn't need the sole porch light to see Megan's cheeks redden. "No, not really." Megan looked down at her lap and shifted the folder just enough to clue Claire in to the presence of a second, slightly different colored packet. "Okay . . . maybe a little."

Reaching across Megan's arm, Claire liberated the top folder from the pile and flipped it open. "Roaring Brook . . . That's the one on this side of town, right?" She took in the colorful marketing brochure that featured a curbside shot of a quaint grouping of moderately sized homes.

"Keller and Sons has been building over here for years, from what our Realtor tells us. They've built a good, solid reputation for building good, solid homes." Megan tapped at the floor plan on the right side of the folder Claire was viewing. "See that one right there? That's the house we'll build if we buy in Roaring Brook."

Claire removed the floor plan from the folder and held it into the light. "Oh, Megan, this house is gorgeous. The kitchen is so spacious! And" — she squinted closely at the drawing — "that playroom on the second floor? It's huge!"

"I know. The boys will love it."

She eyed Megan across the paper. "So why are you hesitating?"

Bobbing her head to the left and then the right, Megan lifted a piece of hair from around Claire's ear and made a face. "Hmmm . . . Is my husband coaching you on what to say through some sort of ear thingy or something?"

She laughed. "No. It's just me."

Megan sunk back against the swing and sighed. "I know this place is nice. I know this builder has been around for a lot of years and that much of his business is repeat buyers, which is good — great, even." Her voice took on an almost monotonous tone as she recited reasons Claire suspected had been recited many times over the past few days, both in Megan's head and to her husband. "I also know the boys would love the house and that we'd make a lot of wonderful memories there."

"But . . ." Claire prompted.

"Wow. I'm here, what — just over a week — and you know there's a *but,* already?" Megan flicked a hand through her hair then handed the second folder over to Claire. "Serenity Falls is just different — the walking trails, the fitness stations, the playground with the little wooden stage for the kids who'd rather be creative than physical . . . all of it. And it's on the Amish side of town."

"Why does that part appeal to you so much?"

Megan drew back. "You mean being on the Amish side? Have you seen how calm it is over there? How quiet? I *need* that. I *want* that."

"I get that." And Claire did. Feeling the doldrums lapping at the edges of her soul at the notion of having to leave Heavenly, Claire made herself take the second packet from Megan. Inside were the same pictures she'd seen just two days earlier. "Trey Sampson," she read aloud. "Has he been building around here for a while, too?"

"He's built condos closer to Breeze Point, but this would be his first real dip into single-family homes."

"Sounds more like a full-fledged jump to me." Claire pulled a magazine-quality pamphlet from the packet's left-side pocket and stared down at the thirty-something man who smiled back at her from the full-color cover. "Nice looking guy."

"He's driven, too. He's all about making Serenity Falls an almost-prototype for a new kind of neighborhood built around old-fashioned values." Megan took the magazine, opened it to the third page, and then handed it back to Claire. "He even picked the brain of some fancy Italian architect when he was in the early planning stages of Serenity Falls. He wants to do this right. It's how he wants to make his name in this business."

Claire let her gaze play across the picture of children blowing bubbles on the steps of one beautiful home while a father and son shared a glass of iced tea on the front steps of another. "It certainly *looks* good."

"Which is what Kyle keeps saying. It looks good, but he doesn't want to view it all from inside a closed house." Megan blew a frustrated breath of air through her otherwise closed lips. "Kyle is right. I've got to let this go." Then, with the Keller and Sons folder firmly in her grasp, she stood and gestured toward the door. "I'll leave you to the quiet daydreams you were enjoying before I crashed the party."

"Trust me, you were a welcome distraction." Then, realizing she was still holding the Serenity Falls packet in her hand, she held it up for Megan. "Don't forget this one."

The pull to take the information was powerful as it moved across Megan's face. But, in the end, the young mother simply waved it off. "Why don't you keep it? Maybe one day, if things change, you can build a house there and invite me over for a cup of coffee."

"If I was able to do that, it would mean that . . ." Claire shook her head, determined to start living in reality instead of hanging on to the same wish-I-coulds and if-onlys that had her facing an uncertain future once again. "Let me know when you've signed the contract on the Roaring Brook house, okay? We can celebrate *that* over a cup of coffee before you have to head back to Chicago."

"You're on." Megan took two steps inside the inn and then turned to wave good night. "Oh, and Claire? I know I've been rather preoccupied at dinner the past few nights, but I want you to know how much I love your shop. It's so . . . *you.* So wonderfully, perfectly you."

Claire was grateful when the door finally closed and she was alone with her thoughts and the tears that were less than a blink away. Megan was right. Heavenly Treasures was her. It was everything she'd ever wanted for herself in terms of a career.

And now, because she'd moved too quickly, she was about to lose her career and her home in one swoop . . .

"Claire?"

She did her best to hide her disappointment as she turned toward the familiar voice and scrambled to find the closest thing to a smile she could offer along with her greeting. "I'm sorry, Aunt Diane, I should have come in a long time ago to see if you needed anything."

Diane stepped onto the porch. "You most certainly shouldn't have come inside. I told you a week ago that tonight was your night off."

Lifting her hand from the back of the swing, Claire pointed at the rectangular wooden box in her aunt's left hand. "What do you have there?"

"It's Harley's."

Claire stopped the swing and rose to her feet. "Harley's?"

Diane started to nod but then stopped. "Technically, he made it for Patrick, but he hadn't gotten around to giving it to him just yet. That's what he planned to do that next day."

A sweet smile crossed Diane's face as Claire watched her aunt peer down at the box in her hand. "He was so excited for Patrick to have it. He even planned how he was going to give it to him."

Claire waited for her aunt to continue then hung on each and every word that was said when she finally did. "That last day, he deliberately hung on to the hammer he'd given Patrick knowing full well he'd come back looking for it at some point over the weekend. He had me put it inside the tool-box and leave it, with a note, on the front porch for Patrick to find." Diane lifted the box onto a small table to the left of the swing and shook her head, sadly. "When I heard about Harley's death, I brought the box inside so nothing would happen to it. I remembered it again this evening, while I was making dinner."

"So he really was looking for a hammer last night," Claire whispered. "Jakob and I didn't believe him."

Diane released her hold on the toolbox and turned to study her niece. "Patrick was here? Last night? Why didn't you tell me?"

Why indeed . . .

"Jakob and I — we didn't want to worry you."

"Why would Patrick being here worry me, dear?"

Claire did her best to explain her decision, reaching out for her aunt's hand as she did. "Because Patrick carries a lot of anger. And when I saw him sneaking around outside the inn at midnight, I was worried. Especially when he could very well be a suspect in Harley's murder."

Diane's eyes widened with shock. "Patrick Duggan could never have hurt Harley. He cared far too deeply for that man."

"Cared for him?" she echoed. "But from what he said last night, it sounded like he only started working with Harley as a way to get out from under his mother's watchful eye."

"In the beginning that may have been true. But Harley won him over because he had no expectations for Patrick. He simply wanted to be that young man's friend in a way no one else really had since Carl was carted off to jail."

CHAPTER 24

She stood sentry at the large front window, counting the buggies that followed one behind the other through the Amish countryside. For a man who had been preceded in death by his spouse, his parents, and his brother, there was no lack of a turnout when it came to Harley Zook's funeral procession. Cousins and other family members had come from Amish communities to the west to pay their respects alongside the man's many friends in Heavenly.

When she reached a count of sixty, she made herself turn away, the sad reality of Harley's murder weighing on her heart. It was hard to understand how such a peaceful group of people could be the target of things like hatred and crime.

As a rule, the Amish weren't confrontational or competitive, they didn't seek revenge for wrongs inflicted on them, and they preferred to take care of things quietly.

So why would Carl Duggan throw away his freedom to end the life of a man who would never have done him any harm? Why would his son, Patrick —

She shook the thought from her head as Diane's words from the previous night all but pointed the finger of guilt solely back in Mose Fisher's direction.

"Hey, Claire, you have a second?"

She paused, mid-step, and turned back toward the front of the store, Jakob's presence just inside the doorway catching her by surprise. "Jakob! I didn't hear you come in."

He pointed at the string of bells just above the door and managed a halfhearted smile as he did. "They rang . . ."

"Oh. I didn't notice."

"Yeah, I saw you standing at the window a few minutes ago." Jakob stepped farther into the store. "For what it's worth, if we'd been standing closer to the actual procession, you wouldn't have had to count."

"I'm not sure I could have helped myself. I've never seen that many buggies in one place at one time."

Jakob nodded. "It's not uncommon to have as many as three hundred lined up behind the body. Fortunately for those standing closer than we were just now, you can gauge how long the line is by the chalked number on the back of each buggy."

She leaned against the counter and allowed herself a moment to take in the man standing less than two feet from her, the same man who'd been making more frequent appearances in her dreams at night and leaving her more confused than ever about the path she'd come to envision for her life. He tended to show up in her dreams anytime she was apprehensive or uncertain, like her subconscious mind knew he'd keep her safe.

And she could see why. The detective's broad shoulders and confident stance emitted an aura of protectiveness that made a person feel secure. And the dimples she knew were hiding just below the surface only added to the overall warmth and honesty that was as much a tangible part of his makeup as his sandy blond hair and amber-flecked hazel eyes.

When she felt him eyeing her curiously, she made herself reengage in the conversation. "What do you mean by a chalked number?"

"Usually a few boys — in the twelve- to fourteen-year-old range — are tasked with writing numbers on the back of all the buggies. The number given correlates with the driver's relation to the deceased. The closer the relationship, the lower the number."

She tilted her head toward the window as a memory tickled its way to the front of her thoughts. "You know, now that you say that, I think I passed a buggy on a country road a few weeks ago with a fifteen written on the back. But there weren't any other buggies around at the time."

"That just means it hadn't rained since they'd attended that funeral." Jakob took a deep breath before continuing. "So we talked to Mose again last night. In a more official capacity this time."

"He *talked* to you?"

His laugh was void of any humor. "Uh, no. But we knew that, didn't we?" He breezed on in a wooden voice that did little to keep the pain from dulling his eyes. "So, rather than get nothing out of him, I had one of my fellow officers asking the questions while I watched and listened from the other side of the two-way mirror."

She pushed away from the counter to stand closer to Jakob, her gaze searching every facet of his face for something to indicate the outcome of the questioning. But there was nothing. Just the same sadness she always saw whenever he talked of his family. "Did he say anything helpful?"

"He said only that he did nothing wrong."

"Well, that's good, right?"

"I guess that depends on whether he thinks killing Harley was wrong."

The swallow he took in reaction to the feel of her hand on his face was unmistakable, but still, she didn't stop. She cared about Jakob and, as a result, hated to see him in pain. "If he did this, Jakob, that's on him. Not you. Remember that."

He covered her hand with his own and allowed his eyes to close for a brief moment. "My father wasn't always so bitter. When I was growing up, Dat wasn't a demonstrative man, but few Amish are. His encouragement came in quiet ways — a quick pat on the shoulder, a slow nod of his head, that sort of thing. I remember wanting to see that nod come in my direction just so I could know I'd pleased him. But it didn't come my way all that often."

She thought of Benjamin and his admiration for Mose, their contrasting memories of the same man hard to hear let alone understand.

"For a long time, I believed it was just Dat's way." He used his hand to press hers more tightly against his skin. "When I saw him with Benjamin, I knew it wasn't."

"Jakob, don't," she whispered.

294

He moved his head just enough to whisper a gentle kiss across her palm, a slight smile skittering across his mouth at her responding sigh. "I guess I'm afraid that the outcome of this investigation will somehow prove to Mose that I wasn't a good son."

"How he could look at you as anything other than a blessing is a mystery to me."

Her hand shook inside his as he met her gaze and held it tight. "Claire, when this is all over, when this case is behind me and you've found your replacement for Esther at the shop, I want us to talk."

The shop . . .

The mere mention of the shop and the future it didn't have was like a bucket of ice water atop Claire's head. She staggered back, pulling her hand from his in the process. She knew she should tell him Heavenly Treasures would be closing in January, that she herself would probably be moving on shortly thereafter, but she couldn't.

Not yet, anyway.

Somehow, saying the words aloud to Jakob would mean they were true, that her dream job in her dream town was about to go up in smoke.

"Claire? Is everything —"

The ring of her cell phone from its temporary spot beside the register saved her from having to tiptoe around the truth. She nearly sprinted to pick it up, ignoring the unfamiliar number on the display screen in favor of the reprieve it offered. "Hello?"

"Hi, Claire, it's me, Megan. I hope you don't mind, but I asked Diane for your number just now and she said it would be okay to give you a quick call."

She made a mental note to pick up a piece of Shoo Fly Pie for Diane on the way home just before she shrugged an apology in Jakob's direction. "No, no, it's fine, Megan. What can I do for you?"

"I was hoping I could entice you into meeting me you-know-where in, say, a half hour."

"You-know-where?" she teased. "I thought you said you weren't going to talk about that place anymore."

"Well . . . things have changed."

She tried to concentrate on the voice in her ear, but it was hard when Jakob was pointing toward the door in silent signal of his exit. The call had certainly brought a welcomed end to an uncomfortable conversation, but if the sudden heaviness of her heart was any indication, she wasn't ready to see him go.

"I'll check back in with you soon," he

whispered.

"I look forward to it."

She followed him with her eyes as he disappeared through the door, the pull to follow him undeniable.

"Claire? Are you still there?"

"What — oh, yeah, I'm sorry. I was just saying good-bye to someone." She wandered aimlessly around the shop, the listlessness she felt in the wake of Jakob's presence impossible to miss. "So what's going on?"

"I am going to burst — absolutely burst — I'm so excited! Kyle, of course, is in meetings all day today and probably won't check his phone before he gets back to the inn tonight. But I need to tell *somebody.* Can you meet me out there again this one last time? Please?"

She checked the clock then peeked at her to-do list. "Make it an hour and you're on."

CHAPTER 25

This time, when Megan Reilly arrived on the grounds of Serenity Falls, Claire was waiting beside her car on the very lot that had a stranglehold on the Chicagoan's heart. Shielding her eyes from the late-afternoon sun, Claire waved a greeting to the woman now picking her way across the hard-packed earth with a smile wide enough to offset the sinking sun.

"Hey, Megan," Claire called as she, too, parted company with the side of her car to split the remaining distance. "I knew you were happy when we spoke on the phone a little while ago but, wow — that smile! What's going on?"

"Remember how I told you that Kyle was leaving the final decision to me?"

"Yes . . ."

"Well, I've decided." Megan threw her arms out to the side and slowly spun around in a little circle before coming to rest in her original spot with a little celebratory jump. "Welcome to our new home . . . or, rather, the *site* of our new home."

"You bought *here*?" She heard the confusion in her voice and instantly felt remorse. "Wait. I didn't mean to sound like that. It's just that, well, I thought you decided last night to build in Roaring Brook. I thought you were going to put down your deposit today."

The hum of work trucks on the other side of the development softened the edges of Megan's squeal. "I did. But then, this morning, I came out here to say good-bye. I needed to make peace with my decision, as silly as I know that sounds."

"No. I get that." And Claire did. Because not too deep down inside, she suspected her aunt would have to drag her out of Heavenly Treasures the day she turned her key back over to Al Gussman.

Megan continued, her voice breathless. "Anyway, I came out here, got out of my car, and . . . nothing. It was gone!"

"What was —" She stopped, straightened her stance, and inhaled. "Oh. Wow. You're right. What happened?"

"I don't know. And I really don't care. All I know is that Kyle can open his windows and I can live in that fairy tale that's been

299

torturing me almost nonstop this past week." Megan's smile disappeared momentarily as she gestured toward the truck sounds. "Now, all I want to do is make these last few months of the school year fly by this one time so we can bring the boys here. They're going to love the house, the playground, the trails, the horse and buggies everywhere, and all of the construction vehicles that are a part of any new housing development of this magnitude."

"Sounds like a perfect fit for two little boys."

Megan's smile returned, tenfold. "It does, doesn't it?" The woman reached into her purse, fished out a camera, and held it out to Claire. "Would you mind taking a picture of me standing here? I know there's not really anything to see except dried mud and a few utility hookups in the background, but still, I want to show them something when we get home."

Claire held the camera close to her eye and pointed it in Megan's direction. "If I zoom out a little, I can get a tiny part of that bulldozer over there in the frame, too."

"Definitely. Bulldozers are always good with the male population."

Shifting her position once or twice, she snapped a few decent pictures and then handed the camera back to Megan. "You've also got those brochures and stuff. Those will certainly help the boys picture their new home, too."

"Actually, I gave those to you, remember?" Megan deposited the camera back in her purse, the last of the sun's rays making her eyes shimmer. "But I want you to keep those. I'll get new ones from the sales office before I head back to the inn, and you can hang on to yours in the event you want to be neighbors one day."

"I'm thinking this place will be sold out long before I'm in a position to buy a home," she quipped, intentionally bypassing the truth about her store. This was Megan's moment, not hers. "Besides, the floor plans you showed me in the folder are way too big for one person."

Megan draped her purse across her shoulder and laughed. "They wouldn't be too big for you and that extremely handsome guy you were sitting on the front porch with the other night."

"Guy?"

"I think Diane said his name is Jakob?"

She felt the instant flush to her face and turned away, moving her head from one side of the tree line to the other to buy herself some time. "Jakob is a friend, that's all."

"If my male friends looked at me the way that guy looks at you, Claire, my husband would go insane."

There was no doubt there was a part of her that wanted to question Megan's read on Jakob's feelings the way she would have in her high school days. But she couldn't. Somehow, hearing someone else back up what Benjamin, Diane, and Martha already believed was more than she could take. Instead, she did her best to laugh it off while searching for a ready-made conversation changer.

"I imagine they'll keep these trees here, yes?" She pointed to the back of the property.

"They'll have to replace that one there, of course." Megan nudged her chin in the direction of the lone struggling tree and the gap its miniscule size offered between her future home and the farm. "But if a new one still doesn't take, I'll be okay with that. After all, it's the chance to be closer to the Amish that made this spot so hard to ignore for me in the first place."

"I wonder who will move in there now that Harley is . . ." Her inquiry vanished from her lips as a flash of movement on the gravel driveway in front of Harley's farmhouse caught her attention. She moved her head to the left just in time to catch a glimpse of a dark blue flannel shirt and a crop of thick brown hair.

"Patrick?" she whispered.

"Patrick? Who's Patrick?"

"Megan, I've got to go." She took off in a half jog, half sprint toward the break in the trees, calling back over her shoulder as she did. "Congratulations on the new home! I hope it's everything you want."

When she reached the gap, she stopped, maneuvered her way between the branches, and stepped onto the edge of Harley's driveway, her ears listening for anything her eyes failed to see. Yet, strain as she might, she heard nothing other than the faint hum of the bulldozer and a barking dog somewhere in the distance.

"Hello?" she called out. "Is anyone here?"

When the only response she got was silence, she moved farther across the driveway, the unsettling message on the side of Harley's foundation propelling her feet away from the house and toward the barn, instead. As she walked, she couldn't help but notice the empty metal trough and the ability to breathe through her nose without her eyes watering.

It was as her aunt had always said: the Amish pulled together in rough times. They helped one another raise a barn after a fire, collect money to offset the cost of a lengthy hospital stay, and, so it seemed, tidy a deceased brethren's farm in order to prepare it for sale or auction.

Claire's footsteps grew heavy as she neared the barn, and the reason wasn't hard to pinpoint. Even though she hadn't really known him beyond an occasional street passing, she identified with Harley Zook. Like Claire, the Amish man had only recently allowed himself to pursue a line of work that interested him in the way Heavenly Treasures did her. And just as Claire's past life had made her connection and proximity to Diane all the more important, Harley's had resulted in him developing a bond with the only other living creatures on his farm. Each cow had been given a name and each had obviously held a special place in his life from things Diane had said.

Aware of an invisible weight pushing down on her chest, she pressed her body against the main door of the barn and stepped inside, the sound of a hushed voice on the other side of the cow pens stopping her dead in her tracks.

"I promise you, Molly, I'll stay close by until that family comes back and gets you, too. No one is going to hurt you on my watch."

She ducked down beneath the railing line and peered past the back legs of the cow closest to the door, the same dark blue flannel pattern she'd seen through the tree line now in plain sight. Only this time, the odd sense she'd had as to the identity of its owner was confirmed mere seconds before the fear kicked in.

She tried to turn around, to quietly retrace her steps back to the door, but it was too late; he'd caught sight of her in her haste to leave.

"Hey! What are you doing here?" He was beside her and grabbing hold of her upper arm before she knew what was happening, the intensity of his grip making her howl in pain.

"Patrick, stop!"

He loosened his grip enough to allow himself an opportunity to step back and take her in from head to toe, the last of the sun's rays through a back window providing sufficient light to shore up her identity. "Wait. I know you. You were at my house the other night . . . and again outside Ms. Weatherly's place when that detective was badgering me."

"Ms. Weatherly is my aunt." When he let

go of her arm, she stepped closer to the door, rubbing the spot where his fingers had pressed against her skin. "I'm Claire. Claire Weatherly."

"Sorry. I guess I thought maybe you were the one."

She allowed her gaze to travel past him just long enough to take in their surroundings and the presence of only one cow. "Are the rest of Harley's cows in the pasture?"

"No. They're gone."

"Gone?"

"Some Amish family has been bringing them over to their farm. Each day they come and get a few more. Yesterday, they came and got all the rest 'cept Molly. She's going later today, I think."

"And the milk cans with all that spoiled milk?"

Patrick nodded. "We took care of that day before yesterday."

"We?" she echoed.

"Me and that kid . . . Luke something or other."

"Luke Hochstetler." She looked around again, her gaze falling on the matching patches of paint halfway up the wall just as a memory from the last time she saw Patrick surfaced in her thoughts. "I thought you said you'd never been out here before."

He took a step back only to recover it just as quickly. "I never said either way. I just said that as a kid, I'd never been allowed to step foot on an Amish farm no matter what my grandparents said. That was the truth. But I ain't a kid no more. I can see what's true with my own two eyes now, and there ain't a whole lot either of them can do about it." He pointed toward the source of light near the back of the barn. "See that window right there? That's where my father's bullet came from. The one that killed Harley's brother. He stood on a rock in my grandfather's yard and took the shot. Only took one from what the papers said."

She searched for something to say but came up short. Patrick's manner of presentation had made it so she wasn't entirely sure whether he was saddened by, or proud of, that fact.

"The papers said he fired that bullet out of ignorance and they were right. My father spouted all this hatred against the Amish all the time, but he wasn't right. I know that now." Patrick's gaze lingered on the window for a moment before finally turning back to hers. "I also know that hatred can wear a black hat just as easily as no hat at all."

She shook her head in an attempt to make sense of what he was saying. "I'm sorry,

Patrick, I don't understand. What was that about hatred wearing a black hat?"

"Amish people. Some of them can hate just as much as some of us. And their hatred can do bad things, too." Patrick slumped against the barn wall and raked his hand through his full head of hair. "Sometimes even to their own people."

Something about his words, and the way in which he said them, rewound her ears back to the moment he released his death grip on her arm.

"What did you mean earlier? When you thought I was 'the one'? What one?"

He jammed his hands into the front pockets of his pants and sighed. "I thought you were that one who used to lurk around here all the time. But when I stopped long enough to actually see you, I realized you were a girl . . . and that you weren't wearing all that Amish stuff."

"Amish stuff?"

"Yeah. That Amish guy was always letting Harley's cows out and messing with our workday. And when he wasn't, he was yelling at him or just hanging around."

It was her turn to grab his arm. "Wait. You've seen an Amish man lurking around here?"

"I haven't this past week, but before . . .

when Harley was still alive . . . yeah."

Steeling herself for an answer she didn't want to hear, she asked the only question she could. "Do you know this man's name?"

"Nah. Harley would just say it didn't matter. That this guy lost someone special to him, too, and was acting out the way I used to before Harley came along."

She knew she really didn't need the confirmation. Harley's description to Patrick virtually filled in the answer all on its own. But, still, she hoped she was wrong. Hoped she could spare Jakob the added pain of locking his father up behind bars.

"Would you know this Amish man if you saw him?"

"You bet I would."

CHAPTER 26

Claire glanced across the center console and tried to imagine what was going through Patrick's head now that they were in her aunt's car and headed toward the main road.

"It's hard to imagine this place actually being something one day," he finally said as they bounced along with the car on the way out of Serenity Falls.

"Have you seen the brochures? It's going to be a really *nice* something by the time this Trey Sampson fellow is done with it." She winced as the left side of the car dropped lower than the right only to recover as they reached the development's exit. "One of the guests staying at the inn right now is getting ready to build in here. She's got two little boys and she's beside herself over the playground and walking trails that will be part of the community when it's finally done."

"Think it'll bother them living so close to the Amish?"

"That's one of the reasons Megan wanted to build here in the first place. She envies their peaceful lifestyle."

When Patrick said nothing, she peeked in his direction once again. "Are you okay?"

Pressing his forehead to the passenger side window, he shrugged ever so slightly. "I guess I'm just thinking what it would be like to be one of those kids."

"One of Megan's kids?"

Again, his shoulders lurched upward. "Yeah, the one you were just talking about. Sounds like she's more open-minded than what I come from."

She heard the hurt in his voice and wished there was something she could do to make it better. Unfortunately, short of having a time machine with redo capabilities, all she had to offer was a listening ear. "It's been rough being without your dad all these years, hasn't it?"

"For the past sixteen years, I thought that, too." He shifted his head from the window to the headrest and released a long, weighted sigh. "But then I met Harley and I started to realize the part before my dad went to jail wasn't much of a picnic, either."

"How so?" She slowed the car in an effort

to buy them a little more time to talk. Somehow, the conversation unfolding between them was preferable to watching him point to Jakob's father as the man behind the incidents at Harley's farm.

"Little kids are supposed to be curious. It's how they learn, ain't it? But I didn't get to be curious. I just had to take what was told to me and accept it as some sort of gospel truth even though it wasn't." Patrick's jaw tightened noticeably. "Can't really understand why people with so much hatred are given a kid to raise while a man who lived his life with an open mind had cows. Seems kinda backward, you know?"

How could she argue? It was something she'd pondered on her own many times over the years, especially when she considered her childless aunt Diane. But there were reasons for everything, even if they weren't always obvious at first. She said as much to Patrick.

"If Harley had his own children, he might not have had time to reach out to you." She let her gaze wander toward the Fisher farm, her worry about what Patrick might say when he finally saw Mose making it difficult to stay in the moment. Still, she tried, even going so far as to pivot her upper body toward the young man in the passenger seat.

"And maybe you needed him more."

Patrick studied her closely, his eyes taking on a misty quality that hinted at the tears he was trying valiantly not to shed. "I still do. But they can't take away the things he taught me. Those things are inside me now."

She reached across the console and squeezed his forearm. "You're right. They are. And those things he taught you were his gift to you. It's up to you what you do with them from here on out."

For the first time since they'd met, a smile played at the corners of Patrick's mouth just before a lone tear escaped down his cheek. "Making things with his hands made Harley awfully happy, and I think I'd like to do the same thing. For him."

She pulled to the side to allow an approaching horse and buggy to pass then turned to look at Patrick once more. "I think Harley would be the first person to tell you to do what makes *you* happy. Life is too short to follow someone else's dream."

"Are you following yours?"

It was her turn to blink back tears as she gave the only answer she could. "Right now, I am. And it's made me happier than I've ever been. But trying to keep your head afloat with a shop on Lighted Way isn't always easy. Especially when you can't pay the rent."

He considered her words then peered out the windshield toward some distant point. "I liked *painting* the things Harley made."

"Then maybe that's your thing. Either way, you'll figure it out." She looked again toward the Fisher farm and knew the time had come to see what Patrick remembered. "So? Are you ready to take a walk?"

His answer came by way of a nod and the sound of his door unlocking. When they met up on her side of the car, he pointed toward the white farmhouse at the end of the next driveway. "Is that the place?"

"I don't know. I guess that'll depend on whether you recognize anyone you see as the man from Harley's farm."

Hooking her thumb in the direction they needed to go, she set off, Patrick falling into step in rapid fashion. Together they walked, the fine gravel of the main road making a soft crunching sound beneath their feet.

"You know the people who live here?"

"I do. And so do you."

Patrick stopped mid-step. "I do?"

"You met Isaac, right? The other man Harley was bringing on to work with the two of you?"

"Oh. That guy." Patrick resumed his previous pace with his hands jammed into his front pockets. "I never met him. He just started working with Harley about a week or so before the murder. Harley sent him out on different jobs than the ones we did."

"Did he tell you much about Isaac?" They rounded the corner of the driveway and headed toward the barn and the tapping sound that drifted through its open door.

"Not really. 'Cept one time, when we drove out to fetch Mary, or maybe it was Molly . . . I can't really remember. But I do know that Harley was saying something about Isaac's dad wasting his life on anger." Patrick's feet slowed as they neared the barn. "Looking back, I guess he was trying to warn me not to do the same thing, but I can't be sure. Next thing I knew, we got busy coaxing that cow back to the barn."

They stopped and peeked inside, the last of the day's natural light making it difficult to gauge the identity of the shadowy figures on the other side. "Hello?" she called. "Isaac? Mose? Are you in there? It's Claire Weatherly."

The taller of the two figures straightened just before a hand shot into the air in greeting. "Hello, Claire." Isaac crossed the barn and stepped outside. "Is there something I can do for you?" Then, seeing Patrick, he nodded quickly. "I am Isaac. Isaac Fisher."

Patrick shot out his hand and waited for Isaac to shake it. "I'm Patrick Duggan, Harley Zook's apprentice."

"Harley Zook has passed on!"

Claire held her breath as the second figure strode toward them with purpose if not anger, each step he took in their direction increasing the dread she felt growing in her heart. Somehow she knew Isaac's suspicions about Mose were about to be confirmed by Patrick. Yet still, she hoped.

She hoped that Isaac was wrong about his father.

She hoped Patrick wouldn't know Mose.

And she hoped with everything she had that Jakob would be able to cross his father off the suspect list once and for all.

"There is no need to speak of that man again." Mose pushed past his youngest son to stand beside Claire with folded arms. "The Lord has called him home and he has been laid to rest —"

With one distinct gasp, Patrick ripped every last bit of hope from Claire while simultaneously confirming what she already knew in her heart to be true. "That's him . . . I mean, you!" Patrick's arm shot into the air guided by the finger he pointed at Mose. "You're the one who fought with Harley! You're the one who nearly got Molly killed by a car two weeks ago! You're the one who wrote those awful things in Harley's barn!"

With each accusation that passed through his lips, Patrick's voice got angrier and angrier, the pain he felt over the loss of his mentor unleashing itself with a frightening furor. She tried to calm him with a quiet touch, but it was no use; the accusations kept coming fast and furiously.

"You might put on that black hat every day and fool everyone around you into thinking you're different, but you're not! I know you're not! I've seen the things you've done to Harley, and you're going to pay, just like my father did!"

CHAPTER 27

At first glance, the Heavenly Police Department looked like any other building along Lighted Way. It boasted the same clapboard siding, the same wide front porch, and the same tastefully written sign above the front door. In fact, the only noticeable difference that set it apart from the shops and restaurants that surrounded it on three sides was the lack of Amish coming and going through its doors.

Here there were no black hats and aproned dresses, no suspenders and head caps. Instead, police uniforms mixed only with English attire as the door leading inside opened and shut throughout the course of a day.

Taking advantage of Esther's Saturday morning shift, Claire crossed Lighted Way and headed down the block to the station, her heart heavy. She'd felt awful calling Jakob the previous night, Patrick's words finding their way through her mouth in a series of starts and stops that, in hindsight, had probably made the retelling harder for Jakob to digest.

All night she'd tossed and turned as she'd recalled Patrick's accusations again and again and again, Isaac's failure to defend his father making the whole thing even more surreal. But it was the unmistakable sadness in Jakob's voice when she called that had driven her from bed before dawn with a feeling of unease she'd been unable to shake ever since.

She stopped outside the station to catch her breath, then pulled the door open and stepped inside, her destination, if not her reason for being there, crystal clear.

"Is Detective Fisher in?"

The weekend dispatcher — a fifty-something balding man — nodded and added a slight smile for good measure. "Ms. Weatherly, right?"

"Claire," she corrected, not unkindly. "I'd love to have a minute of his time if he's available."

"I'll check."

Five minutes later, she was making her way down the locked hallway toward Jakob's office, the sight of his sleep-deprived face peering at her from his doorway stirring up a potpourri of emotions best left unanalyzed in the present. "You look like you got as much sleep as I did," he said by way of a greeting. He touched his hand to the small of her back and guided her into his office, shutting his door to the prying ears of his fellow officers the second she crossed the threshold. "I'm glad you stopped by. It's been a long night."

She took the chair he indicated as he perched on the corner of his desk closest to her. "Did you have to bring your father in last night?"

"I thought about it. Even had a few of our officers at the ready to do just that, but then I decided to have them hold off. Mose isn't going anywhere. He's far too bullheaded to even think about leaving. Besides, the Amish don't run."

It was on the tip of her tongue to say they didn't murder, either, but she let that go. Jakob, of all people, knew there were exceptions to every rule. After all, he himself was one of them. Instead, she allowed herself a moment to take in the dark circles beneath his eyes, the beleaguered bent to his shoulders, and the unfamiliar lines that accompanied his equally unfamiliar frown. "So were you just up all night thinking, then?" she finally asked in lieu of the instinct that made her want to smooth his hand-tousled hair from his forehead.

"I was walking around Zook's farm with a flashlight."

"The cows have been moved to the Hochstetler farm for now. Though, as of late yesterday afternoon, Molly was still there."

"She's gone now, too." He palmed his mouth only to let his hand slip back down to the top of the desk. "I saw the message on the side of the house."

"You hadn't seen it yet?"

"I sent my officers out to take a peek and check the surrounding area for any clues the same night you reported it, but with the funeral and everything else going on with the investigation, I hadn't made it out there to see it myself until last night."

"Chilling, isn't it?"

"More like eye-opening."

There was something about the way he replied that caught her attention and made her sit up tall. "Did you find something?"

He pushed off the edge of the desk and wandered around his office, the room's relatively small dimensions making him turn almost as much as he actually walked. "When I saw the words with my own two eyes, it took me all of about two seconds to know my father didn't write them."

She followed him with her eyes as he paced his way back and forth between the door and his as-yet empty whiteboard. "How can you be so sure?"

"The use of a contraction. Most Amish don't use them in speech and certainly wouldn't use them in something they've written. That alone screams English to me." She, too, stood, the potential elimination of Mose from the list of murder suspects making her wonder why Jakob still looked so sad.

"That's great news, right?"

He leaned against the whiteboard and tapped its clean surface with his knuckles. "The problem is that with the exception of the graffiti, Mose still looks good for the crime."

She looked from Jakob to the clean board and back again before reclaiming the same chair she'd just vacated. "When Walter Snow was murdered, you had all sorts of things written on that board. And it was the same thing with Rob Karble. So what's different this time?"

"Because I couldn't stand looking at my father's name with a big red circle around it any longer. It's in my head nearly twenty-four/seven all on its own. Seeing it there just made it worse somehow."

"The motive you had for him was revenge, right?" At his nod, she stood again and crossed to the whiteboard and its metal sill of dry-erase markers. She plucked a purple one from the lineup and pointed. "May I?"

He parted company with the board, a flash of amusement adding a much-needed spark to his hazel eyes. "By all means."

"So how do you break it out again? Suspect? Motive? Means? Is that right?"

"That works."

She rose up on tiptoe and carefully wrote each of the three categories across the top of the board. When she was done, she capped the purple marker and retrieved a green one, instead. Then, with a quick glance over her shoulder, she stepped to the left and the suspect column. "So other than the graffiti, you still sort of have your father, right?"

"Yes."

She wrote Mose's name then moved to the motive column and wrote, Revenge/ Anger. "Which leaves us with means . . ."

"Harley's body was found propped against a shovel in the middle of my father's corn maze. You don't get any better *means* than that."

With corn maze in the means column, she stepped all the way to the left once again. "I suppose we could keep Patrick on the list for a while, too."

"You suppose?"

"He cared for Harley way too much to be the one who killed him."

She turned in time to see Jakob studying her with an odd look on his face. "You sound so certain."

"After talking to him yesterday and listening to everything he had to say, I kind of am."

"And his sneaking around the inn the other night? That doesn't shake your resolve a little?"

"Diane called you about the hammer, right?"

"She did."

"Well, then, you know that alone backs up the reason he gave us for being there." Still, she wrote his name under Mose's. "I'll put him up here anyway, because there's always a chance he's a gifted actor." Under the motive column she put ditto marks, and under means she named his role as Harley's apprentice.

Slowly, she stepped away to study her work, her shoulders drooping almost instantly. "Two suspects — each of whom is beginning to fall apart under closer scrutiny. That's not really much to go on, is it?"

He settled back against the desk, crossing his arms against his chest in contemplation as he did. "That's the problem with a crime against the Amish. They're quiet people. If they have any dirty laundry to speak of, they keep it to themselves."

She looked again at the motive column and thought of Carl Duggan and the crime he committed against Harley's brother sixteen years earlier. "What about hatred as a motive? Not the kind of personal hatred your father may have had for Harley, or even any lingering hatred Patrick may have had toward the man he saw as helping to put his father away . . . I'm talking about the bigger, broader hatred toward the Amish in general."

"Other than the stuff going on at Harley's farm, we've not been seeing any acts of aggression toward the Amish in our area for quite a while. And other than the graffiti, we can pretty much tie the loose cows to my father."

"Did he admit to that?"

"He said Harley needed to be tending his cows, not driving past his house in his buggy talking about me or fixing things with Isaac."

"I see." She turned her back to the board and met Jakob's eyes. "So what other kinds

325

of motives might propel a person to kill?"

"Betrayal, robbery, jealousy, a crime of passion, obsession, money — those are the most common reasons we come across in murders."

She began running through his list in her head, stopping every once in a while to ask questions along the way. "Any chance Harley betrayed someone other than your father?"

"Knowing what I know about Harley Zook, I'd have to say no, but I can't be entirely sure unless someone steps up and tells me otherwise."

"Nothing was missing from his home?"

"Again, hard to know, but his possessions seemed to be in keeping with the Amish, and we found his money in his boot — not a difficult hiding place for a would-be robber to discover." Sensing her next question, he headed her off at the pass. "Jealousy isn't really an emotion we see with the Amish because everyone lives the same way. And as for a crime of passion, Harley was a widower. He didn't have any womenfolk he was courting from what Isaac told my officers. All the women his age in these parts have husbands, and he was happy living in his brother's house and caring for the offspring of his brother's herd."

"Which leaves us with what?" She pulled the cap from the end of the green marker and snapped it into place. "The money you already found in his boot, right?"

"Well, money isn't always about the actual bills. Sometimes it's about gain, too. Though that doesn't fit with Harley any more than a wad of cash would." He threw his hands up in the air and shook his head. "It's like it was sixteen years ago when John died. Nothing is jumping up and down as a motive. But I'll find it just like the detective on that case finally did."

She stared at the board as Jakob continued to talk, her active mind swirling around his definition of money.

Gain . . .

Gain . . .

"Claire? You still with me?"

"You said gain could be a motive, right?" she whispered against a mental backdrop that was at first fuzzy but was growing increasingly more clear.

"Absolutely. But other than Mose possibly gaining Isaac back from Harley, I don't really see who else might have stood to gain from Harley's death. I mean, what did the guy have? A run-down farmhouse? A relatively new mobile carpentry business? A herd of aging dairy cows? What?"

Dairy cows . . .

Somehow she managed to stifle the gasp that rose in her throat and cover it with a convincing enough coughing fit, each cough buying her more time to come up with a plan that would get her out of Jakob's office without raising suspicion. If and when she discovered there were actual legs to her theory, she'd let him know. Until then, though, there was no sense in getting the detective's hopes up prematurely.

CHAPTER 28

Somewhere between the police station and Harley's farm, the certainty kicked into overdrive, spurred on, no doubt, by the balloon-laden signs that pointed the way like bread crumbs to the witch's door. Yet now that she had the proverbial map in hand, she couldn't believe she hadn't seen it sooner.

It all fit. And it had all been right there in front of her eyes numerous times over the past week. In fact, not more than two days earlier, she'd stared into the handsome face and instantly recognized the qualities of success — vision, drive, desire, and hunger for recognition . . . all things that had been going to waste because of another man's waning passion.

But no more.

With Harley's death came a second lease on a dream as evidenced by Megan Reilly's about-face and the line of cars Claire now spied lined up around the Serenity Falls sales office — cars that until that day had been noticeably absent.

She knew the reason, yet still she wanted to hear someone else say it, someone who would wrap her theory up with a neat little bow. Turning left into Harley's driveway, she drove up to the farmhouse, shifted the car into park, and pulled her cell phone from her purse.

Two buttons later she was smiling at the voice in her ear. "Sleep Heavenly, this is Diane, how may I help you?"

"Aunt Diane, it's me, Claire." She recognized the breathless quality of her voice half a beat too late.

"Claire? What's wrong?"

"Nothing's wrong, Aunt Diane. Really." She winced at the white lie and hoped the reason for it would offset any guilt that remained after they broke the connection. It was for a good cause, after all . . . "But can you do me a favor? Can you let Megan know I need to talk to her?"

"She's already left, dear. She and Kyle headed to the airport about twenty minutes ago."

She dropped her head forward onto the steering wheel, holding back the groan that followed the best she could. "Oh. I guess I didn't realize they were leaving so early."

"Megan's mother called to say one of the boys had a stomach bug, and they moved up their flight."

"Okay, can you hang on just a minute?" Without waiting for a reply, Claire pulled the phone from her ear and quickly scrolled through her recent calls, the Illinois number that had saved her from revealing too much to Jakob the previous day near the top of the list. "Diane? I just realized I still have her number in my phone, so I'm going to hang up and give her a quick call, okay?"

"Is this anything I should know about?"

"In terms of the inn, no. But I promise I'll fill you in on all the details over dinner tonight."

"I thought maybe you and Jakob might go out for a bite to eat or something, this evening. It's the McCormicks' and the Claymores' last night before they all check out in the morning, and the next round of guests doesn't come in until tomorrow afternoon, so it's the perfect time to do it."

She tried not to grit her teeth, but it was hard. Diane was like a pit bull when it came to her desire for Claire and Jakob to become a couple. "Jakob and I don't have any plans. I'll be home at the usual time and I'll tell you about my phone call with Megan then."

Before her aunt could raise a protest, she broke the connection, quickly replacing the call with one to Megan.

It was answered on the third ring. "Claire! I'm so glad you called. I hated leaving before I had a chance to say good-bye, but Johnny is sick and I've got to get home to him."

"It's okay, I understand." She held the phone closer to her ear as she peeked through the trees that separated her car from the community in which Megan and her family would be living in a year. "I won't keep you long. I know you're on the way to the airport with Kyle right now, but I need to ask you a quick question if that's okay."

"Of course." Megan's laugh echoed in her ear. "I think you're entitled to fire a question in my direction after all the house-hunting turmoil I subjected you to this past week. So go ahead, shoot."

"Yesterday morning you were all set to put a deposit down on a lot in Roaring Brook, but you changed your mind at the last minute and went with Serenity Falls, instead. Why did you do that?"

She could almost hear Megan's wheels turning just before her mouth engaged. "Um, you know why. I like the walking trails, the pond, the playground, the floor plans, and the location."

"No, I get that. But you knew Serenity Falls had all those same things Thursday night when you made your decision to go with Roaring Brook." She stopped long enough to phrase her final question in the clearest way possible. "What I want to know is why you changed your mind again on Friday."

"Because that awful, rancid smell of spoiled milk was gone and the secretary in the sales office assured me it was gone for good."

There was nothing about Megan's answer that surprised her; in fact, it was exactly why she'd tracked the woman down in the first place. But still, having the bow tied by an actual person rather than the voices in her head was comforting somehow, maybe even a little validating.

"And since that was the only reason we had for building elsewhere, it was easy to rip up the check to Keller and Sons and make out a new one to Trey Sampson and his company."

Trey Sampson.

The one man who stood to gain the most by Harley Zook's murder . . .

Claire released the breath she hadn't realized she was holding and stepped from the car, the message on the side of Harley's house and its timing in relation to the man's murder the final piece of the puzzle that still needed to be placed. "Megan? Can I ask you one more question?"

"Sure."

"When did you see Serenity Falls for the first time?"

A muffling of voices in the background let her know Kyle was being consulted on the answer before sharing it with Claire. "Our Realtor took us there on the Friday morning we arrived in Heavenly."

"And did you share your reasons for not wanting to build there with your Realtor that same day?"

"You could say that. I tried to be a bit more diplomatic, but Kyle cut straight to the chase and let her know he wasn't going to spend that kind of money on a lot that smelled like spoiled milk."

She heard Kyle saying something but couldn't make out his words over the car noises on Megan's end.

"Did you hear what Kyle just said?"

"No."

"He said the Realtor wasn't surprised. She told us the only reason she'd even brought us out there at all was because of my interest in living as close to the Amish as possible. She said she quit making it one of her stops when it became apparent the smell was going to prevent her from making a sale."

Claire came around the front corner of the house and stopped, the menacing words painted across the home's foundation making all the sense in the world now.

One more and you're dead.

"Do you happen to know if your Realtor had any contact with Trey Sampson's company that day? You know, to provide feedback on your visit or anything like that?"

She waited as Megan relayed the question on to Kyle; his instantaneous yes was all the confirmation she needed to hear.

It was official; the Reillys had been Harley's "one more" . . .

She waited in her car until the last family emerged from the sales office, the balloons tied to the children's wrists and the starry-eyed faces of the adults a near carbon copy of the three previous families who'd emerged from the trailer over the past half hour. Several times she'd picked up the cell phone while she was waiting, the little voice that had kept her safe and sound throughout her life growing persistently louder with each passing minute.

There was more than enough suspicion and evidence to bring Jakob in to the mix, yet still she hesitated. It wasn't that she thought she was wrong but, rather, because she needed to be sure.

That's why, when the last family finally pulled onto the main road, she stepped from her car and headed across the makeshift parking lot toward the temporary sales office currently housed in a double-wide trailer. She knocked briefly on the glass door, then headed inside, the smiley redhead behind the front desk rising to her feet in short order.

"Oh, I'm so sorry. I didn't hear you drive up. Welcome to Serenity Falls — your one and only forever home." The redhead looked past Claire briefly before turning her smile on full blast. "I take it you're not here with a Realtor this afternoon?"

Claire returned the woman's smile and took the familiar glossy folder from her outstretched hand, barely glancing at it as she did. "No. I'm here alone."

"Well then, I'm Vanessa, your on-site sales associate. I'd be happy to show you around the grounds if you'd like. Makes it easier to envision where everything that's shown in your folder will actually be when the community is complete."

Claire nodded politely then got to the reason for her visit. "Is Trey Sampson available by any chance? I'd like to speak with him if I may."

Vanessa's overly tweezed right eyebrow inched upward. "Do you know Trey?"

"My friend, Megan Reilly, put a down payment on a lot in here yesterday and she —"

"Oh, Mrs. Reilly . . . our first official resident of Serenity Falls." Vanessa clapped her hands together softly. "What a lovely, lovely woman. She's going to be so thrilled to hear we signed her first neighbor not more than two hours ago . . . *and* they just so happen to have a pair of little boys, too!"

"That's wonderful!" Claire let her gaze wander toward the office on the other side of the reception area, the open door and lack of any overhead light virtually eliminating all hope of confronting Trey herself. But Vanessa put her fears to rest with a warm arm squeeze and an invitation to sit and wait.

"Trey should be along any minute. He had to make a quick stop at the bank to sign some papers and pick up a check, and he said he'd be back before it was time to close. Which" — Vanessa ducked her head behind her desktop computer — "according to my little clock right here will be in about twenty minutes."

"Thanks." Claire took a seat in the black vinyl chair and lazily thumbed through the floor plans and marketing pieces inside the same folder that was sitting on the nightstand in her room at the inn. When she'd taken a second and third look at each item, she stood and wandered over to the glass case that housed the basic model of a completed Serenity Falls right down to the playground and walking trails that had helped win Megan's heart.

The phone on Vanessa's desk rang and was quickly answered in a voice that seemed incapable of speaking in anything less than full volume. "Welcome to Serenity Falls, this is Vanessa speaking." Instantly, the cheerleader tone of the woman's greeting took on a frosty edge. "Yes, I know who this is . . . Trey is at the bank now, putting his final signature on the papers . . . I'm quite sure he's not going to make off with your money, Ms. Duggan . . ."

This time there was no coughing spell that could cover the gasp that left Claire's lips and traveled around the room, no easy way to shake off the sudden attention from Vanessa the sound garnered.

"One minute, I have a customer here."

Pulling the phone's mouthpiece to the side of her face, Vanessa lifted her brow in Claire's direction once again. "Is everything okay, Miss — Miss . . . I'm sorry, I didn't catch your name."

"Claire. Claire Weatherly. And no, I'm fine. I guess I was just enthralled by the detail of this model." The lie felt like acid on her tongue, but if it got Vanessa back on the phone and yacking away again, it would be worth it in the end.

"Oh. Okay." The sales agent repositioned the phone closer to her mouth, lowering her voice half an octave. "Yes, Ms. Duggan . . . yes, I know you've been waiting for this first sale to go through, but, as you know, there were mitigating factors beyond our control and . . . yes, yes, we're happy everything can be finalized now as well. Yes, I'll let Trey know you called and that you're at your house waiting for your check in the event your phone call last night and again this morning didn't make that clear. Yes . . . yes, Ms. Duggan . . . Good-bye, Ms. Duggan." Vanessa slapped the phone down on its base and groaned loudly. "Ugh!"

"Tough phone call?" Claire pried.

Vanessa's face reddened just before it disappeared into her hands. "I am so sorry. I don't usually handle calls like that, but that woman tries my patience in ways I can't even begin to explain." She lifted her head and glanced at the ceiling as if in prayer. "But that's over now. She gets her cut of the first land acquisition the way she was promised and Trey is free of her and her former ties to the land once and for all."

"Former ties to the land?" she echoed as the room began to spin to the cadence of Patrick's voice.

See that window right there? That's where my father's bullet came from. The one that killed Harley's brother. He stood on a rock in my grandfather's yard and took the shot. Only took one from what the papers said.

She sucked in her breath a second time as Vanessa confirmed the pivotal piece of information Claire had missed only twenty-four hours earlier. "Part of this property was hers — left to her by her now-deceased parents. Trey could have made this place work without her land, but it would have meant rerouting crucial lines and adding to his costs in the long run."

"And this deal was contingent on the first person he signed?"

"Pretty much, yeah. Unfortunately, as Trey says, when you're dealing with someone with no real cash flow, they can make your life miserable."

Suddenly, everything she'd thought she knew had been turned on its head. Still, though, she asked the question that was more about buying time to catch her breath than anything else. "Why?"

Vanessa checked the time on her computer once again and then began stacking the marketing folders in a neat pile on her desk in preparation for the looming five o'clock hour. "Because they don't have a whole lot of patience the way people with money do."

CHAPTER 29

There was so much about Rita as Harley's murderer that made sense in light of everything Claire'd just learned from Vanessa. Like her husband, Carl, Rita Duggan was no fan of the Amish, either, seeing them as the reason she lost the man she married.

In fact, thinking back to things Patrick had said over the past few days, it was obvious that the hatred he'd been raised with didn't fall on his father's shoulders alone. And if that same hatred was a powerful enough motive to propel Carl to murder, it was more than conceivable that same latent hatred, coupled with a desire for revenge and an opportunity to gain in the process, could have pushed the man's wife to do the same.

The only problem that remained was whether Patrick had known about his mother's intentions. If he had and he'd said nothing, he'd have to live with that the rest of his life. If he'd known and somehow aided her in the crime, he'd be charged as an accomplice. Either way, his life was shattered by hatred — a hatred that had been all but willed to him by the same two people who should have wanted better for their son.

Claire drove through downtown Heavenly, the darkened front window of Heavenly Treasures off to her left a painful reminder of the mess she was trying to avoid by playing detective. Several car lengths later, the sight of the police station on her right reminded her of the phone call she was glad she hadn't made from the parking lot of Serenity Falls. She'd been wrong once already in suspecting Trey Sampson, there was no guarantee she wouldn't be adding yet another mistake to her tally sheet with Rita Duggan.

The motive was powerful and the means every bit as strong for Rita as they'd been for her husband sixteen years earlier. The only piece Claire was having trouble understanding was the location of the body.

Why kill Harley in the corn maze when all Rita had to do was walk across her own property the way Carl had?

She followed the road as it wound its way past Sleep Heavenly and into the heart of the English side of town, the lefts and rights she'd taken with Jakob easy enough to remember. Yet this time, when she stepped from the car, she was aware of a growing apprehension in the pit of her stomach. Something about Patrick had spoken to her the previous day in the same way she imagined it had spoken to Harley.

Accepting the fact that the man had been murdered out of hatred and greed was hard enough. But finding a way to wrap her head around the very real possibility that Patrick may have been involved in some way made the whole thing even more repulsive.

Harley had sought Patrick out in an effort to connect with another victim of Carl Duggan's hatred. The last thing she wanted to believe was the notion that in reaching out, Harley had unknowingly sealed his own fate.

Inhaling every ounce of courage she could muster, Claire made her way up the wide steps that led to Rita's front door and knocked, the answering footsteps on the other side of the door virtually instant.

"I was hoping you'd stop by . . ." Rita's eyes narrowed on Claire. "What do you want?"

She peered past the gray-haired woman and noted the pair of suitcases lined up neatly just inside the front entryway. "Did I catch you at a bad time?"

"As a matter of fact, yes, you did." Rita pushed past Claire long enough to survey the road in both directions, offering up an angered groan in the process. "I'm expecting someone any minute and I really don't have time for unnecessary distractions."

"I'm sure Trey will be along anytime now."

Rita tilted her head to the side yet gave no indication she recognized the builder's name. "If you don't mind, I'd rather shut this door and keep that swarm of little gnats right there from comin' into my house."

The warning bells in Claire's head started to go off, but she turned a deaf ear in favor of finding justice for Harley. She accepted the invitation but kept her body positioned just inside the closed door. "So? Is Patrick here?"

"No."

"Do you expect him back soon?"

Rita's gaze dropped to her suitcases and the single airline ticket that sat on a small end table to their left. "I expect him back sometime after I'm gone."

Something about the woman's voice and the glint in her steel gray eyes sent a chill down Claire's spine. "You're skipping out on him, aren't you?"

"He can fend for himself just fine. I got what I needed out of him."

"What you needed?" she echoed.

"It's the only reason I didn't prevent my son from working with that man." Rita's top lip curled with the kind of ugliness that went far beyond the exterior. "I've been working my tail off these past sixteen years. My parents' land was my ticket out of that life. I needed information in order to make that happen. Patrick provided that. And in doing so I was able to take out two of them weirdos at the same time."

"Weirdos?" She heard a faint click somewhere behind Rita, but if the woman noticed, there was no indication.

"You know who I'm talking about. Everyone knows who I'm talking about."

"You mean the Amish?" Claire heard the anger rising in her voice, even knew on some level that it was probably best saved for when jail bars stood between them, but still, she spoke. "Frankly, you're about the only person I've ever met who has a problem with the Amish. They don't cause trouble for anyone."

"Oh?" Rita took a menacing step forward. "You don't think having my parents going on and on about how polite and respectful those little Amish brats were caused trouble when I was growing up? You think being compared to them morning, noon, and

346

night was easy for a kid?"

Claire thought of Jakob and the issues with his father that pre-dated his decision to leave the Amish, the cop's courage and strength guiding her words. "So you re-group. You make yourself proud."

"What are you? A talk show host?" Rita spat, her face contorting in rage. "I bet you think raising that little brat by myself for the past sixteen years should have been easy, too, right?"

"You were raising him yourself because of trouble *your husband* caused. He killed an innocent man in cold blood. How can you not see that?"

"My husband wouldn't be sitting in a jail if those Amish folks weren't livin' around here!" Rita took a second, bigger step toward Claire, essentially cornering her against the door with no room to run. "Those people made my childhood hell and then, when I was finally with someone who hated them as much as I did, they went and took him from me.

"But wait . . . it gets better. I finally have an opportunity to live a better life and even that almost gets ruined because of those people. Why? Because they won't use a refrigerator like normal folk! So now *I'm* the one taking."

"By killing the same innocent man who reached out to your son and made a difference in his life this past month or so?" Claire stopped long enough to breathe, to realize that the location of the body was all part of the plan. "And by trying to frame a second innocent man for a crime you committed?"

"They made it easy the way they follow each other around," Rita spat. "Wanna know something? I hate do-gooder, know-it-alls like yourself. You throw your convictions around like they're the gospel truth and they ain't."

"They're a lot closer to it than yours!" She lurched forward just enough to try and secure a grip on the doorknob at her back, but it was too late. Rita's closed hand came across Claire's face and knocked her to the floor.

She struggled up on her elbow in an effort to retrieve her cell phone from her jacket pocket, but that, too, was smacked across the room. "You ain't callin' anyone. I'm not goin' down for that man's killin'. That other fella is."

"You mean Mose?" she whispered.

"If that's the name of the fella who was causin' all that trouble at that farm, then that's who I mean. But it don't matter

348

much, that just gave me someone to put it on. What *does* matter is knowin' that sixteen years ago one of them Amish folks changed my life and I wasn't about to sit by while that man's brother screwed it up even more."

"Harley didn't screw up your life, Mom! You did that all on your own!"

She did her best to get out of Rita's way as the woman spun around to face her son, but Claire's reaction time was impacted by the blow to her head. Still, it didn't matter, as Rita's full attention was now trained on the back of the house and the broad-shouldered son who'd found a way out of the hatred.

"Don't you talk to me like that, boy!"

"I've never been more ashamed to be your boy than I am at this moment. But that stops here and it stops now. With me."

She saw Patrick step to the side as another, far more familiar shape burst into the room, gun drawn. "Rita Duggan, you are under arrest for the murder of Harley Zook."

CHAPTER 30

Claire was just plugging the final number into the calculator when she heard Jakob at the door, his faint knock, coupled with the sound of his voice as he called her name through the screen, bringing a momentary lift to an evening with very few bright spots.

Pushing back from her desk, she stood and made her way toward the back door of her shop, the tender smile that broke across his face as she approached warming her all the way to her toes. "Isn't this a nice surprise," she offered as she lifted the locking pin from its holder and welcomed him inside. "I thought I was the only one working this late on a Monday night."

"You are." She saw his gaze harden just before his hand cupped the part of her face that still ached from Rita's hit. "I hate that you didn't call me and tell me where you were going. If you had, this wouldn't have happened."

She felt the burning prick of too many tears than she could afford to cry and blinked them away. "What matters is that Patrick called you and that you got there in time before she got away."

The pad of his thumb glided across her cheek with a gentleness that left her wanting more despite the discomfort his touch caused. "It still hurts, doesn't it?"

At her shrug, he retracted his hand and waved it in the direction of her office. "Diane told me you were here, but when I asked why, she said she didn't know. Is everything okay?"

More than anything in the world she wanted to tell him things were fine — exceptional, in fact. But she couldn't.

Nor could she keep him in the dark any longer.

Something had shifted between them the past few weeks, something that hinted at the possibility of a future together. Allowing him to believe in such a possibility when it simply couldn't happen wasn't right.

She knew this. She really did. But did it matter if she told him now or ten minutes from now? Deciding it didn't, she allowed herself one final moment or two of happiness before she delved back into a reality that was far bleaker than she'd even realized.

"Can you come sit with me for a little while?"

"That's what I was hoping for when I showed up at your door just now," he said, his dimples on full display. "But wouldn't you rather get out of here? Maybe stop at Heavenly Brews for a treat or go for a long walk? It's a gorgeous night. There are tons of stars and just enough of a chill to make it so you'd think I was being a gentleman when I put my arm around you."

"That's because you *are* a gentleman," she said.

"I am, but I'd be lying if I didn't say I'd take just about any chance I could to hold you close."

There was a part of her that wanted nothing more than to take that walk, to feel the increased beat of her heart when his arm came around her shoulder as they set out in whatever direction they chose. But that would only delay the inevitable.

She glanced at the floor and then back up at Jakob, the sparkle of hope in his eyes making it difficult to breathe. "Could we just talk here for a while, instead? I . . . I still have a little work to do before I can call it a night."

He hesitated a beat before the agreement eventually came via a slow, easy nod. "I had no idea that owning a gift shop meant so many late nights."

Determined to enjoy at least a few minutes together, she led the way past her office and into the main room, flipping on an occasional light as they passed. When they reached the counter area, she pulled out the pair of stools she kept behind the register area and patted Jakob over. "Have you spoken to Patrick today by any chance?"

"No. Why? Is he okay?"

She waited until he'd gotten settled then sat beside him with what she hoped was a genuine smile. She wanted to relish this time together, wanted to savor it as the gift it was. "He's having a hard time, of course. How could he not when his own mother robbed him of the best thing that had happened to him in years, if not his entire life?"

"Yeah, I feel bad for the guy. He's got to be feeling pretty directionless right now." Jakob shifted in his seat to afford a better view of Claire.

"I'm sure he is, and I'm sure he'll feel like that for quite some time. But today he got a little bit of a nudge from someone very special." She allowed herself to drift back through the quieter parts of her day as she took a much-needed break to recover from the trauma of Saturday night and the official questioning that had followed the next morning. Patrick's arrival, just before lunch, had netted the kind of poignant moment she knew she'd carry in her heart for years to come.

"What happened?"

"Aunt Diane gave him the box Harley made for him."

"The toolbox?" Jakob clarified.

She felt the smile spread across her mouth at the memory she was all too happy to share with Jakob. "Actually, it wasn't a toolbox. It was a painter's box."

Before Jakob could respond, she continued, her voice thick with emotion. "Harley knew that hammers and nails weren't really Patrick's thing. But he did notice an interest in painting. So he made Patrick a box and filled it with paintbrushes of all shapes and sizes. And at the bottom of it all was a note, telling Patrick he could be anything he wanted if he worked at it and tried his best."

Jakob closed his eyes in time with a deep breath. "Harley said that same thing to me sixteen years ago when I stopped by his farm and told him I wanted to help find the man who killed his brother. And I've carried those words and that validation around with me ever since."

She let Jakob take her hand in his and hold it close. "I suspect Patrick will carry those words and that validation with him through his life, as well. He needs that. From *someone*."

"I'll keep an eye on him, Claire. I promise."

Coming from anyone else, she'd put the likelihood of such a promise being kept at about ten percent. But with Jakob, she knew it would be a hundred percent. That's the way Jakob was. It was the path he'd chosen and a path he understood in a way few others ever could. "I know you will," she whispered.

"We can both look in on him . . . together."

The moment had come. It was time to tell him the truth.

She looked down at Jakob's hand entwined around hers and willed the warmth and understanding she felt there to stay with her until she was done with what she needed to say. "No. We can't. Because I won't be here beyond the end of January, middle of February at most."

His grip loosened only to tighten around her once again. "Come on, Claire, that's not funny."

She swallowed. "I know. I'm not trying to be funny, I'm just trying to be honest . . . with myself and with you."

This time, his grip not only loosened, he let go of her hand completely. "What are you talking about? Where are you going?"

"I don't know yet. Someplace where I can get some sort of a job that will allow me to keep a roof over my head and food on my plate."

"You have that," he reminded. "You have this shop and your aunt . . ."

"In about ten weeks, I won't have the shop any longer, and I won't live off my aunt no matter how hard she's going to try and convince me otherwise. That's not the life I want."

He looked around at the shop and the dwindling merchandise on the shelves around them. "I don't understand. Why are you giving up on the shop? You told me that very first day we met that this place was a dream come true for you. What's changed?"

"My finances." She slipped off the stool and wandered across the shop, stopping midway to turn and face him once again. "I thought I had enough socked aside to stay current on the rent and other expenses, but I was wrong. I just don't have enough big-ticket items to sell to really make a go at this."

He met her gaze and held it tight, the hurt and surprise in his eyes impossible to miss. "No. I'm not going to let this happen. You belong in Heavenly. Everyone here loves you. Esther, Eli, Ruth, my sister, your aunt, *me . . .*" He leapt to his feet and came to stand beside her, his hands finding hers once again. "We're going to fix this. You wait and see."

More than anything she wanted to jump on his bandwagon with all his best intentions and heartfelt words, but she couldn't. Her shop and its financial burden were her cross to bear, not Jakob's. "No. I won't take money from you and I won't take it from Aunt Diane. This was my dream to realize — on my own. I fell short, Jakob. It's time to move on."

"Maybe there's another way, Claire. But we're not going to find it if you're so quick to give up and walk away."

"But that's just it. It *hasn't* been quick. I've known this was coming for a while now. I just chose not to see it."

Again, he let go of her hands then raked his own through his hair in frustration. "Why didn't you say something sooner?"

"Because I didn't want to admit it out

loud. Especially to you."

He dragged his hands down his face, stopping midway to peer at her across his fingertips. "Especially to me? Why?"

"I guess I allowed myself to get caught up in a possibility I had never really envisioned for myself until just recently." She heard the tears in her voice, knew it was only a matter of minutes before they made their way down her face.

"Possibility? What possibility?"

She made herself breathe as she willed the tears to stay at bay just a little longer. The last thing she wanted was for her heartbreak to result in some sort of pity-driven response. That, she couldn't handle. Especially not from Jakob.

When she was virtually certain she could speak, she answered his question as simply and honestly as she could. "The possibility of a second chance."

At his questioning eyes, she filled in the rest of the sentence, her voice breaking on the final word. "At love."

Footsteps in the back room brought them both up short, and they turned in time to see Eli, Benjamin, and Al Gussman step into the room, their hands folded neatly in front of them. "Claire. Jakob."

She swiped the back of her hand across

her eyes in an effort to rid them of the tears she felt slipping past her best efforts. "Is — is everything alright?" she finally asked when she was sure she could trust her voice.

"Well, we were kind of hoping you might be able to tell *us* that," her landlord said, stepping forward. "Benjamin, here, told us what's going on and we're here to help."

She turned an accusing eye in Benjamin's direction. "Benjamin, you told me you wouldn't say anything."

"You told *him*?" Jakob questioned.

"A few days ago, yes." She kept her eyes on Benjamin even as she addressed Jakob. "It was either that or explode." Then, bringing her verbal focus in line with her gaze, she dressed Benjamin down in a way she never had before. "You gave me your word. How could you go back on that?"

"You asked that I not tell Esther. I did not tell her. I told only Eli . . . and Mr. Gussman."

Al stepped between Benjamin and Claire waving his hands in the air as he did. "If Benjamin hadn't told me what was going on over here, I wouldn't have known where to put the money."

"What money?" she asked.

"The money that showed up in the mailbox of the general store this morning with a note saying only to use it to pay the rent of a needy business owner this coming year."

She staggered against Jakob and was grateful for the strength she found there. "You can't be serious . . ."

"I can and I am."

"But . . . but where did it come from?"

"I don't know. The note didn't say."

This time, when she looked at Benjamin, the anger was gone, in its place the kind of gratitude that was nearly impossible to express. "Benjamin, I can't accept that kind of money from you."

"It is not from me."

"But who else knew?"

"One of your wishing stars, perhaps?" Benjamin's suspenders pulled taut against his chest as his shoulders rose and fell in a shrug. She felt Jakob studying her, knew he was watching to see if there was something more than friendship between her and Benjamin. But there wasn't. The friendship they shared was more than enough.

Eli took a step forward. "I have something to show you, Claire. It is in the alley."

Shifting her focus from one Miller brother to the other, she fell into step behind her best friend's fiancé. When they reached the back door, Jakob held it open and waited to follow until everyone was outside.

"I will soon have a family of my own. I must support them the best way I can. I hope you will help me do that." Eli stepped around the back of the shop and gestured for Claire and the others to follow. What she found there made her gasp.

"Eli . . . it's beautiful."

"I made this for Esther. It is for her to keep blankets, or dresses, or anything else she sees fit."

She ran her hand along the beveled edges of the handcrafted wooden trunk, the exquisite workmanship that went into the piece obvious. "I had no idea you could make things like this."

"I would like to make more. For you to sell in the shop. Benjamin said they will bring good money for you and for me."

It was no longer possible to hold the tears at bay. Somehow, in the blink of an eye, everything had changed. And it was all because of the people standing around her at that very moment — people who'd come into her life at a low point and given her hope for a brighter and more fulfilling future. It was almost too good to be true . . .

"Are you going to stop farming when you and Esther get married?"

"No. I will do both."

"But what happens if you and Esther have

to move in order to find land? Trunks like this would be much too big to ship."

"I can put trunks in my buggy. Or you can pick them up and visit with Esther when you do."

"But —"

Jakob's breath warmed her ear as he moved his lips close. "That's what I wanted to tell you earlier — the excuse I was using to track you down here."

She looked up at him and smiled. "You don't need an excuse to see me, Jakob. Not now, not ever."

"Then I guess I'll just tell you. Esther and Eli are staying right here in Heavenly."

She felt the tears as they ran down her cheeks, unchecked. "Staying?" she repeated in a choked whisper. "Are you sure?"

"Yah. I am sure."

"But how?" She turned her attention toward a smiling Eli. "I didn't know there was any land around here for you to farm."

"I will farm Harley's old land and make it my own."

She opened her mouth to speak but closed it as Jakob draped an arm across her shoulders and whispered a kiss across her temple. "So if your shop can get a second chance, maybe you can get yours, too?"

ABOUT THE AUTHOR

While spending a rainy afternoon at a friend's house more than thirty years ago, **Laura Bradford** fell in love with writing over a stack of blank paper, a box of crayons, and a freshly sharpened number two pencil. From that moment forward, she never wanted to do or be anything else. Today, Laura is a bestselling mystery and award-winning romance author. She lives in Yorktown Heights, New York, with her husband and their blended brood. Visit her website at laurabradford.com

The employees of Thorndike Press hope you have enjoyed this Large Print book. All our Thorndike, Wheeler, and Kennebec Large Print titles are designed for easy reading, and all our books are made to last. Other Thorndike Press Large Print books are available at your library, through selected bookstores, or directly from us.

For information about titles, please call:
  (800) 223-1244

or visit our Web site at:
  http://gale.cengage.com/thorndike

To share your comments, please write:
  Publisher
  Thorndike Press
  10 Water St., Suite 310
  Waterville, ME 04901